Who's That Knocking On My Door? · LOWER THAN

NOAH AND THE ARK · El Ci· · OF

Dragon · The Maypole · ·nce

The Cherry Tree · Greek Myths · Over The

STORIES FROM THE BALLET · Cowboy Jess

·RE · Blue Moo · PETER PAN IN SCARLET

·E DAY THE WORLD BEGAN · The Quest of Isis

·PPER ROUX · LITTLE ANGEL · Cowboy Jess Saddles Up

·r and the Round Table · LOVESONG · FOREVER X

·l Goddesses · Princess Stories · Unicorns Unicorns!

·E · Starry Tales · Casting the Gods Adrift

& NELLY · Too Big! · Hope on a Rope

·ephant · God's Kingdom · A PILGRIM'S PROGRESS

·CRACKER · The Hay Cart · What Am I For?

·ries From British History · My First Oxford Book of Stories

·tlers · BRAVE MAGIC · GRANDMA CHICKENLEGS

Pioneers At Piano Ridge · STOP THE TRAIN

·Y HOUSE · Jalopy · The Jesse Tree · NOT THE END OF

·seus · Dog Days · DANCING THE NIGHT AWAY

·he Questing Knights of the Faerie Queen · Doctor Quack

·HINK AGAIN! · MO · Noisy Neighbours · FATHER

THE STOPS · Monacello · ROBIN HOOD, GEORGE

·HER STORIES · Pittipat and the Saucer of Moon

POSITIVELY LAST PERFORMANCE · THE MIDDLE OF

The
Positively
LAST
PERFORMANCE

The Positively LAST PERFORMANCE

GERALDINE
McCAUGHREAN

OXFORD
UNIVERSITY PRESS

OXFORD
UNIVERSITY PRESS

Great Clarendon Street, Oxford OX2 6DP

Oxford University Press is a department of the University of Oxford.
It furthers the University's objective of excellence in research, scholarship,
and education by publishing worldwide in

Oxford   New York

Auckland Cape Town Dar es Salaam Hong Kong Karachi
Kuala Lumpur Madrid Melbourne Mexico City Nairobi
New Delhi Shanghai Taipei Toronto

With offices in

Argentina Austria Brazil Chile Czech Republic France Greece
Guatemala Hungary Italy Japan Poland Portugal Singapore
South Korea Switzerland Thailand Turkey Ukraine Vietnam

Oxford is a registered trade mark of Oxford University Press
in the UK and in certain other countries

British Library Cataloguing in Publication Data

Data available

ISBN: 978-0-19-273320-7

1 3 5 7 9 10 8 6 4 2

Printed and bound by CPI Group (UK) Ltd, Croydon, CR0 4YY

Paper used in the production of this book is a natural,
recyclable product made from wood grown in sustainable forests.
The manufacturing process conforms to the environmental
regulations of the country of origin.

For The Theatre Royal Margate
and the wonderful people, past and present,
who helped to write this book.

A proportion of the proceeds from this book will go to
The Theatre Royal—Margate's greatest asset
—except, of course, for its inhabitants.

G. M.

PROLOGUE

S adly, the Royal Theatre had not seen a paying audience for two years. What with thick chains on every door, and the windows whitewashed over, the building had the look of a blind convict, waiting on the corner of the square to be carted away to prison. Indoors, the walls were black with mould, the brass coat hooks and door handles blotched with verdigris. Hinged seats, once upholstered in scarlet, were darkening too, to the colour of dried blood. Damp does that. Cobwebs hung in swags from the dusty chandelier high in the centre of the ceiling. The Box Office had been shut long enough for the word CLOSED to have faded to a blank.

A sorry fate to overtake a stately old building. But neither the tip-up seats nor the mice squealed in protest; the seats, because no one sat on them; the mice, because there were no mice. Mice fear three things in this life: cats, nervy elephants . . . and ghosts.

Every theatre has ghosts, of course. The Royal had more than its fair share. A whole host of ghosts. Over the years, their number had gradually increased—ancient and modern swept together into the one dark corner, a motley assortment, but all devoted to the theatre and the shelter it gave them. Had they been paying customers, they would have counted as a good audience for a matinee. The sorry state of the building did not trouble the resident ghosts. The Royal Theatre had seen better days, but then so had they. It suited them nicely.

❧

So it is not quite true to say that *no one* sat on the plush seats of The Royal. It is just that the resident ghosts, no longer heavy enough to keep a sprung seat from tipping up, chose to sit on the broken ones that had flopped down. (Everybody knows it is an indignity to get folded up inside your own chair.) Alternatively, they perched on the seatbacks, or the edge of the stage, or straddled the rail around the orchestra pit. The Twins preferred the opera-boxes jutting out of the side walls of the auditorium: there were armchairs inside, little lamps, and somewhere to rest elbows. The boxes did not give a very good view of the stage but they were swanky to a degree.

The Dress Circle was strictly out-of-bounds, though, since the cracks had started to appear. Eugenius Birch said it was no longer safe.

Chapter One

Seen BETTER DAYS

Eugenius Birch climbed a ladder once used to service spot-lamps, and peered up at the underside of the Circle. Impossible to judge how far the cracks had spread, or whether the nasty downward bulge in the plaster had got worse. But, to an engineer's eye, there was no mistaking the sag in Row C.

'Oh, do take care, Mr Birch!' called Miss Melluish.

'The risk is small, madam,' said Eugenius leaning out from the rungs by one hand. 'What is the worst that can befall me? I do wish those electricals had not been turned off: I can see almost nothing.'

On the stage, Lily Oliver eased the laces in her bodice in readiness for singing. It was a habit she had formed in her days of deep breathing, and she had never bothered to break it, even though she did not (strictly speaking) breathe any more. It seemed to raise the men's spirits to see her loosen her laces and to know a song was on its way. 'What would you like to hear next, gentlemen? Ladies?'

Mikey the Mod put his jacket over his head and his ankles on the seat in front. Up in the Royal Box, the Twins rested their chins on their fists. Florence Melluish frowned a little, thinking that Mr Birch's worries about the Circle deserved everyone's full attention. Maurice tuned his banjo to the key of A. Lily always started in the key of A.

Lily usually sang a medley of songs before joining her actor husband Roland in a scene from a play. Comedy on Mondays and Fridays; tragedy on Wednesdays; burlesque on Saturdays; in between any script Roland could still remember from his days in repertory.

'Could it truly come tumbling down, Mr Birch?' whimpered Miss Melluish.

'One day it certainly will, dear lady. The works of Man are fleeting ... But perhaps we shall be spared for a year or two more.'

'Ladies and Gents!' boomed Lord George striding on stage. 'We at The Royal are delighted to bring you your very own songbird—Lily Oliver, singing ... '

An immense **bang** shook dust from the great decaying curtains.

Eugenius fell off the bottom rung of the ladder; Mikey slid down between seats, and the music died on the songbird's lips. Everyone took it for the Dress Circle finally collapsing, but it was only the slamming open of the side doors. Like some mediaeval siege engine, great slabs of daylight forced their way into the gloomy auditorium. Vandals?

❧

'You'll see the potential at once,' said the man from the Council stepping indoors. 'Nothing to look at on the outside but one

4

step inside and there's the full glory of it . . . I keep telling the Development Committee: Seashaw *needs* the Arts. The Arts are the key. You've got to have the Arts, or where are you?'

He ushered in his guests: a big man with curly hair and red trousers, a slight woman who moved as if the wind had blown her over the doorsill, and a child who was all eyes and patchwork dungarees. They stepped directly into the theatre from the pavement outside: Mr Letts wanted to show them the auditorium first, rather than the dismal little foyer: first impressions are so important . . .

He had shown others around: developers, photographers, historians, investment consultants, fellow Councillors . . . But he was placing his best hopes in these theatricals. Young though they were, they had a youthful optimism, an energy that he had not seen in any of the others. Living in Seashaw, Mr Letts had almost forgotten there were optimists and dreamers left in the world.

'The whole building seems to be holding its breath!' whispered the woman.

'That'll be the smell,' said the man.

❧

The ghosts let go their pent-up breath. Not vandals, then. Vandals had broken in once, and Miss Melluish had needed her smelling salts afterwards. The Residents had been obliged to watch the yobs jumping up and down on the seats, emptying out the property baskets, letting off the fire extinguishers before brawling their way out again because none of them had remembered to bring a spray can or a decent knife.

These people were not vandals.

❧

'Who are *they*?' said the child, pointing directly at Jim and Joanie up in the Royal Box.

Mr Letts pointed at the selfsame moment. 'The lion and the unicorn, you see,' he said of the gilded mouldings on the front of the box. 'Royal emblems. That's where the queen would have sat. Or the king.'

'Terrible view,' was the man's reaction. 'You look straight into the wings, and you can't see anything happening stage-left.' But he looked around with joy at all the other gilded stucco mouldings decorating the theatre—Greek helmets, angels, harps, swags of flowers, cupids and masks. As he did so he rubbed the top of his curly hair, as if to soothe some inner agitation. 'What happened to the walls?' he asked.

'Skin deep! We've had it looked into,' cheeped Mr Letts, but could not suggest either a reason or a cure for the acne of black mould. It coated every wall and ceiling, and had dyed the curtains a darker red.

'How are the certificates?'

'Oh, early days, early days.' Mr Letts's heart was already sinking. Always 'the mould', always 'the certificates'. Could no one look beyond the problems to the sheer history—the romance— of this noble old building? In all probability, The Royal would end up as an apartment block or a nightclub. But Mr Letts was Seashaw born and bred, and he wished, with a wistful, weary, washed-out longing, that the town's theatre could somehow survive the march of Progress. Throughout its long life it had been

6

open and closed, open and closed, as one owner after another ran out of money, lost heart, or died of overwork. Only three years ago it had been struggling along, getting by, almost making ends meet. Surely it could reopen one last time? —even stage the kind of shows he remembered seeing there as a boy!

Mr Letts had hoped these young, arty types might share his dream. He had hoped they could forgive The Royal's little imperfections and the jaded, faded town that no longer loved it.

'Any other questions before we press on to the Administration area?' he asked, shuddering at the thought of the dingy foyer.

'Any ghosts?' asked the woman.

'*Ghosts?*' Mr Letts let out an explosive laugh. Mould he had no answer for. Structural decay left him floundering. But ghosts? 'No! No, no! No ghosts! Ha ha. That's one thing we haven't got to worry about!'

❧

Behind them, Roland Oliver had climbed on to a chair, so as to examine the top of the younger man's head for signs of balding.

His wife Lily watched, her organza dress riffling in the breeze from the open doors, and thought how long it had been since audiences had streamed out into the alley at the end of a play, talking about the actors or humming one of her songs.

❧

'So what do you think?' said Mr Letts dejectedly.

'What do we think?' the man in red trousers repeated to his wife. Both hands were in his hair now.

7

'We'd beggar ourselves doing it up, and have no money to put on shows,' said his wife.

'There are always grants.'

'It will be the death of us,' she countered blithely.

'Yes, but what a way to go!' The whole family laughed.

Taken aback, Mr Letts laughed too, uncertainly, because theatre people are always a bit unnerving. But he so *wanted* them to mean it.

'And Gracie?' said the man.

The girl's mother spoke even before the girl could: 'Gracie's idea in the first place, wasn't it?'

Mr Letts almost skipped for joy. Could it be true that The Royal might yet tuck up her skirts and dodge the bulldozers? That the great curtains might one day swish and swash again, rather than burn in a skip? That the orchestra pit might fill up with music, rather than concrete? He knew he ought to warn them: the dream was impossible. But that's the point of theatre and actors, isn't it? They are the stuff that dreams are made on. The party of visitors shut the side doors and herded out to the foyer; the swing doors clip-clopped to and fro behind them.

❧

'What do you say, fellow incumbents?' asked Eugenius Birch.

'I scent a theatrical,' said Lord George.

'I also.'

'Too young to pull it off,' said the actor decisively.

'Just because he has a full head of hair . . . ' said his wife.

'A man who has not outgrown his hair has not yet grown to wisdom,' said Roland Oliver pompously (and not for the first time).

'Wise man or fool: is he going to save us or sink us?' said the Lifeboatman, his oilskins dripping noisily on to his boots. 'Will he end by wanting to demolish the place, like all those others?'

Miss Melluish began to cry discreetly into a lace handkerchief. Songbird Lily Oliver decided it was time to cheer everyone up with a song. She sang a jaunty little number about charabancs and outings to the seaside, about people putting on their best clothes and leaving the city in favour of sunshine and fun. Maurice played his banjo; the man in the pit ran his fingers over the keys of the silent piano; Jimmy and Joanie clapped in time and, one by one, the assembly was persuaded to join in with the chorus. No risk of the visitors hearing, of course; who can hear ghosts singing? For years and years the occupants of The Royal had been entertaining themselves without a single complaint from the neighbours.

'All aboard for sunny Seashaw
There let us our hearts combine.
Warm upon the limpid lee shore,
I'll be yours if you'll be mine,
In the sunny summertime.
You'll be mine and I'll be yours,
On Seashaw's sandy sunny shores.'

The song fell silent, but the Twins' enthusiastic clapping went on. At least, they took it for the Twins' clapping.

But it was not. The girl in the patchwork dungarees was standing at the brink of the Circle clapping with all her might.

The ghosts drew in breath as one. A pat of mould peeled off the wall and fell with a splat on to the stage.

But of course! The child was not clapping their song: she was simply experimenting—clapping so as to hear the noise of it echo through the big auditorium. It is one of those things people do in a big hollow space, isn't it? Eugenius Birch was the first to realize this and put their minds at rest. Pure coincidence. The child had not heard a note.

'That was lovely!' called Gracie. 'Sing another one!'

Mikey the Mod emerged from under his coat. Roland Oliver dropped his script. Maurice held tight with both hands to the cracked brim of his straw boater. A man in overalls came out from the wings holding a spanner.

'She can see us!' said Joanie.

'I said before, she was pointing at us. I told you,' said her brother. 'Did I not say?'

'*Can* you see us, young lady?' asked Eugenius Birch, uneasily fingering the stud of his wing collar. 'I hardly think . . .'

'Of course I can see you!' said Gracie, beaming.

The ghosts were aghast. They turned to each other, bewildered, panicky.

'*Why?*'

'*Is she a new one?*'

'*Is she one of us?*'

but Gracie only hooted with laughter.

From somewhere in the dark recesses of the wings came a weary, wary *uh-oh* . . . Or perhaps it was just a very hollow laugh.

Chapter Two

OPENING UP

'I'm Gracie,' said Gracie, joining them in the stalls. 'Isn't this the best theatre anywhere? I like it better than all the others. Who are you?'

They continued to stare at her, some with fear, others with open hostility.

'Theatrical blood. Didn't I say?' said Lord George. 'We have been scented out by a fellow theatrical.'

'So can she not see *me*, then?' asked Mikey the Mod. 'I'm not showbiz.'

But Gracie could see them all. She walked up to Miss Melluish (who was closest), meaning to shake hands. But although the librarian felt obliged to offer the gloved fingers of one hand, Gracie could feel nothing to grip.

'Those people you came with . . .' said Miss Melluish.

11

'Mum and Dad—oh, and Mr Letts from the Council. We're going to open up the theatre again. If they let us.'

If she had clattered a stick along the bars of a lion's cage she could not have stirred up such a roaring and growling and restless unease. Mikey's eyes darted here and there as if looking for somewhere to hide. Douglas Douglass threw his sou'wester on the floor with a noise like a wet plaice hitting the slab. The Twins hugged each other. The librarian tottered. The banjo player took off his straw boater and laid bare a strip of white forehead above the shiny blackness of his face.

'We do not mean to be rude,' he said, 'but we would rather . . . '

'We would as soon your good parents went and saved some other theatre, in some other town,' declared a voice from the pit.

'Move along now. Move along, please,' said a policeman in riding boots, and signalled with his old-fashioned truncheon for Gracie to leave.

But thanks to her parents' line of work, Gracie had attended many schools. She had entered many playgrounds on her first day to be confronted by hostile faces and a closing of ranks. She knew that the trick was to hold your ground and keep talking; sooner or later people got over hating you for being a stranger.

Anxious and pale, nervous hands clasping her husband's elbow, songbird Lily Oliver was at least trying to picture The Royal open to the public once again. 'Imagine, Roland! An audience! It is a fine, heartening sight, an audience.'

'You've got *us*,' said Douglas Douglass sulkily.

'Yeah,' said Mikey, 'you got us.'

'Sadly, I fear the task of reopening will be beyond the means of your excellent parents,' said Eugenius Birch, because he was a gentleman and always civil.

'There are grants,' said Gracie. (That was as far as her understanding went of business, but her father said it often, whenever he added up the cost of his dreams and it came out 'impossible'. 'There are grants.') 'Thought you'd be pleased. Lots of plays and pantos and concerts . . . I don't suppose ghosts need to buy tickets, do they?'

But the Residents of The Royal did not think of themselves as ghosts. The very word made their faces stiffen like drying dishcloths.

'We found sanctuary here, child,' said the florid man with the shiny top hat and long side-whiskers. 'What manner of sanctuary is a place whose doors stand open to the four winds?'

'Draughty is what,' said the forthright Douglas Douglass.

'What's a sanctuary?' said Gracie. 'I went to a donkey place called a sanctuary once. It was great.'

They were offended at being likened to donkeys, but a shabby, bent figure in the corner of the orchestra pit, wearing a painter's smock and an awful hat pinned round with cloth, spoke out of the deeps. He spoke without ever turning round to look at her. 'A sanctuary is somewhere to seek out shelter. We all had need of that. It is the *single* thing we have in common.' He said it pointedly, as if to make clear that he could not be lumped together with the others. (Gracie noticed the artist's canvas set up in front of him was clean, untouched; perhaps he was stuck for an idea for what to paint. Why did he not turn round? she wondered.)

'Shelter? Why?' she said. 'It's not raining.'

The ghosts writhed in their blood-coloured seats, in their gauzy clothes, in their diaphanous bodies. 'Not shelter from the weather; shelter from a dangerous world,' said the earnest young man with the blackened face.

'Why?' said Gracie again. 'What's dangerous about it?' she asked them, one after another, knowing she should not pester, knowing how many times she had been told not to make a nuisance of herself. Unfortunately, knowing it was wrong never made a shred of difference. Her father liked to say there were stories in everyone if only you could prise the lid off and get a look inside. And Gracie liked stories. One by one she asked them. One by one they said that they did not remember, could not remember. 'You must have terrible bad memories,' said Gracie.

❧

Gracie's memory was excellent. She could remember a train journey when she had slept in the luggage rack. She could remember a house with curtains over the doors to keep out the draught, and how they moved as if someone was lurking behind them. She could remember a caravan, the rain so loud on its roof that it sounded angry. She could remember catching sight of the sea between two hills; a pub with a boat suspended from the ceiling. Every year of her life, the Walter Family had taken their annual holiday near Nanna Glossop's house in Seashaw. They did not stay *with* Nanna Glossop since she seemed not to like them very much and said they upset the cats. (Nanna re-homed cats, and the older she got the bigger the cats became: obese moggies that filled whole sofas, so that there was no room left for visitors.) Even so, year by year the Walters dutifully spent their summer holiday visiting Nanna, and keeping out of her way as much as possible so as not to irritate her. And what tremendous fun they had had leaving Nanna in peace!

Being in a theatrical line of work, they had quickly tracked down The Royal. Gracie remembered every show she had ever seen there. Stage sets hung in her memory like so many handkerchiefs on a washing-line—drawing rooms, gardens, railway stations, fire escapes, blasted heaths . . . She remembered a Captain Hook with hair down to his waist; a puppet ostrich who flew through space to live on an asteroid with a duck. Caravan holidays do not allow for babysitting, so she had been taken along to all sorts of unsuitable, adult plays. Looked at askance by the ushers for bringing a child to see *A Streetcar Named Desire* or *King Lear*, Ellie Walter would say, 'Don't worry: she'll go to sleep if she's bored.' And it was true . . . though generally Gracie would pick up the story-line before dozing off: who was in love with whom, and whether it would turn out well. King Lear rather reminded her of Nanna Glossop, except that he kept a hundred fat, lazy knights instead of a hundred fat, lazy cats.

Gracie was vague as to what Nanna had died of in the end—a surfeit of crossness? Or had she gone one step too far and re-homed a tiger and got eaten? The need to visit Seashaw passed, along with Nanna. But by then, Gracie had grown so fond of the place that she did not want to go anywhere else on holiday, and kicked up a terrible fuss at talk of Spain or Scotland.

The year they arrived in Seashaw to find The Royal had closed down, Gracie cried all week. She would rather the Isle of Wight floated away and sank (she said) than that the Theatre Royal be gone for ever. Only her genius idea—that they could one day reopen it and run it themselves—had been enough to console her.

Without Gracie's bright idea, would Mr and Mrs Walter have looked twice at the advertisement in *The Stage*? Perhaps. Would they have left jobs and home and travelled far afield to view a derelict and bankrupt theatre? Probably not. But Gracie had a will of steel. Sometimes (she had been told) it made her a bit of a bully. But as she said in her own defence: a person can't help what their will is made of, any more than what height they turn out to be.

❧

A terrible thought visited Gracie, just as she sat herself down in one of the red velvet seats, and she jumped up again.

'Nanna Glossop isn't sheltering here, too, is she?'

The Residents looked at one another uneasily.

But no (Gracie decided on reflection): alive or dead, Nanna Glossop would never have taken shelter in The Royal. She had always hated theatre, and nagged her son-in-law to get himself 'a proper job'. Gracie felt safe to go on:

'*One* of you must remember why you took shelter! You're not old enough to have forgotten *everything*,' she persisted.

In the end, like townspeople besieged by a dragon, they looked around for a volunteer. When no one volunteered, they all stepped back, leaving Miss Melluish in the firing line.

Miss Melluish whimpered.

Gracie beamed. 'Tell me all about you,' she said, with the ruthlessness of a thrush thrashing a snail against a rock.

Chapter Three

Quite Enough Excitement

Miss Melluish needed the longest memory of all if she was to think back to her days as a librarian. For she had seen two hundred years come and go since her death. She was tall and bony, her coat wrapping her round like a flag round a flagpole. Apart from the fact that, under the coat, she was dressed in her drawers, she seemed a very respectable lady.

Sadly, Florence Melluish herself believed she fell far short of respectable, which was a blow, since she had been brought up to think respectability the only thing that mattered. When she said, 'I ran the circulating library in Pump Street,' she might have been confessing to theft or a kidnapping. 'My family's circumstances were very much reduced, you see, after dear Papa died.' She winced as she said it.

'Wassat mean?' asked Mikey.

'They were short of the necessary,' said the actor in a stage whisper.

'*Poor*, if you will have it so!' Miss Melluish burst out, on the verge of tears. 'A life of gentility was no longer open to me. My aunt found me . . . oh dear . . . *gainful employment*.'

'She means she had to get a job,' Douglas Douglass translated brutally, and Miss Melluish winced again.

Gracie pitied Miss Melluish for losing her father, of course, but not for working in a library. It had to be wonderful, to be surrounded by books all day. Not that she could quite picture what a circulating library might be: did the building slowly revolve, or was it on board a bus, touring around Seashaw full of people reading books until they got back to where they started? 'I love books,' she said eagerly, in case Miss Melluish thought that books had gone out of fashion since her day.

The librarian's lower lip trembled. 'Oh so did I. *So did I!*' she wailed.

🌿

On the morning of 14th January 1808, Florence Melluish set off for the circulating library despite the fact that it was Sunday. No one at all was on the streets; the rain was raining sideways. Like flights of silver arrows, it barraged the town, tearing holes in roofs. Miss Melluish said a prayer for any fishermen caught out by the storm, any gardeners whose handiwork was being demolished. Seashaw saw more than its fair share of storms, but this was out of the ordinary. The sky was green. Carts had been blown askew across the road. Somewhere, a pig was squealing. The houses along the seafront would take a terrible hammering when the tide came in later . . . There was no view of the sea from Pump Street, but she knew it was low tide from the quantity of sand in the wind.

Florence wondered what phase the moon was in—such things matter in a seaside town, because the moon says what the tides will be doing. But for days the moon had been hidden by rolling cloud. Such things matter to a sentimental librarian, too. She would like to have made a wish on a new moon or the first star of evening. She would like to have wished . . .

It was all she could do to shoulder her way through the wind. It seemed to be trying to push her backwards, to stop her reaching the door. The library occupied one end of the chemist's shop, but had its own front door. She had to fight the wind to pull the door open. Despite gloves, her hands trembled, and not only with cold but with unseemly excitement. She was warmed by a burning sensation near her stomach. She tried to put it down to a stimulating breakfast of bread and butter, but there was no mistaking: it was excitement. Her heart fluttered.

Ridiculous. To be excited by the prospect of a Sunday in Seashaw Circulating Library.

Her hair came loose and stood straight up from her head. She laughed out loud. Indoors, she had to tame it all over again, cramming it back into a bun, nailing it down with hairpins. She thought, Even my hair is excited today.

And yet just one year before, she had first entered this windowless room like a damned soul re-entering its tomb at dawn. The shame of having to find work, the shame of being poor, of seeing the family home sold and the furniture on sale in the

Auction Rooms had turned her from a buxom plump-cheeked girl into a knobbly twig of a spinster. She spent her evenings at the lodging house taking in the seams of all her clothes, by the light of a stained and cracked oil lamp.

For the first few weeks she imagined everyone who came into the library was smirking and whispering about her. *That's the Melluish girl. Did you hear? Her father got into debt before he died.* But either the people did not recognize her or they did not despise poverty as much as Mama did. Florence's mama had gone away to Sheepsgate, determined to die of shame. Sheepsgate had an excellent tailor of mourning clothes, and Mama believed a lady's appearance was more important than anything.

Was it? Lately Florence had started to wonder.

The men who carted away the furniture to the Auction House had had to struggle with three large wardrobes and four crates of clothes, but not a single box of books. They had actually commented: 'No books—that's a mercy.' Of course, Florence could read perfectly well—both magazines and sheet music—but had grown up without any book but the Bible in the house. A young lady of respectable family and passable looks did not need an education beyond deportment and playing the piano or cards. As for novels—well, novels were simply not respectable.

Whatever had possessed her aunt to find her a post as a librarian when she knew nothing whatsoever about books? Simply to hide her ignorance, Florence Melluish had begun to read the books on the shelves. Adventure. Romance. Travel. People . . .

And her life had filled up with delight.

Soon she barely saw the customers who drifted through from the chemist with their bags of potions and pills to borrow books.

For under her desk, within the secret shelter of her lap, were camel trains bound for Samarkand, soldiers charging into battle on horseback, villains carrying off maidens, and lovers swimming the Hellespont. Ships foundered, explorers ate lizards, pagan souls were saved, and saints were skewered.

To her amazement she found that the chemist's customers were also shamelessly fond of books, and eager to talk about the ones they were returning, the ones they wanted to borrow. They did not 'cut' her on the grounds that her dead father had got the family into debt: they were too busy talking about books. Soon, Florence was recommending titles to her visitors—she no longer thought of them as customers—and they were recommending them to her. The chemist was pleasantly surprised when his trade improved. Now people tended to come in through the library door and drift through to the shop rather than the other way round.

Florence wrote out little reviews in her most respectable handwriting, and shut them inside the covers so that visitors could see at a glance the merits of a book. She never reviewed poetry, though, because who was she to pass judgement on the sublime?

'Poetry is so very . . . *everything,*' Miss Melluish remarked to the vicar next time he was borrowing a book on gardening.

'As is gardening,' remarked the vicar.

So, although she had no garden, Miss Melluish began to read about pricking out and potting on, about grafting and pollinating and how to train grape vines and espaliers. 'It is not like training dogs,' she told the grocer's wife, who smiled and said she had guessed as much.

When Florence unfastened her hair that night, it bushed out from her head so that she looked like a *taraxacum officinale* ripe to shed its seeds. Of course that might have had something to do with the weather: her hair always frizzed when it rained, and for days it had done little but rain or snow or spill roof tiles and thatch-straw over the town. When she looked out of her attic window, the darkness was littered with seagulls and noisy with the sea's roar. Somewhere, an inn sign fell from its hinges. Sand hissed against the windows—and she lived a good half a mile from the beach.

That was when Miss Melluish had decided to go in to the library next morning, for fear sand had found its way in among the books. Pump Street was much closer to the sea than her little rented room, and sand is so damaging if it finds its way indoors.

❧

Even at low tide the sea was roaring, howling, and braying like a menagerie. There would be no visitors to the library, of course, but that was all right. She would sit at her desk and read poetry and plays while the storm raged. She would be among friends. The strangest seething, indigestible warmth was humming under her ribcage: the promise of marvels and impossibilities awaiting her inside each buckram cover.

As fences keeled over and dry stone walls collapsed, gutters overflowed, and puddles formed knee-deep in the dips, Florence Melluish sat in her library amid a welter of words: a thousand rose petals raining (it seemed) from between the pages of her beloved books. The sound of the wooden groynes being swept away was drowned out by the incoming tide. She did not recognize the sound of the stone harbour arm cracking, for who has ever heard such a sound? She did not hear the roof thatches migrate, like giant flying hedgehogs, out of town.

Somewhere mid-morning, she found herself gathering books into her arms, holding them, like frightened children, to her breast, soothing the fears of the characters within them. For Moll Flanders had never seen such a storm. Evelina and Roxana had never heard such destruction outside of war. Even Robinson Crusoe was becoming concerned for his coconut crop and canoe. The Ancient Mariner had plainly seen worse things happen at sea . . . but then the circulating library did rather feel to be at sea, for all it was four furlongs inshore.

Miss Melluish went to the door. It seemed to be locked, but it was only the wind bolting it shut. She barged her way into the street, and the door slammed so instantly behind her that it trapped her skirts. For a whole minute she was pinioned in place, looking down the length of Pump Street.

A sea view. Never before, but now . . . a sea view.

Rampant, maned with spray, armed with the rubble of every building it had demolished, the ocean itself was roaring towards her—a watery beast delivering the End of the World.

After dousing her from head to foot in icy foam, the wave spent itself at her feet. It slurried back down the hill, porridgy with sand, mud, wattle, plaster, plants, and dead birds. A child, knocked off his feet, snatched from between running parents, was being dragged downhill by the tide of rubble. Unfastening and stepping out of her skirts, Miss Melluish escaped the library doors and ran—slow motion in the wind—to grab the boy by one flailing foot and drag him clear.

She could make no sense of the townscape in front of her: a rick-rack jumble of roof-ridges, boulders, carts, and trees. The End of the World is too big to fit sensibly inside anyone's skull. Only one string of words found room in hers: *Miss Melluish was seen wearing her drawers in the street at noon.*

Everyone was running to save themselves—but so discreetly, in silence, without uttering a word. How strange. How bizarre. How courageous. Then she realized that their screams too were part of the flotsam being swept away by the noise of the sea and the hiss of the rain. A nearby building toppled in seeming silence.

Her employer, the chemist, barged into her, skidding on the slippery cobbles. '*Run! Run!*' he mouthed, face red with shouting. She waved a vague hand towards the retreating salt-slime. *But it has gone now*, the gesture said. How fortunate that the freak wave had stopped short at the library door. A miracle, for otherwise the books might have been soiled.

'*The tide is but halfway up!*' bawled the chemist, pummelling at her with both fists. (His hands were full of money from the till; he could not grab hold of her arm.)

'But the books,' said Miss Melluish mildly.

It was all very well, you see, for the chemist to grab up Saturday's takings and run for high ground. When one has been put in charge of twelve shelves of books, what is one to do? Must *The Orphan of the Rhine* swim for her life? Must the tales of King Arthur's knights be tossed into deep water and lost for ever like the sword Excalibur? Must Peregrine Pickle drown?

24

Besides, one freak wave did not signify. Almighty God had distinctly promised there would be no repeat of the unpleasantness in Noah's time. The sky might be as dark green as seaweed; the lighthouse and jetty might be gone, but a second Flood was out of the question.

She battled her way back through the library door and bolted it against the storm. Then she set about taking the books off the shelves. She apologized for disturbing them. She explained the need to evacuate the building. She found herself putting them into piles, not according to size, but according to love: those to be saved first, should the wind break in and start to tear page from binding. Those she did not greatly care for—Walpole and Cobbett—she left on the shelves. The little volumes of lyric poetry she slipped into the pocket of her coat, which she put on over her sodden bodice and drawers. It stopped her body juddering with cold: 'Not because it is wool,' she told herself, 'but because it has poetry in the pockets.'

The storm paused for breath. Miss Melluish smiled round at her seventeen stacks of books, her seventeen pillars of wisdom and joy.

Then a second wave punched in the windows. The ground shook. The backwash scraped the library wall like the scaly flank of some lumbering dragon circling the building. It scoured the ground from under Andrew Street and left the houses there hanging over space, their contents spilling out like the insides of a gutted fish.

Miss Melluish sat down at her desk and picked up a book she had never read. Indeed, she could not remember ever seeing it on the shelves, or the name on its flyleaf. She opened it at random and read out loud:

> *'I have since written what no tide*
> *Shall ever wash away, what men*
> *Unborn shall read o'er ocean wide . . .'*

She turned the page.

> *'Death stands above me, whispering low*
> *I know not what into my ear:*
> *Of his strange language all I know*
> *Is, there is not a word of fear.'*

The third wave broke down the door, hungry for Literature.

❧

'They say the sea came in as far as Tivoli Park,' said Eugenius Birch and thus, in his gentlemanly way, drew the stares of the others away from Miss Melluish.

'Never! That's got to be half a mile!'

'I seen some storms close up,' said the lifeboatman. 'Nothing the like of that.'

'Oh you poor lamb!' groaned the actress, and went to stroke Miss Melluish's hair which, during the telling of her story, had sprung loose, dripped wet and was now expanding into a halo of frizz.

'Did the chemist come back and save you?' asked Gracie, desperate to know the end of the story. 'He did, didn't he!'

The other residents of The Royal turned as one, and she knew she had said something truly stupid. It came to her in a rush, like a winter sea: Miss Melluish had not been rescued.

❧

As the tinctures and potions, lotions and remedies tinkled from the chemist's shelves and swirled together, purple, red, and lemon-yellow, another nameless colour had escaped the mouth of Florence Melluish to be swallowed by the ocean. She was swept out to sea, her body never found, her death barely noted among the hundreds of others along the storm-battered coastline.

❧

Gracie knew she should not ask, but her curiosity was ravenous. 'Why did you choose to live here? After, I mean. Why The Royal?'

'Was it the operas you liked, dear?' suggested Lily Oliver. 'You being so classy.'

Florence pulled a book from her coat pocket and rocked gently forward and back, clutching it to her chest. Its pages were a solid, unreadable wad of paper pulp.

'Do we not think Miss Melluish has been sufficiently upset for one day?' asked Eugenius Birch, doing his best to spare her more pain.

But Florence, having said the worst, seemed able to say more. 'For a time, I dwelt in the Bettison Library on the other side of the square,' she said. '*Such* an elegant establishment. The ceilings so high that there was a need for ladders to reach the books and for servants to climb them! A thousand and one books! Beautiful.

Tea was served there, and dainty little cakes. Card games every afternoon. People went there to be seen in their most fashionable clothes.' Wistfully she looked down at the drawers protruding from under her coat. 'A thousand and one books! Mr Bettison had *such* perfect taste. He became manager here for a time, you know? When his library was pulled down, I came here. It was close by, and Mr Bettison must have thought it respectable or he would never have bought it.' She added as if struck by it for the first time, 'Some theatrical plays are almost as exciting as books.'

The ghosts murmured their agreement, and briefly wished they had been alive (or even dead) in the age of Bettison's Library & Tea Rooms.

'I never been in a library,' said Mikey the Mod, and mentally added the fact to his list. Mikey had a long list of things he had not done before dying. It helped him to stay angry.

Gracie replaited one of her plaits. She buttoned up all the flap buttons on her pockets. She retied both her trainers. But it was no good. Curiosity was still chewing on her like a puppy.

'Do *you* remember the flood?' she asked the man in the oilskins.

'What do you take me for, Noah?' said Douglas Douglass.

'Well what *do* you remember?' she persisted. Like a squirrel with a nut, she instinctively knew that inside an awkward outside there was always something worth getting at.

'Nothing I wouldn't sooner forget,' said Douglas Douglass.

Gracie replaited her other plait. She unbuttoned all the flap buttons on her pockets. She got out her handkerchief, folded it and put it away again. But it was no good.

'Have you *really* never asked before?'

She could feel them trying to ignore her. She could feel them all trying to shut the doors to keep out a sea of trouble.

'Have you *really* never told each other your stories before?'

Pale glances met and glanced off one another.

'We do not . . .' began Eugenius Birch.

'We have never . . .' began Roland Oliver.

'Who cares?' said Mikey belligerently. 'I don't.'

'None of our business,' said Douglas Douglass.

The splendid Lord George expanded his chest; his stiff shirt-front crackled and buckled with the weight of the words behind it. He gripped one lapel. 'This charming abode is all any man needs! What has the world to offer better than music! Drama! Spectacle! Comedy! It is the very stuff of merriment and gaiety. Why, if I had my beasts still . . .' Lord George stalked up and down the centre aisle flapping frilly shirt cuffs at the stalls and circle. 'When we came here, we left behind our toil and sorrows! We left behind differences of birth and rank, our fears for the future, our past failings! We united in merriment. In song! In sensation! We are become a brotherhood of merrymakers! The Past is . . .' (his hands urged the others to join him in saying it) '. . . PAST!'

Gracie looked around her at their faces, sepia coloured, like old photographs (except for the lad in the bent strawboater with his face painted black). Merriment was not the word that sprang to mind. In the corner of the pit, the painter's paintbrush scratched drily across the canvas and left no mark. Again that subhuman noise sounded from backstage: a bellowing yelp tailing away into a shriek. No one but Gracie turned a hair.

Then the rear doors banged open and everyone flinched. Their heads were still full of Florence's story and they were half expecting the sea to spill into the auditorium. Instead, the head of a ladder intruded. An electrician had come to check the wiring.

'I'm going down to the sea,' Gracie told the ghosts. 'I promised myself. The sea every day. The sea from Day One.'

'Nice,' said the electrician dully.

'Want to come?' said Gracie to the ghosts.

'You're all right,' said the electrician sourly, and thought what a pain children were, always telling you things you did not want to know.

They flickered. The ghosts actually flickered, like guttering oil lamps.

'We could go to the library if you like!' Gracie persisted.

'Do I look like I got the day off?' snarled the electrician.

Miss Melluish had put her fingers in her ears, shaking her head at the thought of stepping out-of-doors.

Eugenius Birch placed himself in front of his fellows. 'We do not go out of this place,' he told Gracie, and his low whisper was more convincing, more final than all Lord George's booming talk of merriment.

❦

So Gracie walked down to the sea alone. It was a glorious summer day, the sunlight hazy, gauzy, a-glitter. The sea was still and steely flat: she tried to picture it gathering itself into a single fist to punch the lights out of Seashaw. She tried to picture all the seafront buildings flattened or in ruins. Impossible. All her life she had been coming to this town, with its beach and shops and caravan parks and happinesses. Now it was home. That was impossible to imagine, too. Something nudged her—something large and damp nosed.

'Oh! Hello, donkey! Have they started the donkey rides on the beach already? Wonderful.'

The light was so strange that the wind farm, miles out at sea, appeared to be floating in mid-air, like countless tiny angels. Impossible.

Perhaps ghosts too were impossible, thought Gracie—a mirage, like wind turbines floating in mid-air,

Chapter Four

A BREATH OF HAPPINESS

'There are grants,' said Gracie's father.

'For mould? Mouldy grants?' His wife was unconvinced.

'The Council come free if you're infested—bed bugs—rats. Why not mould?'

'Mould isn't an infestation. It's just a stinky nuisance,' said his wife.

'It's a health risk . . . I should think.'

'So should I!'

'So! There are probably grants!'

Every morning the argument was raked over and brought back to life. Whatever problems The Royal faced—and there were plenty—the oozing, weeping, furry, stinking mould in the auditorium was the worst. It cankered the white-and-gold beauty of the place: an acne of mould. And it smelt with an unwholesome, rotting smell. 'Like a whale with bad breath,' said Gracie's mum who had spent an hour scraping it off with a plastic picnic knife and treating it with anti-fungal wash. All she had to show for it was a bucketful of black strands and a grey patch of wall one metre square. 'Like mange on a cat,' as she put it. Gracie's mum was disheartened. She tried not to let it show, but how could they invite an audience into the realms of magic when the realms smelt like a mildewed fishmongery and felt so clammy cold? 'It's manure backstage,' she observed.

'Manure?'

'Horse manure. Trust me; I have a nose for smells. I am a connoisseur of stinks. I could rent myself out as a diviner of pony poo—a horse whiffler.'

Gracie watched the bright cheery faces her parents put on while they bickered, and was not fooled for a moment. They were worried. Everything was riding on this: hopes and savings and careers. They were certainly too busy to talk of ghosts or floods or angel turbines floating between sky and sea. Besides, even if Gracie had been able to get their attention, she was no longer certain of her facts. Perhaps she had simply dreamt the ghosts.

Sure enough, the next time she tried to visit them, she slipped into the auditorium and found . . . no one. No lifeboatman in oilskins, no lad in black greasepaint, no Miss Melluish fumbling with her hairpins and buttons and words. The street doors were open and somewhere a dustbin truck was emptying a bottle bank: the noise of hopes being dashed.

The stage doors must have been opened up, too, because the big red curtains were bellying out in the draught. Another of her parents' attempts to be rid of the smell.

'Anyone here?' she called. Crash went the bottles and jars into the droning truck. Gracie felt empty and a little foolish. Had she truly imagined them all? How could her brain have invented such a motley bus-queue of ghosts? And given them names she had never even heard before? To solace herself she decided to try on some costumes. During the grand theatre tour, Mr Letts from the Council had shown them the maze of rooms and cubbyholes under the stage, and one of them had still been crammed with costumes. She climbed on to the stage and down the steep steps into the understage, all cobwebby and cluttered. And when she opened the costume-cupboard door . . .

. . . there they all were.

Shoulders sagged and faces fell as, once again, the residents of The Royal realized Gracie could see them. Their cloak of invisibility had been ripped wide open.

'We ought not to go in a draught,' said the Twins, their faces palely gleaming like two silver spoons in the gloom. 'It's bad for our cough.'

'You don't have a cough,' sneered Mikey the Mod.

'That's only cos we stay out of the draughts.'

'Move along please,' said PC Nixon, pointing his truncheon at Gracie. 'Disturbing the peace is a criminal offence.'

'Did the theatre always stink?' Gracie asked in reply. 'I've been here often when it was open: I don't remember the stink.'

The company sighed. They had been hoping they had imagined the little patchwork intruder, but no: here she was again, poking at them with her prying offensive questions.

'You get used to it,' said Mikey the Mod sulkily. 'Get used to anything after a bit.'

'Just a drop of damp,' said Douglas Douglass, his oilskins still dripping as they had dripped for seventy years. 'A drop of damp never killed anyone.'

Gracie resisted the urge to mention Miss Melluish and the Flood. Instead she asked, 'Is it time for a show?'

At once their faces relaxed, their hands unclenched. Lily Oliver beamed and led the way upstairs from the understage. With her dress bunched up in one hand, she made light work of the steep wooden steps. Gracie closed all the big doors (to spare them the draught and noise) and darkness settled back over the auditorium like a damp shroud. The pianist returned to his pit and struck up silent music. Maurice the Minstrel tuned his banjo to the key of A. Lily and Roland sang 'I Dreamt that I Dwelt in Marble Halls', baritone and soprano breathing new life into an old ballad.

❧

The electrician did not know what he was missing. As he balanced on his ladder, dismantling lamps, checking fuse boxes and unscrewing light switches, the Olivers performed *The Comic Opera of Summer Amusement or An Adventure in Seashaw*, playing all eleven roles themselves. For music they had to make do with Maurice on his banjo in white gloves and black greasepaint, and for an audience they had to make do with Gracie and a miscellany of refugee ghosts. But then they had been doing so for a hundred years.

When it came to 'All aboard for sunny Seashaw', Gracie joined in—which first startled the electrician and then annoyed him. He hated kids who showed off.

'I'd clap, but me hands are busy,' he muttered sourly. But for Gracie he was drowned out by the sound of Roland Oliver declaiming, 'The boy stood on the burning deck whence all but he had fled . . .' Throughout the show the watching audience moved their lips, word perfect from hearing it all so often.

The electrician collapsed his ladder and clattered out into the street—'Who closed these doors?'—and Gracie was free to ask at last:

'Do you do the same show every day?'

Lily gave a bell-like laugh. 'Heaven above, no, child! Dear Roland worked extensively in London. His repertoire is simply huge!'

Mikey snorted. Roland ran a hand over his hair and, feeling his bald spot, left his hand covering it. The fact was, to the ghosts of The Royal, every scene and song and verse and joke was as familiar as an episode of *Poirot* or *Friends* repeated on TV for the thousandth time.

'Why don't you take turns?' asked Gracie. 'Everyone could put on their own show.'

The actors stared at her as if she had suggested striptease or juggling with scorpions. 'What, *amateurs*? Get you to the Hippodrome!'

'We cannot do owt, us,' said the Twins.

'Boring in't it,' Mikey the Mod sneered. 'I tell them, but they keep on going at it. Same thing day after day.' Everyone was accustomed to Mikey's rudeness, though, and had learned to ignore him. They ignored him now.

'People must keep within the bounds stated,' said the policeman. 'Everyone in their right and proper place. According to the by-laws.'

36

The man in the shiny top hat clutched the lapels of his tailcoat. 'There was a time when I might have brought before you strongmen and fire-eaters, tigers and pythons ... contortionists, orchestras one hundred strong, acrobats and coconut shies ... But the Glory Days are gone, Miss, and we must rest content in the Age of Drab.'

They glowered at her now: the little patchwork thing who dressed like a boy and jangled their hard-won peace.

'You could each tell your story,' said Gracie. 'Dad says people are as good as books if you know how to read them. Look at Miss Melluish.'

At that, Miss Melluish seemed to try and fold herself away like a deckchair in a gale. She should never ever have spoken up. The others plainly agreed with her. Their mouths set into straight, obstinate lines. But Gracie was undaunted. She had played this game at parties and in playgrounds: getting people to speak who have zipped shut their mouths. Fixing her gaze on the Twins, her eyes wide, her face a picture of eagerness, she asked them, 'Was it really, truly *wonderful* back then?'

✿

Joanie and Jim were alike in every way. They both liked bacon cooked crispy, and the colour red, playing dominoes, and popping seaweed by stepping on it. They both hated the skin on custard, earwigs, writing right-handed, and taking medicine. They both had brown hair and pointy chins and one eyebrow higher than the other. They both had tuberculosis.

That is how they both came to be patients at the TB Hospital. Some people came willingly to visit the Sea Bathing Hospital and lie in tubs of warm saltwater and snuff up the good sea air: in short to have a pleasant rest. Joan and Jimmy would not have chosen to go to the Tuberculosis Hospital. Until someone discovered a cure for TB, it was like sitting in a draughty station waiting room waiting for that black and gasping steam train, Death. The beds were hard; the truth was harder. Soon Joanie and Jim would be dead. Meanwhile, all around them, the joyous world of Seashaw waltzed on, riotous with a fun they had never even tasted.

On summer nights, the beds were wheeled outside on to the veranda and the patients could lie on their backs watching the dark and surging sea, deep and hungry as Death. Meanwhile, stars turned handsprings overhead, and behind them blazed the great sputtering glitter of Seashaw: largest constellation in the Fun Nebula. Music. Fireworks, train whistles, and charabancs. The fun fair. Wild animals. Wilder people. Laughter.

Laughter was not encouraged at the TB Hospital. Not that the nurses were killjoys, but laughing stirs up the mucus in the lungs and can lead to coughing fits. So laughter could end in tears.

But Joanie and Jim were ten years old. They had never eaten fried fish out of a newspaper parcel. They had never danced the Lambeth Walk or gone carol singing. They could neither of them swim or skip or join a team (unless it was a quiz team). And they had missed so much school that they were as ignorant as fleas, so a quiz team was probably out of the question as well.

❦

'This death business,' said Joanie one night, from her bed on the veranda. 'Don't wanna go on my own.'

'That's why I come along,' said Jim. 'We stick together, you'n'me, right?'

There was a long silence during which a tram took a bend too fast and everyone on board let out a happy shriek. A policeman's horse galloped down the road.

'Know what I want, Jimmy?' said Joan as the noise of the Scenic Railway rumbled in the distance like thunder. 'Wanna ride on a Galloper. That would be grand, wouldn't it?'

It was the longest sentence his sister had spoken for a week, and long enough to coil itself round Jimmy's heart two-and-a-half times at least. 'That's what we'll do, then,' he said and sat up in bed. The night was as warm as tepid tea. The moon was a silver shilling spun into the sky for a bet. 'We'll do the lot.'

They thought everyone else was asleep, but Nelly the Nabob was watching, as usual. Now she put a finger to her lips and beckoned him closer, 'Where are you off to, scallywags?' Jimmy had hardly begun to explain when Nelly unearthed from her bedclothes the vast handbag she never let out of her sight. She brought out a white five pound note and told him: 'Ride the Galloper for me, eh?'

They thought to use the hospital bed for transport, but the veranda steps were too steep. Just as well, because a hospital bed being wheeled through the street would have attracted attention. But parked outside the Eden Dell Temperance Hotel stood a wicker perambulator—the kind holidaymakers could hire for the week. It seemed like a gift—a sign—an omen.

'First the fiver, now the pram. It was meant, that's what.'

Joanie climbed in and her brother pushed.

❧

'We was down at the Hall-by-the-Sea quick as any goat-chaise.'

'It was like getting to Heaven.'

'It was all lit up: hundreds of lanterns, all different colours. Never seen a rainbow at night before.'

The man on the door was accustomed to peeling penniless children off the windowpanes and kicking them on their way. But Joanie and Jim had the money to get in. They had something, too, in their ashen faces, their sunken glittering eyes, the twig-thin hands that thrust the money at him
—'And how am I supposed to change that?'—
that persuaded him to let them in free. They must not pass through the ballroom, he said—there was a dress code and it was not nightshirts—but they might visit the pleasure gardens beyond. 'Just don't get ate,' he advised.

The sign painted along the front wall of the Hall bore the words

Beasts and Reptiles
from all parts of the Universe

amid paintings of jungle, desert, and mountains. The gardens behind were neither jungle nor desert nor mountainous, but a parkland of fountains and statues and fishponds. It was all the more mysterious for being gas-lit and empty of people. There were parrots flying free, and monkeys in cages, and in a glass tank a green coil that looked to be a hosepipe until it unwound and looked at them, tongue a-flicker. *Deadliest of Snakes*, said the sign.

The lion cage was empty, which Jim thought a shame and a gip until he saw the look on Joanie's face. She got down from the pram and touched the bent bolt, the cold black bars.

'He got away!' she said, and looked up at the starlit sky as if the missing lion must have headed straight for its rightful hunting ground among the stars.

When Joanie and Jim came upon the bears it was a shock: a jet of golden droplets falling gently on to Joanie's hair.

The wall rose up sheer. The cages were set into the wall, bars cemented into the brickwork. And there, like prisoners shaking at their prison bars, stood two great bears. Their yellow eyes rested now on two children in nightshirts and shawls. Ribbons of silver drizzled from their nostrils and, when they opened their jaws to roar, the noise was like millstones grinding. Leathery palms banged at the bars.

'We will get you out,' said Joan. 'I promise.'

It occurred to her that there must be an entry to the cages behind the wall; somewhere the keepers could throw in food or remove the bears while their cages were cleaned. 'We have to get round back,' Joan told her brother. Jim tried to reason with her, but she had promised the bears rescue and a promise is a promise.

'Bears are foreign: they don't know what you said,' Jim reasoned.

'But *I* know,' Joanie said. 'I promised.'

As the two children searched for a way through, over or round the wall, the bears swayed from foot to foot, slapping at the bars. 'S'pose they eat us?' said Jim.

'What's the difference?' said Joanie.

'S'pose they run through the town and eat a baby. Or go up the hospital and eat Nurse Marge.'

41

And then Joan started crying, which had to be stopped, because crying can rattle the lungs about just as much as laughing. So Jimmy suggested, 'Least let's find the Big Galloper 'fore it stops for the night.'

They left the Hall-by-the-Sea, and Jim wheeled Joan along the seafront. Reaching the pier, they took it in turns to sit in the speak-your-weight machine, which said that Jim weighed three stone. But Joanie weighed so little that the machine refused even to venture a guess. They went down the pier a way, to see the model railway and hear a minstrel band singing on the bandstand. But the wheels of the pram kept catching in the planks. And the sight of the black sea swilling below them, the *thought* of the black sea, churning and cold, sent them back to the promenade and the Big Galloper.

Red and gold and topped off with a roof like a wedding cake, the carousel blared out enough music to scare a regiment of horses. But the noble steeds with their streaming manes and tails and harlequin saddlecloths only flared their nostrils, bared their teeth, and galloped joyfully round and round.

'You expect me to change that?' said the roustabout, looking at the white five pound note. And he let them on free. And Jim was in the Light Brigade charging the Russian cannon, and Joan was the Queen riding to Banbury Cross. The touch of the coarse mane, the cold of the glossy flanks, the soft leather reins, the hard golden studs around the saddle, the barley sugar spiral of the pole: she felt them all, as if her entire skin was brand new on and had never felt anything ever before.

'There was blood on its mane, poor thing, but I wiped it off,' said Joanie. 'And then we come here. And that was best of all.'

'A wheel come off the pram and it was too far back for Joanie to walk without a rest. So we come inside The Royal.'

'And you sang to us!' Joan pointed at Lily and laughed. 'And there was two little plays and Mr Roland was in one wearing a crown. And there in another was a villain with hair oil, and a demon come out the floor. And after, there was a sing-along, and we sung, didn't we, Jimmy. We sung all evening.'

'After, we went down on the beach, and there it was: the lion from the open cage, and this woman was taking it for a walk on a lead!' said Jim.

'She said we could stroke him. His name was Lionel.'

'Lionel liked the feel of the ripples going over his paws.'

'Had eyes the colour of piddle, and his mane was all sandy where he been rolling. He licked the blood off my hands.'

'Never went back up the Hospital,' said Jim. ' . . . Well, only to give the money back to Nellie, as we never spent any. In't that right, Joanie?'

His sister nodded vigorously. ''Tain't true 'bout laughing. We sung all evening—and laughed! Didn't cough. Haven't coughed ever since, have we, Jimmy, and we kept on being well right up till now!'

❧

The faces in the stalls and on the stage wore the strangest array of expressions. Miss Melluish was silently weeping again. Lily Oliver covered her mouth and turned away. The closest anyone came to laughing was Mikey the Mod, who gave an unpleasant snort and flicked the back of his hand. 'Codswallop,' he said. 'Little fibbers.'

The radiant smile slipped from Joan's face. She looked round for someone to back her up. 'You was there, Maurice!' she said to the lad with the blackened face. 'You was singing on the pier! You saw us!'

Maurice squirmed, eyes very white within the greasepaint. 'We Nightingales . . . the pier was not our patch.'

'What pier?' said Gracie, trying to change the subject.

The policeman took off his helmet and rapped on it nervously with his knuckles. 'I am sure no member of the constabulary would permit children in nightclothes to roam the streets at night—not in a stolen perambulator leastways . . .'

Joan's husky voice became thin and high. '*You* saw us, Lily! You looked straight at us and said, "Sing up, songbirds! Sing up!"'

'When the houselights are down, child, we see nothing of the audience,' said Roland Oliver, answering on his wife's behalf.

'How come you got in here without paying?' jeered Mikey. 'And you "ran", did you? Her on her last breath, and you *ran* . . .'

'Be silent, boy,' barked Eugenius. 'Keep quiet if you have nothing helpful to say.'

But happiness clearly disagreed with Mikey the Mod. '*Lion on the beach.* Yeah. Little fibbers.'

'*Jimmy! Tell them!*' pleaded Joan.

But before her brother could back her up, the flamboyant gentleman in side-whiskers, waistcoat, and shiny top hat broke in, commanding as a ringmaster's whip, and declared, 'It is all true!'

'The Hall-by-the-Sea was mine. Finest emporium of pleasure anywhere on the globe! Eighth modern Wonder of the World!

In winter, when the circuses were not on the road, there were elephants! tigers! pythons! horses! In summer there were only the zoologicals—and, of course, those performers retired from the ring. Lionel was there in his declining years taking a well deserved retirement. Gentle as any lamb, Lionel. My wife was wont to walk him on the beach in the small hours of the night. I had almost forgot. To think it! I had almost forgot. Far from being a lie, I would say that the meeting with Lionel is proof incontrovertible! These children are speaking the God's own truth.'

The smile returned then to everyone's face. They had not wanted it to be a lie, and now the lion was proof. Unlikely as it sounded, two children, wasted and weary, sick and sorry, really had gone out one night and plundered the world of enough fun to last them a lifetime. More than a lifetime, in fact.

❧

Gracie waited patiently until she felt it was safe to ask her question again: 'What pier?'

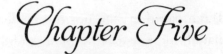

Chapter Five

PIERLESS
PERFECTION

'There is no pier.'

One by one, the ghosts turned to look at her.

'Silly girl. Do you not have eyes?'

'You cannot overlook the pier! It is two-thirds of a mile long!'

'With a bandstand in the middle.'

'A little concert hall at the end.'

'Where the steamers dock?'

'What steamers?' said Mikey. 'I never saw steamers.'

They knew, of course, that modern day Seashaw did not look the same as when they had left it. The audiences who had filled and emptied the auditorium, like tides filling and emptying a cave, had shown them changing fashions, manners, tastes, and haircuts. But it was impossible for any of them to imagine Seashaw without a *pier*.

Eugenius Birch paced up and down the aisles. 'It is no matter. No great matter,' he said, terse, sensible, and then—'What no pier at all?' Finally he turned on Gracie, hands clenched into fists: '*Show me, for God's sake!*'

So, almost by accident, one of the residents of The Royal was persuaded to venture outside. At the last moment, the policeman went along too (perhaps in case the pier had been stolen).

Appalled, the others watched them go, Miss Melluish sniffing at her smelling salts. Douglas Douglass warned them against landmines on the beach, and Mikey shouted, '*Shut the door! Keep the door shut, can't you?*'

'Just going to look for the pier, Mum!' called Gracie as loudly as she could in the direction of the office. Eugenius Birch flinched from the noise.

Outside, looking around the square, he took comfort from the tall town houses, the grassy little park around which they stood. Nothing had changed much. But beyond the square he began to stumble. Traffic queued at the junction: he gagged on the petrol fumes. He pondered over a litter bin cram-full of food cartons and paper cups. He watched the traffic lights so fixedly that his eyes turned from red to amber to green. Eugenius Birch, as an architect and engineer, could picture the future and change better than most. But nothing like this.

❧

He first laid eyes on Seashaw from the sea, arriving aboard a sailing boat. In mooring alongside the old wooden jetty, the boat set the whole structure swaying. The stumpy wooden pier was rickety-legged and broken-backed, buffeted by storm and tide, beardy with seaweed and slime. Eugenius had been hired to build its replacement.

He had built many piers around the coast of England, reaching out into the sea, straining, striving to grasp the horizon and draw it closer.

❧

'Piers beckon to the world,' he told Gracie. 'They say—*Come closer! Come! See this wonderful town of ours!*'

❧

Within months, he had planted the sea with saplings of iron— an avenue of iron trees flourishing curly, fronded brackets. Soon, these metal struts supported a platform, a deck longer than any ship in the world.

'I lived for many years in India, and I believe it may have coloured my soul, for my piers had many a dome and minaret. My paintwork was exotic.'

Beyond the shallows, beyond the sheltering harbour, beyond the reef, beyond the line where the sea changed from blue to brown, stretched Birch's elegant pier. It ended in a fist of iron with landing stages at three different levels. Here the steamers could tie up whatever the time of day—high tide, low tide, mid-tide.

❧

'And here they came!' cried Eugenius Birch. 'Three, four, five boats a day, puffing down from London in six or seven hours, crammed with people bent on joy! As they streamed ashore down my pier, the whole town lay ahead of them. Minstrels sang, bands played, performing dogs and hellfire preachers barked, photographers flattered . . . At first they could not hear the sounds of the town for the swashing of the sea. And the ladies would look down at the water below and shriek, "Oh I am afraid!' so that their young men would have an excuse to put an arm about them.'

Eugenius Birch walked faster and faster; Gracie had to run to keep up. He strained to see ahead. Finally he flung his hand in angry despair at the huge white building blocking his view. 'What is this—this—this slab?' he asked. 'It blocks the view of my beautiful—'

He was running by the time they descended Marine Parade and passed the silted harbour. A clutch of schoolboys went by, practising spitting like footballers. A thin, contemptuous rain spat in Eugenius's face, too, as he stared across the water, along the coast, out to the horizon, tears ill-concealed by a large silk handkerchief.

'I'm very sorry your pier is gone,' said Gracie.

'*I have laboured in vain, I have spent my strength for naught, and in vain.*' He shook his head and turned back to face the way they had come. 'The people. What do the people do? Fifty-thousand souls walked ashore from my pier in a single summer . . . Do they no longer come, for want of a pier? Or where do the steamers dock? The harbour is silted up! Why does no one dredge it?'

The policeman drew out his notebook to list everything that had been taken away without his permission. But there was too much: the great hotels, the stalls and marquees, the ranks of horse-brakes . . . 'Where are the bathing machines? Where are the trams?'

Gracie shrugged, embarrassed. She had no idea what they were talking about. 'Sorry,' was all she could say.

The return journey was no better. They passed the Ivory Tower, a high-rise block of flats that stood where once the Hall-by-the-Sea had boasted 'Beasts and Reptiles from all parts of the Universe'. A clutter of little shops and lock-ups had been marked for demolition, and men with crowbars were busily smashing hinges, locks, windows, shop signs. There was a hoarding saying who the developers were, but a swearword had been written across it in spray paint, so it was impossible to read.

'The lido used to be here,' said Eugenius, pointing to the beach.

'It still is,' she told him eagerly. 'Sort of. Bits of it.'

'And yet not the people? There are so few people!'

Gulls had sliced open a black plastic sack of rubbish and spilled the contents across the pavement.

In search of crowds she led the way back through the town centre. But so many of the shops were for sale, so many were boarded up. There was a pool of vomit outside the Indian restaurant. To PC Nixon's chagrin, the old police station had been turned into a museum. The museum was closed. For some reason, the sight of bald, naked shop dummies in Primark's windows sent him into such paroxysms of rage that he went rigid, and they had to lean him against a wall like a stepladder and wait for him to recover. So Gracie headed back towards the seafront.

And still Eugenius Birch went on asking: 'Where are they? Where are all the visitors? Has the world lost its need for happiness? What has happened to this town?'

'Gone to the devil, plainly,' said PC Nixon.

Gracie was offended on the town's behalf. 'But it's *beautiful*, look,' she insisted, surveying the beach and sea and ghostly host of wind-farm angels floating between sky and sea. 'And now I live here, it's *mine*.' She reached out an arm in front of her and looked along it, pretending it was a pier stretching far, far out to sea.

And Eugenius Birch was moved to tears all over again. 'I fear, child, there is something I should tell you about The Roy—' But seeing the obstinacy in her face, he left it unsaid.

'Nothing is what it was,' lamented PC Nixon.

'No! It's *better!*' declared Gracie and stamped one foot. 'I'll show you! You haven't seen my best places yet. There's the Joke Shop and the Arcades and The Cup Cake Café. There are the Caves and the . . . and oh look! Donkeys on the putting green!'

The policeman placed a weightless hand on her shoulder. 'No need, Miss. We have The Royal. Isn't that right, Mr Birch sir?'

Eugenius Birch stretched out his arm towards the horizon and peered along it. 'For now,' he said soundlessly into the sleeve of his coat.

Chapter Six

YES WE CAN!

On the way back, Gracie introduced Mr Birch and PC Nixon to the world of the Tin Can Man:

> ### THE GRAND CAN-YON
> #### YES-WE-CAN!

'It's all he sells, look!' she said. 'Things that come in cans. Isn't that the coolest thing? Dad calls him Tintin, but his name's Bob really. See how the paint cans are arranged by colour, like a rainbow?'

They stood outside, noses pressed to the window, until a film of white turned the glass opaque. Then they sidled inside.

PC Nixon was frankly appalled by the idea of vegetables and fruit in tin cans and said that beer in cans was an abomination. Cat food was a mystery to him as well—'The meat of cats?'—though he felt a sneaking admiration for the orderly system of stacking.

Eugenius Birch moved among the ziggurats and pyramids of cans, soothed in his grief for the lost pier. He was a man who built in iron, and it comforted him to know that another man felt the same passion he did for a column of shining metal.

'A tin can is like a little suit of armour, isn't it, Bob?' said Gracie to the man behind the counter.

'Uh-huh,' Bob grunted without looking up from his copy of *The Grocer*. 'Keeps out the arrows of germ and rot.'

'There, you see?'

Bob glanced up for signs of a third person, but seeing no one other than Gracie went back to his magazine. He did not much like customers: they were messy and disorderly and thought it was funny to take the bottom can from a stack. But he did have a certain soft spot for the child who visited him every school holiday to wander among the displays asking annoying questions. She might not buy anything, but at least she did not take the bottom can from any of his displays. Not that Bob let his soft spot show. A man in the tin-can line of work shuns softness of any kind.

Artichokes and asparagus, lychees and lighter fuel, coffee and condensed milk, Irn-Bru and Epsom salts, shaving foam and sardines, talcum and tyre repair kits: they lined the 'Yes-We-Can!' in alphabetical order, with outcrops of oddities such as triangular corned beef, and commemorative biscuit tins. Bob told people that he stocked canned goods because they were cheap to buy, easy to stack and slow to pass their sell-by date. But secretly he simply adored cans—the aluminium cylinder in particular. Up in the loft, he had an aluminium coffin for every member of his family in which he fully intended himself and them to be buried *immediately* after death: eight suits of armour tailored to keep out germs and rot.

'I like the picture, Bob,' said Gracie. 'That's new.'

He glanced over his shoulder at the French poster stuck askew on the wall. 'The daughter sent it at Christmas. Why's a mystery. Dancing girls? Still, you got to look grateful, haven't you. Is it me or is it cold in here?'

Eugenius Birch gave a low woof which he tried to disguise as a cough. 'It depicts a dance renowned in certain Paris nightclubs. The mesdemoiselles are dancing the can-can.' Again the woof-woof of a laugh, so loud that Gracie felt sure Bob must hear it.

'Are they dancing the can-can, maybe?' Gracie asked Bob tentatively.

Bob's day was made. He laughed so much that he fell off his aluminium stool with a clatter. 'The can-can! 'Course! Why didn't I—' and he snatched up the phone to tell his daughter he had just got the joke, and to ask her round for dinner.

�

Back at the Royal Theatre, PC Nixon was quick to pour out tales of germ and rot—the vomit, the half-naked women, the vandalism, the buildings gone, the deserted promenade . . . The listeners shuddered in their broken seats, knowing they were right not to have gone. They bewailed the disappearance of the pier, the destruction of the Hall-by-the-Sea, the decline and fall of Seashaw.

'Are *they* still out there?' was all Mikey said, eyes wide, fists sunk so far into his pockets that the linings tore.

Eugenius Birch did mention the fascinating contents of 'Yes-We-Can!', but by then it was too late: everyone's worst fears had been confirmed.

'Nothing's what it was,' croaked the Oldest Inhabitant.

There was no dimming Gracie's faith in Seashaw, though. She was determined to win them over to her point of view. If her ghosts refused to venture out in a pack, then she would have to lure them into the open one at a time and pick them off with her sharp arrows of happiness.

Chapter Seven

Taking THE PLUNGE

'I'll wager one thing has not changed!' said a voice straight from the East End of London. A man wearing gaiters, a smoking jacket, and a woman's hat sucked on a pipe that had not been lit for a hundred years. 'I'll wager Philpot's Bathing Rooms still have the finest machines on the beach. Ah! Philpot's was the place. Civilized as Rome and Clacton put together. Civilized as Buckingham Palace was Philpot's.' And he pushed out his chest like a self-satisfied pigeon.

'I divine our Mr Bodkins is a Philpot man,' said Eugenius Birch wryly.

'I do have that honour, sir, 'deed I do. And I'll wager Philpot's still has more machines than any other on the beach!'

The news came as a terrible blow to Mr Bodkins: not only were the Bathing Rooms gone from the promenade, but there was not a bathing machine left on the whole coast. The shock shook from him a stream of language that was very far from 'civilized'. PC Nixon laid a hand on his shoulder as if he might be about to arrest him for it, but in fact it was a startling gesture of friendship. A more unlikely pair of friends than PC Nixon and Bodkins it was hard to imagine.

'There must have come another flood,' was all Bodkins could think. 'Surge must've took them. Smashed 'em on the rocks. Tragic.'

'Ah! The bathing machines!' said the photographer, a seedy little man with chemical-stained fingers. A black cloth draped one shoulder of his shabby suit. 'I gained all my work down among the machines. That was my territory, and a tasty territory it was. What a scantness of clothing! What a deal of pulchritude.'

And then, to everyone's astonishment, the policeman punched him.

❧

A heatwave had spilled trippers by the thousand on to the beaches of Seashaw. The heat had sipped up so much sea and turned it into mist that the beach was all but fogbound. PC Nixon was finding it difficult to patrol the sands. His horse was in danger of treading on holidaymakers, and it was almost impossible to spot naughtinesses.

It was PC Nixon's duty—his object in life—to stop naughtinesses. Young single men must only swim from one end of the beach, young ladies from the other. Between them sat families sweltering in a no-man's land amid a clutter of spades and parasols. Public morals demanded that even fully clothed courting couples must not sit too close together. The by-laws prohibited canoodling in public, and PC Nixon was a stickler for by-laws. He was also a prig.

'Mind where you're going!' complained a voice out of the mist.

Already Nixon's horse had stumbled into a hole, kicked over a boy's sandcastle and trodden on a picnic. Bathing machines loomed out of the mist like small houses on the move. What if a pickpocket was working the beach? Or some tramp was begging? Or sweethearts were stealing forbidden kisses, hidden behind these curtains of white mist?

To add to PC Nixon's troubles, his horse Reg had recently developed a liking for Rosie, one of the mares pulling bathing machines in and out of the sea. Always before, he had been able to rely on Reg to steer a straight course up. Now Reg was inclined to *drift* diagonally in the mare's direction. Just to be on the safe side, he shouted into the fog, 'Stop that unseemly behaviour this minute! I can see you!'

Just as he reached the waterline, Reg collided with a ghastly figure—black and headless. A photographer was crouching over his tripod and camera, half hidden under a black cloth. As Reg breathed down his ear, he fired his flashgun in surprise.

The flash spooked the mare standing peacefully between the shafts of a nearby bathing machine. She reared up and lunged forwards, jerking the reins out of her driver's hands and plunging into the sea. A pile of clothing tumbled out of the back of the van, a fusillade of swearwords out of the front. The photographer scrambled to his feet, but instead of running to catch her bridle, rammed in another glass plate, reloaded his flash, and tried for a photograph of the runaway horse.

The mare might have steadied down. But as her owner struggled to recover his reins, the second flash saw her rear up again and set off for France, her brown eyes a–dazzle with exploding magnesium. Instead of a slow waddle out to her usual spot, she plunged like a rocking horse over the surf and into deep water. The bathing machine floated off the bottom, and Rosie the mare set off to swim, nose up, eyes rolling. She swam powerfully, knees clipping her bottom jaw, while spray foamed up behind her and welled over the driver's footboard.

Police horse Reg ploughed into the water after her: a four-legged, lovelorn lifeguard. For it was Reg's beloved Rosie who was striking out for the Continent towing half a ton of prime oak behind her.

'*Stop in the name of public safety!*' shouted PC Nixon drawing level with the driver of the bathing machine. 'I might have known it would be you, Bodkins, causing a disturbance!'

Both horses were swimming now, and PC Nixon was wet to his waistband from the bow–wave that swept round Reg's broad chest.

'I done nuffin', you Bow Street sand-jockey. Fool fires off a flash-bang and 'fore I know it Rosie's up to her oxters in the oggin. If she drowns I'll swing for that happy-snapper, so 'elp me.'

Rosie was not yet showing signs of drowning. There could be no turning back, though: one big wave might roll over both bathing machine and horse. All sight of the beach was soon swallowed up by the sea fret, all sounds of the beach by the swash of the waves. When they emerged suddenly into bright sunshine, they might have been in the heart of the ocean.

Reg drew level with the cart shafts. PC Nixon leaned out of the saddle and tugged loose the buckles and straps that hitched

Rosie into them. She swam clear, ears flat against her head, veins bulging in forehead and neck. Describing a wide circle in the glittering sea, she set off the way she had come, eyes rolling in the direction of her owner as if to say *enough's enough*.

❧

'I had to make a split-second decision!' PC Nixon told a rapt audience of Residents. 'If I was to render assistance to Bodkins here, I had to dismount and climb aboard the machine!'

'What d'you mean "*dismount*"?' jeered Bodkins, baring a set of teeth as handsome as a whelk stall. 'Your 'orse dumped you in the oggin and took off after Rosie!'

❧

Nixon felt the weight of his boots the moment he hit the water. His head went under and he feared he was set to patrol the seabed for ever and a day, blowing his whistle at turbot and having to shine his boots with seaweed. But catching hold of one wheel of the bathing machine, he managed to clamber upwards. Bodkins did not appreciate having his smoking jacket wetted by the man who slumped down beside him.

Thus the two found themselves at the prow of a drifting oak boat: no keel, no oars, no tiller, just a sort of gypsy caravan rising and falling on the swell. For ten minutes they waited—to see if it was going to sink—to see if the tide would carry it ashore again. Not a word passed between them. The only sound was the chattering of PC Nixon's teeth and the squelching of his boots. He would like to have told Bodkins he was under arrest, but could not think of a suitable offence to charge him with. That upset him: some people memorize the Bible; Nixon had memorized the Statute Book and all the local by-laws.

'*Why do you go about like that?*' he burst out with sudden irrational spleen. PC Nixon was a dapper man, a proper man who prided himself on being smart at all times. Something inside him curled up like a hedgehog at the sight of Bodkins in filthy cricket flannels, gaiters, smoking jacket and lady's hat.

Bodkins glanced down as if he had never given his clothes a thought before. 'Lost property,' he said. 'I pick 'em up at the Rooms. Yer day tripper leaves all sorts at Philpot's and never comes back for 'em. Hat, coats, shoes, trowsies—I ask you, how can you go home without your strides? But they do. Waste not want not, I say. A fing of shreds and patches, me.'

' . . . of ballad songs and snatches!' cried PC Nixon delightedly. 'You are a Gilbert and Sullivan man?'

'Love it like bread and jam. See *Pinafore* at The Royal, did you?'

'The best yet!—after *The Mikado*, of course.'

''Course. And *Pirates of Penzance*.'

PC Nixon decided then and there to treat the incident not as a crime but as an accident. No fan of Gilbert and Sullivan could possibly be capable of a wrongdoing. He took out his notebook to write an account of his 'rescue of bathing machine 34' . . . only to find the paper sodden and his pencil gone.

'Fanks,' said Bodkins gruffly.

'Huh?'

'For cutting Rosie loose.'

'Oh, I er . . . ' said Nixon.

'Love that 'orse,' said Bodkins.

'So does Reg.'

'*I say! Is it time yet?*' asked a third voice.

❧

Clarabel had spent the morning in Philpot's Bathing Rooms having a jolly time and trying to pluck up the courage to go swimming. She knew that Seashaw was a little *vulgar*, but sea bathing was not. Sea bathing was fashionable.

At parties in London people often said, 'Living so near the sea, you must often bathe, my dear?' It was tedious to keep saying she did not. They might start to think her a coward or—worse still—behind the times.

So after a morning at Philpot's, listening to young men trying to play the piano, and reading old copies of *Punch* magazine, Clarabel made that steep, scary climb down the cliff steps and (despite the mist) found her allotted bathing machine, Number 33.

At least she thought she had. She found, instead, Number 34.

The driver was already up on his driving seat at the front. Clarabel did not address him (hated speaking to the lower orders) but simply ducked under the drop-canopy at the back, climbed inside and took off her clothes. Folding them carefully, she rested them on the top step, along with her flounced and woolly bathing costume and matching hat.

At that very moment, the bathing machine set off with a lurch, toppled her off her feet, and splashed forwards into the sea. Clarabel, being a first-timer, had no way of knowing anything was wrong. She clung on grimly to the wooden bench against the wall. A damp towel hanging from a peg slapped her rhythmically in the ear. And she waited for the machine to reach a suitable depth of water and to stop. She dared not attempt to struggle into her costume; it was complicated enough in daylight and when the floor was not heaving.

It would soon be over. No one would see how nobly or ignobly she took the plunge: the patent fold-down back-canopy would hide her from everyone's eyes but God's.

In fact no one need ever know whether she even ventured down the ladder into the chilly water or just stayed where she was and rode back to shore looking damp, pink-cheeked, and invigorated. Clarabel pinched her cheeks and looked around for her clothes. Surely she had set them down somewhere near the door?

She had not realized that bathing machines actually *left the bottom* when they drove into the sea. To think she had never noticed them rocking and bobbing behind their stocky horses. Clarabel's stomach began to object to the swaying motion. Ridiculous to feel seasick thirty yards from the beach! Surely the wretched driver would call out to her when the machine was in place—when it was time to begin the silly rigmarole? Ridiculous that she did not even know whether the wretch had stopped. Ridiculous that she could not find her own clothes—or even her bathing costume—in a space the size of a coal hole.

'*Is it time yet?*' she called, in tones as regal as a lady can manage who is wearing nothing at all.

❧

Bodkins looked at PC Nixon. Nixon looked at Bodkins.

'*You have someone aboard?*'

'Sounds like it.'

'*Who?*'

'Gawd knows. A stowaway.'

There was no hatch between the driver and the compartment behind him. That would never do: a driver might stick his head into the van and see what he should not. But without a hatch, Bodkins could not stick his head in and reassure his passenger either. '*You just sit tight, lady!*' he bawled. 'If I was you I'd give swimming a miss today. There's jellyfish around.'

There was an unhappy gulp from the van and then a tremulous: 'Very well. You may take me ashore again.'

'Very good, ma'am.'

The machine perched for a moment on a foam-tipped wave, then slithered down it and sailed on, revolving slowly.

PC Nixon boggled at him. 'But she must be told!'

Bodkins shrugged. 'She ain't noticed this far. What the eye don't see, the 'eart don't grieve over.'

'But her life is in peril!'

'You tell 'er, then. Climb round and break the bad news.'

So PC Nixon clambered over the roof of the bathing machine—only to find the drop-canopy was down. Fold by fold, spoke by spoke, he laboriously raised the heavy canvas awning and fastened it with its straps.

Down in the van, daylight flooded in as the canopy rose. Clarabel was confronted, slice by slice, with a view of the ocean. Nothing else. Just the ocean. No sign of land.

And then a pair of wet riding boots, a pair of wet legs, were lowering themselves down from the roof. And then a man in

64

uniform was standing on the threshold, looking at her with the oddest expression on his face.

Clarabel screamed.

❧

Five minutes later, PC Nixon rejoined Bodkins on the dashboard. He was unwilling to talk. Bodkins too was quiet. Clarabel was talking enough for both of them.

'*My father will make you pay for this! I would have you know that my father is a director of Bobby's Departmental Store! Father will make you sorry! Father will see you drummed out of the Police Force! Father will take away your licence!*'

'I tried to explain,' whimpered Nixon. 'I tried my best.'

Bodkins shrugged. 'Uppity-tuppity, hoity-toity mare.'

'*My father will inform the Chief Commissioner of Police! This is kidnap! This is abduction!*'

PC Nixon tried to explain that it was, strictly speaking, False Imprisonment and not Kidnap, but the lady in the bathing machine was not listening.

They drifted into another patch of mist. A falling tide had carried them out to sea; they were firmly in the grip of off-shore currents, floating out of the jaws of the estuary and into the Channel, starting to turn south, drifting and spinning. Bodkins wished he had a pair of reins to hold: he always felt better with a pair of reins in his hands. 'A man can swim to France from Dover,' he observed. 'Been done.'

'So . . . which way's France?' asked Nixon.

'Gawd knows.'

'*Take me ashore! This is an outrage! My brothers will horsewhip you!*'

'Maybe we'll fetch up in 'appy 'Ampshire. I got a cousin there.'

Then something happened which was as British as beef and onions, as awe-inspiring as the National Anthem. A British Navy battleship loomed out of the mist, its prow a giant cleaver of grey steel swinging their way. The ship had no idea they were there, and swept them aside on her bow wave.

❧

'Were you all killed?' asked Gracie while the others were still holding their breath in suspense.

'Nah, fank the Lawd,' said Bodkins, 'just bleedin' petrified. Nixon went over the roof—to see if the bizzom was drowning or just screaming to pass the time. She was down on her knees, promising to fit churches up with bells an' feed the starving an' all sorts, if she was spared. Nixon comes on with the comfort and cheer, and gives 'er his jacket . . . and by the time we got ashore, his goose was cooked.'

'There was nothing for it,' said PC Nixon in a doom-laden whisper.

'As they steamed off, the Navy spotted us, fank the Lawd,' said Bodkins. 'Put out a gig to take us off. They put a rope on Number 34 'n'all—tried towing 'er back, but she broke loose.'

'Whereas I did not,' said Nixon, his voice cracked with sorrow. 'Clarabel told me we were engaged even before we got back to Seashaw.'

Bodkins did not understand. But then Bodkins had never been troubled by Propriety or Respectability, whereas Clarabel and PC Nixon knew the whole unwritten rule-book for being a good Victorian. An officer of the law who sees an unaccompanied lady without her clothes on, while floating in a bathing machine down the sea lanes of the North Sea, is absolutely honour-bound to marry her.

'She made my life a misery,' the policeman lamented. 'Wanted me to sit around all evening in a suit and a cravat. Got me promoted to Sergeant, then to Inspector. Got me a medal for the rescue. Had me living in the family house up by Quark Park. In the end, she told me I had to give up the Force and join the family business—Bobby's Departmental Store.'

Nixon looked around him to see that they all understood the enormity of this crime. He drew out a postcard from his breast pocket and showed it to each person in turn: a portrait of a dozen policemen, their helmeted heads displayed, like coconuts on a coconut shy, above the words

Seashaw's FINEST
Wish you a happy visit
To Seashaw by the sea

'I loved my job. Law and Order is what I am. When I refused, Clarabel turned snippy. *Nag nag nag.* Night and day, *nag, nag, nag.* Next year she went silent instead: spoke not a word to me. Silent nagging. Could not even bring herself to *like Gilbert and Sullivan!* Said she would not be seen dead at The Royal!' (Lily Oliver let out a gratifying gasp of horror.) 'Right! Can you imagine? Culture? Art? Drama? Not she. So I came along on my own. Safe haven. Met up with Bodkins. *The Mikado* again, I think it was.'

Bodkins nodded. The pianist in the pit hummed a few lines of '*He's gone and married Yum Yum*', stroking the keys of his silent piano.

Henceforth, PC Nixon—when not patrolling the town on Reg—had spent each evening at The Royal, hiding from his dreadful snob of a wife.

To everyone's surprise, the elderly painter volunteered one of his rare comments.

'Bodkins should have blinkered that horse of his. Then she would not have been startled.'

A tear crept into PC Nixon's eye now, as he thought how different his life might have been if Rosie *had* worn blinkers. Or if the photographer's flashgun had failed. Or if they had all been born into the twenty-first century, where young women did not seem to care who saw them walking about half naked.

Bodkins had fonder memories of his bathing machine than of any wife or child. He smiled fondly now, as he thought of Number 34. 'Came right back, she did. Like a n'oming pigeon, Washed up under the pier. Was quite an attraction for a while. I'd sit up top, and point her out through the planks. "That there's the machine I drove to France and back in the Great Bathing-Machine Cross-Channel Race of 1875," I told the trippers. Gullible saps. Many's the beer they stood me, for my heer-o-ical escapade.'

The pianist struck up silent music. Maurice the Minstrel tuned his banjo to the key of A. And they all sang a song called 'I Married a Mermaid', which had a great many verses. Gracie thought she caught the sound backstage of tap-dancing: *clippety-clippety-clip*, but decided she was being ridiculous.

Chapter Eight

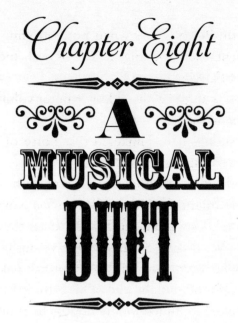

A MUSICAL DUET

Finding a secret horde of ghosts is quite as thrilling as locating an abandoned sweetshop. At night Gracie savoured the thought of unwrapping them, like chocolates, and tasting their pasts. While her parents made an endless round of banks, solicitors, council offices, and building firms, she persecuted the Residents.

'I think you should all get up on the stage and tell your stories!'

This time, when they ignored her, she stood on the brink of the orchestra pit and harangued the man who every day sat in front of the carcass of an old upright piano. Its back was gone, its workings were hanging out, like a skeleton falling out of a wardrobe. The candle-holders on either side of the music stand wagged to and fro like the windscreen wipers on a car. And though his fingers expertly roamed the keys, not a note of music ever sounded.

'What's your name?'

'Shadrach, Miss.'

'I think your piano is broken, Shadrach. I can't hear anything.'

'But I can,' said Shadrach. 'Inside my head. Beethoven would testify: the best music is heard inside one's head.'

'Who's Beethoven?'

'Beethoven was a deaf pianist.'

'Are you deaf?'

'I am a pianist. Inside my head I am a great concert pianist. In life, however . . .' If he thought he would be allowed to stop there, he had underestimated Gracie's barbarous curiosity.

'Go on. What did you do? Tell us. We won't tell anyone else. Miss Melluish told. Bodkins and the policeman told. What did you do?'

Shadrach gave a shudder. 'In life, I supplied music for people to *eat* by. I was a pianist at the Assembly Rooms. I played music for people who cared more for a chop than for Chopin, more for their choux pastry than their Schubert. I gained my release one November night when the Assembly Rooms caught fire. I played until my arpeggios burned in the air like embers. The last music I heard in life was the timpany of falling chandeliers and the clamour of a fire engine.'

❧

Several of the Residents glowered at Gracie as if to say, *Happy now?* What did she suppose she had achieved by reminding Shadrach of a ghastly death a hundred and twenty years before?

But the lad with the banjo and the blackened face reacted quite differently. He sat down on the edge of the pit, like a swimmer by a swimming pool, and reached his banjo towards Shadrach.

'You can play this if you care to, sir,' he said. 'I could teach you.'

Shadrach eyed the boy's shoes and spats dangling into his little underground preserve. Grudgingly he plinked a string, and the banjo (being itself a ghost of a banjo) gave a satisfying *ping*.

'Did you ever work the Assembly Rooms?' Shadrach asked, stiffly polite.

'Not me, sir. It burned down before I was born. The Blackbirds were strictly hotel lawns and beach. But lordy, we pulled the crowds!'

'Wage or hats?' asked Lord George, drawn into the conversation despite himself.

'I beg your pardon, sir?'

'Were you paid a wage, or did the Blackbirds pass round a hat?'

'Ten hats!' said Maurice proudly. 'One would not have held a morsel of what we took on a good day! I was on one-per-cent-of-the-takings-and-bring-your-own-banjo.' At the news of this paltry pay, all the show people threw up their hands in dismay, but Maurice would not hear a word against the Blackbirds. 'I would have played for nothing, I would. The Blackbirds were better than any niggers in Seashaw.'

Gracie gave an audible gasp. 'You can't say that!'

'Why?' A spark of defensive pride lit Maurice's eye. 'Who was better?'

'I liked the Hurly-Burlies, misself,' said Bodkins.

'The Dixielanders were smartly turned out,' said PC Nixon. 'But I do confess the Blackbirds were good. Only time I ever saw *Iolanthe* sung by niggers.'

'Stop it! No one uses that word who's halfway decent!' said Gracie stamping her foot in fury.

'Did anyone ever see the Dandycoons?' asked the photographer, unwisely. Gracie scooped a handful of sand out of a fire bucket and threw it at him.

Maurice and the photographer looked around them for someone who could explain what they had done wrong, but the others were just as bewildered by Gracie in full battle cry. '*How would you like it if someone called you names like that?*'

'Nothing unsavoury about my Swanee Minstrels. They were a quality act,' said Lord George. 'I found them in Bromwich while the circus was touring.'

'Where's Bromwich?'

'I've never been there, wherever it is,' said Mikey the Mod.

'Good public houses. Terrible audiences.'

'I said *how would you like it?*' raged Gracie.

'Bromwich?' squeaked Maurice, fanning himself with his straw boater, trying to cool his blushes.

Mikey champed on a wad of imaginary chewing gum. 'She thinks you're insulting niggers, Maurice.'

Again that pleading look—an appeal to the assembly for understanding. 'But how can I insult a nigger? I *am* a nigger! A nigger is the best thing you can be!' Both he and Gracie had reached the brink of tears.

'No you're not. You're a thick idiot dressed up to look like . . . like . . . ' She tried to remember which words were allowed and which were not: the rules kept changing.

'Shakespeare's *Othello*?' suggested Miss Melluish, trying to be helpful.

'Are there minstrels in *Othello*?' said Roland Oliver anxiously. 'I do not believe I ever saw it staged with minstrels.'

❧

Maurice Hopper was only thirteen when the Great War broke out. Born on the day King Edward came to the throne, he entered the world to the music of the National Anthem being played outside the nursing home, by the Seashaw and Sheepsgate Silver Band. It may have been that which put music in his soul. Or it may have been the banjo he inherited from his Uncle Savile.

By 1915, the boy could be seen every Sunday sitting on the sea wall trying to play along with the various troupes performing on the promenade and the beach. Maurice had set his heart on becoming a nigger-minstrel.

At first his plucking trailed behind the band, finishing several seconds after they did. It so annoyed the Leader of the Blackbirds that one day he took off his straw boater and skimmed it like a discus at the boy on the sea wall, catching Maurice a slicing blow across the neck. The St John's Ambulance Brigade had to staunch the blood. The bandleader was so appalled at his own sin of temper that he prayed on his knees for Maurice, outside the first-aid hut. Afterwards he let the boy keep the straw boater. Next to his banjo, that hat was Maurice's most prized possession. He determined to become not only a minstrel but a Blackbird Minstrel. Before his fifteenth birthday he was wearing spats over his school shoes, a striped blazer, and was standing on the lawn of the Metropole Hotel performing 'I wish I was in Dixie' to a crowd of eighty. The hotel guests sitting about under parasols drinking lemonade and fanning away the bees were clearly so wealthy that

73

even his father was impressed. His mother could not quite recognize which of the Blackbirds was her Maurice underneath the greasepaint, and congratulated the wrong lad, but he had not the heart to put her right.

There were a lot of ladies holidaying alone that year. Their beaux were away at the Front, soldiering, having a jolly time—or possibly not. By the following year many of the white muslin dresses had given way to black crêpe. Their beaux would not be coming home. By 1916, the Blackbird Minstrels were made up entirely of schoolboys and men over fifty, but went on performing, keeping people's spirits up.

The war was a far distant monster, a murderer who only got in touch by telegram:

WE REGRET TO INFORM YOU ...

Young men returned home maimed, or not at all. But the war was not actually happening in Seashaw. Even in 1917 it was still a shapeless, faceless misery which sobbed on the other side of the English Channel. And Seashaw was (as ever) the remedy to gloom and fright and weariness. It was Happiness-on-Sea.

Then the bomb dropped.

On a sunny day in August, Maurice was upstairs in the bedroom of his house in Windsor Avenue prodding away at a bowl of sand to toughen up the skin of his banjo-plucking fingertips. He heard the drone of an engine. British aeroplanes had become a familiar sight and sound. This was a different noise altogether. Maurice pushed open the sash window and stuck out his head. So he was in time to see the Gotha biplane grumble and rumble

74

eastwards over the town. It did not so much as peck or shudder as it shed its last bomb.

The bomb landed on Number 39. The blast broke windows all along the street, like a skipped stone shattering the shine on a pond. Maurice saw it happen as in a Newsreel at the cinema—silently—since the explosion had temporarily deafened him. The air around his head swarmed with familiar objects—roof tiles, curtains, a suitcase handle, the pages of a book, a sock. For whole minutes nothing happened. Then all that was left of Number 39—three teetering walls—crumpled inwards. Everyone's gas lamps flickered as the gas main ruptured, and then the pile of rubble went up in flames.

While his father fretted over the insurance forms next day, Maurice polished his church shoes, and taking his banjo for moral support, went to the Army Recruiting Office to join up. If the German Bosch could bomb Number 39 Windsor Avenue, there was nothing they would not sink to.

The recruiting sergeant asked Maurice about his banjo. For one terrible moment, he thought he was being told he had to leave it behind. But the sergeant was only sharing a passion—'I'm a ukulele man myself. Always good for morale, a sing-song.' He was in a jolly mood: the bomb in Windsor Avenue had already brought eight new recruits.

The next day there was a concert at the Royal Theatre to raise funds for the bombed-out family. There were one-act plays, magic-tricks, and patriotic speeches. The Blackbirds led the community singing. And standing on the stage, looking out at a white and gold auditorium echoing with cheers, Maurice shed tears of pure joy that cut channels through his black greasepaint. When he came home, he would be a professional minstrel, on two per cent of takings. But nothing would ever match his pride at singing 'Way Down upon the Swanee River' in the Royal Theatre, to a sea of waving, sandcastle Union Jacks.

For an encore all the minstrel bands joined together to sing 'I Wish I Was In Dixie', and for the first time Maurice did not wish himself anywhere of the kind. Seashaw seemed the finest place in the world for any boy to become a man.

⚜

The trenches had nothing to offer of white or gold. Already the mud had slurped down every colour, along with several million lives. Nothing but brown remained: mud and pain and fear and rats and orders, flowing like sewage along the endless trenches of Cambrai.

Maurice's banjo was indeed welcome, and for all it would not stay in tune in the damp and cold, the men in his Company did not care. Inside two days he had been made to sing every song he knew. When his banjo case fell apart, the Company captain taped it together with his own puttee tape in return for a rendering of 'Mississippi Miss'.

Maurice stuck up a picture postcard of Seashaw Pier over his bunk but the vibration of the big guns collapsed the mud walls, and Seashaw Pier simply disappeared, along with his bunk. During Maurice's second week at the Front, a story went round which some men believed and some did not: a football had found its way into no-man's-land, and a handful of German and English troopers had declared a truce—just for an hour—so as to enjoy a friendly game of football.

'That old chestnut,' said the captain. 'I heard that story last Christmas. And the Christmas before. It never happened.'

'I heard it from a man whose brother was in D Division and he heard it in the hospital from a nun. A nun wouldn't lie, would she, sir?'

'We should give it a try,' said the Socialist who did not agree with the war.

'We could have a sing-song with Jerry,' said Welsh Taffy. 'Hopper here could knock out a tune.'

'Used to love music,' said the lieutenant with the dirty bandage round his head and began crying again.

After one glass of Finn's whisky—the first alcohol ever to pass Maurice's lips—he too expressed the opinion that War was a bad idea—that the world should be like the Royal Theatre . . . but bigger, obviously . . . with everybody singing along: not the same notes, necessarily, but in harmony.

And somehow, what with the lack of sleep and Finn's whisky and the captain gone to HQ to query orders, and the fear hotter than scalding bathwater, and three unburied bodies watching him, eyes open . . . somehow the wild idea became a wilder reality. Taffy tied a white flag to a rifle and waved it above the parapet. The Socialist snatched Maurice's banjo and tossed it over the parapet, talking about the Universal Brotherhood of Man. Maurice, who had been in the trenches for ten days and not slept above three hours in all that time, went after his banjo like a dog after a bone. Picking it up, he began to tune it—there in the middle of no-man's-land.

'Don't tune it, *play it!*' hissed the Socialist, emerging over the parapet on hands and knees, closely followed by Finn with the whisky bottle. So Maurice played and sang . . . though it came out a bit wrong:

> *I wish I was in Seashaw, hoorah, hoorah*
> *I wish I was in Seashaw . . .*

His hands shook with cold, fear, and weariness. Two more filthy, trembling greatcoats dragged themselves into view. Taffy's flag waved in time to the music.

Hoorah! Hoorah! I wish I was in Seashaw . . .

Then the German machine guns opened up, and the interesting experiment into the Brotherhood of Man came to a messy, mud-caked end.

❧

Maurice had no memory of his return journey to England. Yearning desire, like a stretcher, carried his spirit from the slaughterhouse of Cambrai back to the gilded splendour of The Royal. His banjo was tucked under one elbow, his mud-brown uniform had resolved itself into striped blazer and cricketer's flannels. His face was even blacked as if ready for a minstrel-concert.

❧

After his story was told, all manner of memories blew through the auditorium of The Royal, like a blizzard on a sunny day, as Residents recalled some father, son, grandfather or ancestor swallowed up by the Great War. They all thought they had put it behind them, but something like that—well, it kicks Time so hard that it makes a dent, and thought slips back down into the dent and can never quite escape it.

'Yeah. So why *do* you paint your face?' asked Mikey, insensitively. For him, the Great War was no more than a period of history he had studied at school.

Maurice was bewildered. He had never thought about why he wore the trademark black greasepaint. 'To look like a nigger, of course.'

Again Gracie gasped. 'Don't say it! It's just not ... How would you feel, being called .... being insulted by an idiot like you!'

Maurice put the arms of his striped blazer over his head and curled up in a ball.

'A word is surely only as good or bad as the speaker intends it to be?' said Eugenius Birch. 'A palmful of letters? Surely not. Any word may be an insult, when spoken with loathing. Any word may be foul when spoken by the foul-minded. It is not the word that does harm. A word has nor mass, nor sharp edges, nor venom. Does Maurice use the word with evil intent? I do not believe so. On the contrary ...'

'*What word?*' begged Maurice.

'Ask a black person, why don't you?' Gracie snapped at him.

The minstrel's eyes opened wide. His teeth flashed white in his painted face, and he giggled at her silliness. 'Golly gosh!' he said. 'How would I do that? I never met a real live black person in my whole life!'

Chapter Nine

Play DIXIE FOR ME

So he was easy to persuade. Gracie lured Maurice out of the theatre with exotic promises of foreign music.

Once, a hundred years before, Maurice had dreamed of travelling to America's Deep South, standing on the banks of the Swanee River and listening to real minstrel music while cradling a banjo in his arms as round and shining as a full moon. Life had taken him to France instead and left him face down in muddy carnage.

Now, Gracie led him at breakneck speed through the streets of Seashaw, holding one arm aloft: 'Follow me! Follow me!'

No minstrel band was playing on the beach. The seafront hotels had been turned into flats, and no choir sang on the lawn. No palm court orchestras played. No striped blazers or straw boaters. Nobody rattled spoons against their kneecaps or played a harmonica outside the Mechanical Elephant Public House. There was not a banjo in sight. To a melancholy man, it could have looked as if a flood of years had washed minstrelsy out of Seashaw altogether.

But as he studied the faces in the street—faces of every nationality—Maurice took hold of Gracie's arm so tightly that she could almost believe she was feeling his grip. 'Oh, the music!' he whispered. 'The music must be tickety-boo!'

He was bewildered by the charity bookshop where the owner liked Wagnerian opera and German lieder. Why, he asked, had the man not been shot as a German collaborator? Or at least shut up in an internment camp.

'He does work for charity,' said Gracie charitably.

'But he's a Hun-lover!' said Maurice. 'More niggers, if you please, Miss!'

'Only if you promise never to say that word ever again.'

She took him to the Polski Schlep where, on a big old boom box, Magda Umer was singing Polish lyrics as full of shushes as a lullaby.

She took him to the Bombay Duck where they stood outside the kitchen window and listened to bhangra.

She took him to the Italian ice-cream parlour where the radio was always tuned to Heart FM because Giovanni despised Italian restaurant music. (Also, he liked to annoy his mother-in-law.)

They went to the beauty parlour where the beautician played CDs of lapping water and wolves howling, and had a tattoo on her thigh.

The Goth shop, Dracula Sucks, was sharing its music with the whole street, but its frenzied drumming sounded too much like machine gun fire, and Gracie had to prise Maurice out from behind the wheelie bins and hurry him onwards.

In HMV, Maurice stood transfixed beneath the TV screen and watched singers who made minstrels look like mechanics newly crawled out from under a car. The music pulsed through him, giving him the strangest impression that his heartbeat had been restored to him. His feet could not stay still. He danced soft-shoe shuffle, in time to hard rock. '*Oh Gabriel blow that horn!*' he roared at one point, and the loudspeaker system wowed and crackled for a moment.

Last of all, Gracie took him to the vinyl store, where Nat King Cole crooned tunes about the moon, and Maurice leaned against the speakers so that his hair trembled with pleasure. 'Oh, Miss!' he whispered, eyes closed, 'I fancied the Blackbirds had music! In France I thought the Welsh Fusiliers had music! But I did not know the half of it till today!'

❧

'And there were real live American singers!' he told the Residents when they got back to The Royal. 'Most of the words were sung too loud to hear, but some were in praise of gardening, I think, for they sang a lot about hoes. They were uncommon proud of their hoes . . . Lady minstrel's too, in bathing suits, by golly! The cat's whiskers!—oh beg pardon, Miss Melluish. They were genuine article! Dixie! The real thing!'

The rest of the assembly were dubious. His sad history had reawakened their own memories of the Great War. His sunny, puppyish enthusiasm jarred on them. Or perhaps they were annoyed that, by going out, he had somehow betrayed them.

'I shall go again!' said Maurice, blind to their scowls. 'Gracie says that a band plays on Sundays up at the Fort!'

The Residents looked even more uneasy. What, must they call the little patchwork intruder by name now?

Shadrach the pianist bobbed up in his orchestra pit, like a prairie dog from its hole, and asked warily, 'Will there be Elgar played?'

'Course! Everywhere!' Gracie said, keeping her fingers crossed in case it was a lie.

Shadrach nodded curtly in Maurice's direction. 'I might come along, then,' he said, hands still poised over his silent piano.

Chapter Ten

Remind ME AGAIN

'So do you remember that concert?' asked Gracie of The Royal's very own Songbird. 'The concert before Maurice went off and got . . . muddy.'

Several of the Residents nodded.

'As if it were yesterday,' said Lily Oliver. 'Do you remember, dearest?'

The actress's husband shot her the strangest look, then recovered himself. Laying one hand to his forehead and stretching out the other towards the Golden Past, he declaimed, 'How well I remember! The sea of paper sandcastle flags, the singing, the patriotic fervour!'

'You were in the audience yourself by then, of course,' said Lily stroking his arm with the tenderest affection. 'You quite escaped the War, you wretched man.'

The Victorians and Edwardians turned on Roland demanding an explanation. Had he shirked his duty? Had he refused to serve? Had he ducked conscription?

The actor's embarrassment was plain to see, but he said nothing in his own defence. It took his wife to do that.

'Roly was dead before War broke out,' she said. Her husband's sky-blue eyes pleaded with her to leave it at that.

'Tell us,' said Gracie.

❦

Roland Oliver, as a young man, had a magnificent mane of hair. That was not, of course, the reason he became a star of the stage: that was entirely down to his acting genius. But to hear the chatter in the Stalls bar during the interval, you could have been forgiven for thinking his looks were the secret of his success.

'Such a strong jaw!'

'Such marvellous teeth!'

'That little smile he does . . . '

'Ah yes—and so good in profile.'

'Well, that's the nose. He must come of noble stock, don't you think?'

'Does his voice not thrill to the core?'

'It does. It does. Oh but that *hair*!'

'Well naturally, the *hair*.'

When he was not appearing at the Aldwych or the Savoy in London, he was touring the provinces, and not with one play but with three in repertory, so that Sunderland or Chester might fill the theatre three times over and revel in the genius of Roland Oliver. Tirelessly he bounded from triumph to triumph, from

Shakespeare to Sophocles, from Restoration to operetta. It was said that theatre ghosts (and every theatre has those) materialized especially to see him perform. At least his agent said so.

His Nordic good looks had their disadvantages, of course. Wherever he stayed on tour—in digs and guest houses—the landladies and their daughters would fall desperately in love with him. They brought him breakfast in bed and incessant cups of tea, waited on the stairs so as to brush against him accidentally. They stole his cufflinks and collars for keepsakes. He would even find them hiding in his wardrobe when he went to hang up his suit at night.

In self defence he married, his choice falling on the fortunate Lily Alium for three very good reasons. One: she was playing opposite him just then in *An Ideal Husband* and the publicity did wonders for the play. Two: she had enough talent not to miss cues or draw bad reviews, but not too much to outdo him. Three: she was in the Profession, and actors (like Orthodox Jews) should never marry outside their religion. No one can live with an actor, except another actor.

Since she was a Seashaw girl, they bought a house in Seashaw—though you could hardly say they settled there, for the relentless touring went on—Blackpool, Liverpool, Hartlepool, Poole. As Lily observed wryly, 'The marriage vows of touring actors should be "for Richmond, for Porchester, in Skegness and in Eltham".'

Then came *Macbeth*. The Scottish Play. The Unlucky Play.

Not that Roland was superstitious, of course. (When did you ever hear of a superstitious actor?) Besides, measures can be taken to fend off bad luck. Running three times round the theatre before every performance, for instance. Never speaking the word 'Macb—' . . . *that* word, especially not inside the theatre. No, Roland Oliver laughed—ha ha!—in the face of superstition, as he set off for the auditions. It was a good role and, if he could land it, a grand opportunity to work with The Great Beerbohm Tree.

His first audition was a great success.

'Admirable, dear boy,' the great man said, 'though the hair will not do.'

Astonishing. Never before had Roland's golden mane been anything but welcome. 'It is not authentic, dear boy,' boomed the voice from beyond the footlights. 'The man was not a Viking, he was a Scot. Red hair, dear boy. Red hair.'

And in his eagerness to oblige The Great Tree, Roland hurried off to a pharmacy and bought henna dye.

His wife scolded him next day for not reading the instructions on the box, though Roland knew in his heart of hearts that chemistry had nothing to do with it: the curse of the Scottish Play had descended on his head. His glorious crest—once likened to a 'golden pheasant perched on the statue of a Greek god'—was now scarlet. Vermilion. Pillar-box red.

He went at it with boot black, then with peroxide, but all he succeeded in doing was scalding his scalp. While Lily stitched pieces of suede into 'a sort of a battle helmet any Scots warlord might wear', her husband shut himself in the bathroom, larding his head with cold cream to dull the pain.

In his panic, the script he had so quickly and easily memorized slipped clean out of mind.

At the second audition, The Great Tree admired the actor's lack of vanity in making himself look exactly like a moth-eaten twelfth century warlord. But he lost all patience when Oliver could not remember any of his lines.

It grew back, of course. Within the year, the golden coxcomb was back, flopping across his forehead, curling around his ears. His face appeared on many collectible postcards. His name appeared on countless playbills. And whether he was playing Hamlet or Othello, Jack Worthing or Captain Ahab, Uncle Vanya or Sinbad the Sailor, his hair was never again any colour but blond.

But the gods are pitiless. At the age of thirty-eight, he noticed his comb was often blond, too, that his pillow was regularly threaded with gold. His hair had turned treacherous and begun to desert him. Unable to believe age or peroxide could be the cause, he blamed the curse of *Mac*—, that Scottish Play, and fear struck all over again. When, on stage, he fluffed his lines, he instantly recalled that appalling audition when he had looked inside his head and found all the words missing.

A dreadful notion nudged its way into his skull and would not be pushed out again. He became convinced that with every falling hair another line of script trickled out of his memory. Losing one's hair is bad enough for a matinee idol. Add to that a failing memory and he is lost.

A full head of hair had clearly, somehow, held the words in place. For he could remember knowing the entire works of Molnar and Oscar Wilde, whole acres of Chekhov and as much as anyone reasonably needed to know of George Bernard Shaw. He had known the lyrics of a dozen operettas, and the moves for thirty swordfights. Now he was forgetting everything he had ever known.

Not that he spoke his fear aloud. A true gentleman must put on a brave face, keep his disappointments to himself—but an actor without a memory is like a bird without wings.

The fear undermined him. His nerve failed. He found excuses to turn down plays in London. (Provincial critics were so much more forgiving than London ones.) He declared himself weary of living out of suitcases and staying in dreary northern hotels. He no longer toured so far afield. But at night he regularly suffered the same nightmare: It was opening-night, just before curtain up, and he was running from person to person backstage—'*I have no script! No one has given me a script! What am I to say?*'—until at last someone would take pity on him and hand him a sheaf of paper which he promptly dropped, pages spilling into the pit and down the stage trap. Crawling about the stage, gathering them up, he found every one of them . . . blank. He would wake up wet with sweat.

The fear clenched his abdomen so tightly that his fans commented afresh on his wonderful waistline. Fear squeezed on his brain so hard that his vision darkened and lights exploded in his skull, the little bonfires burning up more and more words! His memory was a leaky boat. His livelihood depended on it, and yet he knew it was sinking under him, sinking lower and lower in the water, bringing him closer and closer to cold oblivion and the deep dark. He lay awake at night and wept.

Roland began to suspect that his fellow actors had spotted his weakness and were 'making allowances'. Take the night he had strayed from *Henry V* and stumbled into *The Merry Wives of Windsor*. Loyally, the rest of the cast dogged his snowy footsteps through *A Winter's Tale*, meeting up with Julius Caesar at Philippi, then on through a Birnam Woods lively with Midsummer fairies. Some young chap, fresh from the Sarah Thorne School of Acting, had even performed an impromptu juggling act until Roland remembered his lines and forged on across the blasted heath to defeat the Volscii and marry Cleopatra, only to founder in *The Tempest*.

No one was so impolite as to mention it afterwards. The audience did not seem to have noticed, so no harm done.

But Roland Oliver had noticed.

He took to wearing hats, in the hope that it would stop the leak. But hats only wore away more and more of his hairline, like the sea eroding chalk cliffs. A monkish tonsure appeared like magic. He tried combing his locks backwards, sideways and forwards, but they only furled outwards again and left the window open for more words to fly away into air, into thin air.

So one night, after 'drying' five times during a performance of *Man and Superman*, Roland Oliver climbed to the roof of The Royal Theatre Seashaw and threw himself off the parapet, to the sound of thrushes whistling in Hawley Square.

❧

Lily was still terribly cross with him for it. 'What did you think you were doing? In the middle of a three-week run? With no understudy?'

❧

For a time, husband and wife had been separated by death—though on some nights his ghost had been clearly visible in the fifth row, especially to the actors on the stage. (Actors have always been more open to The Unlikely than people who lead regular lives.)

Then, during rehearsals for *Peter Pan*, Lily hooked her harness to an overhead wire and leapt off the Upper Circle in an elegant imitation of flying. The wire had not been properly installed and broke like a shoelace, dropping her head-first in among the empty stall seats.

'Luckily, it was early in rehearsals, so it did not matter,' Lily explained. 'They were able to get another actress in time. They did not even need to alter the programmes.'

Reunited by death, Lily and Roland Oliver found a new role at The Royal, entertaining others whose need for happiness had brought them back there for ever and a day. Roland was easier in his mind: this show was likely to run and run . . . and run: any actor likes to know he has the prospect of long-term work. And surely Death had put an end to the thousand natural shocks that hair is heir to? No more would drop out? Would it?

Sadly, the old fears still nagged. He checked daily for new corn circles in his golden crop, even though there was no reflection when he looked in a mirror.

❧

It was not Roland who told them all this: it was his wife. Roland Oliver listened appalled as his secrets were spilled to all and sundry. He could not understand how Lily could do it. He could not understand how Lily *came to know it*, when he had gone to such pains to hide his suffering from her. And why would she want to shame him now, in front of his entire audience—unmask him just because the revolting child had asked to know? He blushed henna red. Such was his humiliation that he might have hurled himself off the roof all over again but that suicide was no longer an option.

To his astonishment, the Residents of The Royal did not greet the story with laughter—well, not once Eugenius Birch had ejected Mikey with the toe of his boot. They understood. They grasped the horror of a failing memory.

'With Beethoven it was deafness,' said the pianist.

'With Joshua Reynolds it was blindness,' said the painter in the corner of the pit.

'With the playwright Mr Wycherley it was the power of speech,' said Miss Melluish.

They all knew how spiteful Fate could be.

In fact Miss Melluish, eager to be helpful, ran to the property cupboard in search of a wig, but the mice had made free with the wig basket and what remained looked like the coconut casualties under a coconut shy.

'I know where we should go!' said Gracie. 'The Bong Shop!'

Mikey the Mod slunk sulkily back to his broken seat. 'I never been to a Bong Shop,' he muttered.

'Who has?' observed the minstrel.

But whether out of sympathy or simple curiosity, several of the other Residents stood up, ready to go.

'Is it not worth a try, my adored one?' said Lily Oliver. 'We do not want to lose any *more* of your repertoire.'

And that decided it.

Roland Oliver allowed the appalling patchwork child to take him outdoors in search of a cure, even though the last time he stepped out had been a century before, by way of a swallow dive on to the basement stairs.

'Best foot forward,' said Lily brightly, threading an arm through her husband's elbow. And though several Residents lost their nerve in the theatre porch, a handful found the courage to tag along.

'*Just going to the Bong Shop, Dad!*' called Gracie through the office window.

But her father did not swivel round in his seat to say, 'I'll come! I could do with some plastic dog poo!' In fact, he did not so much as look up.

An unfamiliar pang went through Gracie—a feeling she had never experienced before. But then never before had her parents been too busy to spare her a smile, a wave, a word. There were many demands on their time, she understood that. All the meetings, the form-filling, the worrying, the camping out in the dressing rooms to save paying rent . . . When The Royal was open again, everything would be different: she knew that. Even so, a trip to the Bong Shop had always before been something she did with her dad and a fistful of pocket money. The pocket money too had been forgotten lately, and she did not like to ask. Every pound was needed if The Royal was to do that phoenix thing and flutter back to life. If Roland Oliver could wear a stiff upper lip, so too could she—especially with the prospect of seeing her friend Tamburlaine again, and the Bong Shop.

But the pocket money would have been nice.

The dad would have been nicer.

Chapter Eleven

Tamburlaine
THE UTTERLY
GREAT

'*Is it not brave to be a king? Is it not passing brave to be a king, and ride in triumph through . . .* some place or other,' said Roland, his memory jogged by the extraordinary name. 'I played *Tamburlaine the Great* in Richmond in 1903, you know. I was a triumph.'

'I don't think this is the same Tamburlaine,' said Gracie, and she was right.

Tamburlaine's shop was in the arcade on Hall-by-the-Sea Road. In fact Tamburlaine owned two shops, side by side, hemmed in by the hammering of demolition workers, because the arcade's days were coming to an end.

The Bong Shop was a haven of oddness in a commonplace world. For a start, the air was hazy with coloured smoke from burning joss sticks. The sticks were clutched by Greek gods, brass monkeys, beatific Buddhas and Kali Goddess of Destruction, and gave off such billowing clouds that other items for sale appeared out of the smog by happy chance—a card shuffling machine, a glass unicorn, a glitter ball, a miniature cage of model finches who had real feathers and sang at the turn of a key. The statue of a mermaid loomed into view wearing a feather boa, oven gloves, and a bracelet of Chinese coins. She seemed to be guarding a set of Ali Baba raffia baskets and some wind chimes made of old thermometer cases. Christmas decorations, paper lanterns, and bunting suggested a year-round, all-purpose party in progress, and the inflatable swimming-rings in the shape of horses, ducks, and sharks gave the impression they had escaped from the fish tank in the corner. Alone in the fish tank, a single spider crab lay suspiciously still.

There were Hallowe'en brooms and garden gnomes, chopsticks and jars of garam masala and celery seed, while, overhead, luminous stick-on stars formed constellations on the ceiling. There were dried rose petals and fossilized sea horses, geodes and seashells and the leftover outsides of a cuttlefish; an electric rat whose eyes glowed pink (batteries not supplied). And in among these, like Sherlock Holmes braving a Victorian fog, sat Tamburlaine, proprietor of the Bong Shop.

If there were 'bongs' to be had, Gracie had never found one among the smoke—or perhaps she had without realizing, because she had no idea if a bong was animal, vegetable, or mineral.

'Hey, Tamburlaine!'

'Hey, babe. How's tricks?'

Despite the Russian fur hat and a vague liking for white leopards, Tamburlaine was nothing like his namesake. He was not a fourteenth-century Mongolian warlord and empire-builder. He was Seashaw born-and-bred, and one of seven brothers whose parents had decided they must all have names starting with T. 'Tonka' Tony ran a stock-car stadium in Sheepsgate, Trevor a dry-cleaning shop in Easterbarn. Terry was in road-haulage, Trelawny did spread betting, and Torquil played darts, but not for a living, because he was not very good at it.

'That's six,' said Douglas Douglass after Gracie explained this. 'Who's seven?'

'We don't talk about Theodoric, do we, Tamburlaine?' said Gracie, and Tamburlaine agreed that Theodoric was unmentionable, wondering why the name had come up at all since he thought Gracie the only customer in the shop.

'You here on holiday again, babe?'

'Nope. Here to stay this time. We're opening up The Royal again. Told you we would.'

'Nice work,' said Tamburlaine. It was not a rapturous reaction, but then the owner of the Bong Shop was, at all times, placid and easy-going. Even the fur flaps of his Russian hat were relaxed. Even his eyelids.

'The theatre's haunted, you know,' said Gracie.

'Don't say.'

'Ghosts.'

'Usually the way with haunting.'

'Lots.'

'Right. Well. Takes all sorts. Live and let live.'

'They're nice.'

'Yeah. Well. They get a bad press, ghosts.'

Meanwhile, Roland Oliver hunted the shop for a cure. There were unguents, gels, and creams made from rose petals, transparent liquor with flecks of glitter, nail varnish remover, lurid bubble baths, and sachets of mud all the way from the Dead Sea. There were labels printed in Japanese, Arabic, and Esperanto. Most of the ghosts had forgotten why they had come, mesmerized by lava lamps pluming scarlet blobs through sealed glass jars.

For years Gracie had been coming here, returning home with some priceless treat: foaming bath oil which (her father said) would make her the most beautiful girl in the world; a sherbet dab which (her father said) you had only to lick to be able to speak swaggaboogie; a kazoo that could summon the tooth fairy in an emergency. Her very favourite possession was a light-up Virgin who granted wishes if you said 'Goodnight' nicely enough and counted backwards from ten. Gracie had utter faith in their magic. Surely something here would restore Roland Oliver's hair!

The Residents were less confident. Regardless of which century they had been born into, they had all seen such lotions and potions on sale before to holidaymakers who had left their good sense at home, but brought along their pennies.

'Flim-Flam-on-Sea!' cried Lord George. 'What a splendid establishment!'

Meanwhile, Lily Oliver had found her way through a beaded curtain and into the adjoining shop. 'Come see! Come see!' she called.

The Joke Shop, too, was part of Tamburlaine's empire. At first sight it had none of the exotic mystery of the Bong Shop— just rows of things in cellophane packets. But on closer inspection, these were just as strange. A pair of pink plastic breasts. A highwayman's mask. A light sabre. A snake. Bottles of fake blood. Cardboard hats and a sonic screwdriver; whoopee cushions and plastic dog poo in a variety of sizes. 'Miss Melluish would not have cared for this place,' said Eugenius Birch in a way that suggested he too had his doubts. Vampire teeth. An imitation wheel-clamp. A Roman breastplate. Slip-on duck feet . . .

Tamburlaine, engrossed in his paperback, did not follow them through from the other side of the bead curtain. He would not have been able, in any case, to see the six ghosts, fingers over their mouths, contemplating the fancy-dress racks, and in particular the wigs.

There the things hung, like an assortment of road-kill, bagged up in polythene: glossy or woolly, brown, yellow, black, or green. Each had a name. Should Roland choose *The Blonde Bombshell? The Indian Squaw? The Elvis Presley? The Incredible Hulk? The Phantom of the Opera?* The decision was unanimous.

'He cannot.'

'He must not.'

'In no wise.'

'Not our Mr Oliver.'

'It would not accord with his moustache.'

'Never mind his moustache! It would not accord with his *person*!'

'Not our Mr Oliver.'

'Not the great Roland Oliver.'

'He is simply too . . . He cannot.'

'In no wise.'

It was a fortunate decision, for how would any of the nylon wigs have balanced on the scalp of a spectre? How would spectral fingers have found their way into a stapled polythene bag? How, without pocket money, could Gracie have paid for any one of the wigs? But she was not one to be defeated by a setback.

She called goodbye to Tamburlaine and then, as they stepped out on to the street, whispered a new idea into the ear of Lily Oliver. The actress's eyes grew wide.

Lily's husband scowled. He was, just then, brimming with affection for his fellow Residents who had never before shown such a touching regard for his dignity. But Gracie he still disliked. He blamed her for laying bare his shameful, secret fears. 'What does The Quilt say?' he asked his wife suspiciously.

'Nothing but nonsense as usual,' said Lily brightly, and hooked arms with him once more. 'Let us walk back among our old places, dearest, the haunts of our courting days!'

❦

Like PC Nixon, Roland was horrified by the 'naughtinesses' they passed on the streets. But for him, the worst crimes were what the young men had done to their hair, shaving it all off or cutting it as close as shorn sheep.

'Head lice,' said Bodkins, who had seen the style last in the nineteenth century East End.

'Fashion,' said Gracie. 'Honest.'

'But their memories?' cried the actor. 'Their memories will all be lost to them!' And at once his hand rose to his hair, palm spread over the pink crown of his golden head.

Lily and Gracie exchanged glances. The actress's fingers flew to loosen her corset as she always did before a performance. 'Oh look, Roly!' she cried. 'The synagogue where we were married! Do you recall?'

The Seashaw Synagogue to which Gracie had brought them held no memories for Roland. It may not even have been built in his lifetime. Luckily there was no date written up on the front of the building.

'Oh, say you remember, dearest!' Lily was chirruping. 'My canopy? The crunch of the wineglass under your foot—oh! Our lovely rabbi?' Lily's face was a picture of happiness. 'All those . . . er . . . fiddlers! Yes! All that dancing! How we danced, did we not, dear heart?'

Roland stared at the building in front of him. His mouth began to form a question. The others were clearly startled. Nothing in the Viking features of Roland, the buttery gold of Lily's hair said 'Jewish'. But with a sweeping glance which had quelled chattering audiences in a hundred theatres, Lily Oliver forbade them to speak one word.

'So . . . we . . . ' Roland began, the agitation so terrible in his eyes that Gracie wanted to call a halt then and there, was sorry she had ever whispered her idea in Lily's ear. But Lily had moved into character, and though her knowledge of Judaism consisted of a week playing Jessica in Hull in *The Merchant of Venice*, she was Jewish now from head to foot, inside and out, body and soul.

'Oh, say you remember, beloved!' she cried ecstatically.

Roland looked inside his memory and found nothing: nothing of his wedding, of being Jewish, of Judaism. As far as he could recall, his mother had been Welsh and his father had been a bachelor. But then his memory had betrayed him so many, many times: his wife never. If Lily said it, it *must* be true. Why, already he could remember Jewish friends, dear friends, clever, admirable colleagues in the acting profession! Augustus Harris! Sarah Bernhardt! Jewish, eh? Already the word tasted sweet in his mouth—strange, but sweet.

Roland Oliver had spent so many years hiding his poor memory from those around him—even from himself. He hid it now.

'The happiest day of my life, beloved,' he said. 'A memory to be cherished. *Mazel tov*.'

At first it felt odd and unfamiliar, like a new suit of clothes. But just as clothes soften and stretch with wear, so a role fits itself around an actor—he grows into it. Within the day, Roland felt as Jewish as Hanukkah, and remembered the lyrics of *Yerushalaim Chel Zahav* and could recite a dozen Psalms word-perfectly. Instead of some nylon wig, a yarmulke appeared spontaneously on the balding crown of his head. By the sheer power of thought, by the miracle of belief, the hole in Oliver's sky was patched with a Jewish skullcap, and he had perfect faith that he would never forget another line.

So what if—occasionally—he still drifted from Marlowe to Molière, from Pangloss to Pericles? Nobody mentioned it, and Roland never noticed. As far as he was concerned, God had kissed the top of his head and healed his memory.

Gracie's success rather alarmed her. 'Do you think God will mind?' she whispered to Lily, who looked at her in astonishment.

'He should mind that we are God-fearing actors?' she asked, spreading wide her hands. Her role too was also shaping itself softly to the contours of her diaphanous body.

Chapter Twelve

The MECHANICAL ELEPHANT MAN

Mr Letts from the Council was dismayed to see the change in those nice young people at the theatre, and he immediately blamed himself for letting them camp out there while their application for the lease was considered; clearly the decayed old building was an unhealthy environment. They had both lost weight and looked haggard, as if they had not slept one night since moving in. They still greeted him with eager smiles and cooked him toast on a primus, but he could see it in their faces: Seashaw Disease: a leeching away of hopefulness and energy; the weariness of bears pushing at the bars of a cage.

'No one ever gives us a straight answer. Is there a grant or isn't there? Can we have a bank loan or not? Can we have the lease or not? We just want a straight answer!'

Mr Letts chewed the side of his clipboard and realized how foolishly much he had been looking forward to seeing them. Foolish to have thought these two might want to talk about Judi Dench and Ian McKellen, about his Theatre Club trips to Guildford. He had forgotten that running a theatre is a business like any other. 'I'm sorry,' he said. 'Wheels grind slow, you know. I do have *some* news.'

Immediately their backs stiffened, their eyes brightened, the toast over the primus began to char. 'Yes?'

'I have fixed a date for the structural engineer to call. To check the building over. For any serious structural faults, you know? It's an important step forward in the decision-making process.'

❧

'*Your* turn,' Gracie told the man in the overalls holding the spanner. He appeared only rarely, always from the wings or the flies or the understage where he tinkered purposefully with ropes and pulleys.

'Who, me?'

'Tell us your story. Quick, in case the inspector men turn up.'

'I don't have a story. I just work here,' he said, then corrected himself. 'Worked.'

Shy and soft-spoken, Frank Stuart showed no sign of fear or sorrow. There was no visible bruising where tragedy had struck. In life he had built scenery and props for The Royal. His work gave him a pleasure that absorbed him one hundred per cent. When working, he would concentrate so completely that no one could get his attention—not his wife, not his children, not Death itself. He had simply looked up one day, from carving a tricky dovetail joint, to find he was no longer in his garden shed but backstage at

The Royal where he had been at his happiest. It was an honour and a privilege (he said), and was grateful that the theatre wanted him.

'Best job in the world. Next to elephants, of course.'

'*Elephants?*' Lord George leapt to his feet, 'You have commerce with elephants? Elephants ravish my soul, sir! Elephants are the mainstay of my circus! Elephants hold high the canvas sky of Travelling Entertainment!' He seemed on the point of offering Frank a job with the Sanger Circus, until he remembered he was a hundred and twenty years too late.

Frank Stuart gave a little shrug and looked shyly around. 'I just built the one. In the garden shed, like. See if I could.'

❧

The fact was, Frank Stuart was a genius: he had simply never noticed. Only his wife had noticed, and she could never get his attention long enough to tell him so. She made allowances, knowing that all geniuses are eccentric—though the Elephant did seem a step towards downright madness.

He was no sooner home from his day-job at the theatre than he was in his shed, banging sheets of metal, machining lengths of canvas, oiling pistons, stripping electric wires. His wife began to worry when a vacuum cleaner went missing, a standard lamp, a sewing machine, her brother's motorbike . . . and then, one by one, all the menfolk down the street. It was as if some monstrous idol in the woodshed was demanding offerings and devouring them to the sound of the Light Programme on Frank's portable radio. But in fact the neighbours were simply standing about marvelling at Frank Stuart's craftsmanship. They left home saying, 'Ha! It'll never work.' They returned home and woke their sleeping children to tell them, 'Just wait till you see it!'

Only one minor hitch arose: Nellie finished was too big to get out of the shed door. The end wall had to be demolished. To the accompaniment of *Your Hundred Best Tunes* on the radio, she emerged into the evening garden aboard a trolley. Her face and scalp were missing (to allow for further brain surgery) and Frank Stuart was carrying her ears, but there was no mistaking the nature of Nellie. Nellie was an elephant—an elephant automaton with seating enough for ten along her steely spine, and a wave-able trunk.

The children, who, in their nightclothes, were lining the garden fence, burst into applause (or tears of terror) and Frank Stuart, shuffling his feet amid the planks of his shed wall, allowed himself a shy, crooked smile and said, 'She's coming on, eh?'

On test runs, Nellie charged along at twenty-seven miles an hour, but the Council did not allow that after she went into operation. Her passengers were mostly children, and parents would not have taken kindly to seeing their little ones disappear over the horizon at the speed of a Ford Popular.

Even at eight miles an hour she was famous, though. Hobby mechanics and model-makers travelled from all over the country to marvel at the pistons in her knees, the hydraulics in her rear, while holidaying children at the trunk end tried to feed her sugar lumps. Grown men brawled for the job of mahout.

❧

'So where is she now?' Everyone wanted to know. It was as if Frank, in death, might have brought Nellie along with him to The Royal and parked her outside for forty years.

But Frank was unwilling to say more. He turned on his heel and retreated to the wooden stairs at the back of the stage. Frank's preserve was up among the cleats and ropes and rigging of the flies—that space above the stage from which back-cloths are lowered like great ships' sails. Two generations of living stagehands and designers had shared the space with Frank's inventive genius without ever realizing it. They had felt no brush with him at all, except perhaps when some fleeting, brilliant idea entered their heads which seemed to come from nowhere.

Eugenius Birch (whose genius was very similar to that of the mechanical elephant man) started after Frank. 'Hydraulics, sir! Pray tell me more of your hydraulics! Hydraulics ravish my soul rather more than elephants!'

But a dark cloud had engulfed Frank Stuart. From the deck of the stage they shouted upwards towards the crow's-nest of hoists and crossbeams. 'Where is Nellie now?' And Gracie started singing 'Nellie the Elephant' which was soon taken up even by the Georgians and Victorians who had never heard it before.

Somewhere in the middle of verse three, in a paroxysm of rage, the inventor came down the staircase again, pushed past them, stalked to the edge of the stage and pointed out into the auditorium at the only person still sitting there.

'*He* killed her. *His* sort. His mindless mob of brain-dead dope-head morons!' and he threw his spanner at Mikey the Mod who let out a scream of pure terror.

Chapter Thirteen

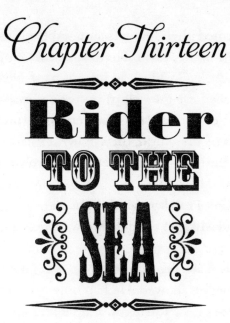

Rider TO THE SEA

Mikey was a Mod—which said all there was to say. No part of his life was untouched by the Mod-ness of Mikey. He wore the parka. He listened to the music. He bought the long jacket with the velvet collar. He bathed in his jeans so as to shrink them to his shape. He had the hair. He dressed for action. Seven mirrors showed him the finished effect, and they were all attached to his scooter. Seven wing-mirrors, six headlamps and a tiger's tail: that was what it took to turn a Lambretta scooter into a war chariot, and Mikey into a lord of the road. He had the good mates. He had the cigarettes. He knew the swearwords . . . and could just about drink a bottle of beer without being sick. He hated Rockers for the very good reason that Rockers hated Mods.

His mother could do nothing with him—which is as it should be when you are fifteen and a lord of the road. Mods (as they informed their parents) are orphans of the universe. They exist on a higher plain. They do not watch *Blue Peter*, they watch *Ready Steady Go*. They do not eat roast-beef-and-two-veg on a Sunday; they eat grey chips out of a newspaper and drink Mackesons out of the bottle. As they cruise their chariots around the battlefields of the world, they draw the stares of pretty girls, because what bird can resist a teenager in velvet-collared jacket and wet jeans?

And on Bank Holidays Mods fight.

'Fight?' said Mikey. 'I thought we were going to pick up dolly birds.'

Luckily his mate Tiger thought he was joking: Mikey hated it when his newness showed. He had only been a member of the Riders to the Sea for a fortnight, and he was still feeling his way. One day, he planned to be Head Stallion of the Riders. In the meantime, he had a thing or two still to learn.

He knew, of course, that Rockers were the Devil's spawn and should never have been born and deserved to be staked out in the desert and eaten by fire ants. But he had not fully realized that the trip planned to Seashaw on Bank Holiday Monday was in fact a prearranged war. The Rockers would go there on their stupid macho motorbikes wearing their stupid biking leathers and duck's arse hair. The Mods would cruise down there, cool as a menthol cigarette, and do battle with them, man-to-man.

'Pell-mell, like the hoplites at Marathon!' said Tiger (who went to Grammar School). 'Take a rounders bat.'

Mikey took a cricket bat (well, where do you get hold of a rounders bat if you don't have a sister?); also a packed lunch his mother had made for him. 'Salmon paste, scotch egg and a Milky Bar. Your favourite,' she said. 'Cricket on the beach. Funland with your friends. How lovely!' and gave him a kiss and a ten shilling note. When the Riders to the Sea stopped for petrol in Ashford, he threw the greaseproof paper and paper napkin away, crushed the sandwich into something which looked as if he might have made it himself, and ate it as though he was biting the face off a Rocker.

The A2 going east swarmed with mopeds. Most had two up: many a Mod warrior had brought his Mod girlfriend. One day, Mikey too would have a girlfriend riding pillion, arms round his waist, gripping tight. It was thrilling. He had not realized that, in joining the Riders, he had joined such a vast brotherhood of right-minded studs. To think! Every one of these dudes had discovered the same truths about life: that it is meaningless and boring; that parents don't belong in a modern world; that nothing matters except the Here and Now, and that the Here and Now both belong to the Mods! Chicks, drugs, music: those are the wheels on which the world runs . . . and Mods run it!

'It's their birthright, right? Police, the Law—they're the sta-bilizers on a baby bike, right?' Tiger told him. 'When you're a man, you do without them, right? There are no rules. Right and wrong? One big lie . . . Two. Two big lies.' Tiger was planning to read Sociology at University.

The road to Seashaw also swarmed with motorbikes: a beetle plague of black leather jackets tattooed with studs and wormy with stupid bits of chain that didn't do anything; boots like sea-divers wear; exhausts noisy as firework night. 'In point of fact,' said Tiger, 'it's illegal not to have a silencer on your exhaust, right?'

Then suddenly, the sea appeared in the distance, like the ultimate wing mirror, and Mikey had to stop himself shouting out, *the sea! the sea!* because on family holidays the first person in the car to spot the sea was the winner. Of course he had put such childish things behind him now. His L-plates were hidden in his panniers and his cricket bat was freshly oiled. He was a Rider to the Sea now, a warrior seeking first blood.

They parked up on the railway station forecourt and headed directly for Funland, a permanent fairground and the chief reason everyone came to Seashaw on a Bank Holiday. From a distance it sounded as if the war had started already, what with the screams and shrieks and clatter, but it was only people enjoying themselves, riding the big dipper and the dodgems and the chair-o-planes. Enjoying being scared. Funland was Mikey's favourite place in the world.

He should not have drunk the bottled beer before going on the swingboat, but he was still managing to enjoy himself at noon. The cinema signalled to him across the acres of rides and booths and noise, its neon sign flashing. There might be birds to sit next to in the dark. 'Go to the pictures, shall we?' he asked.

'We should get to work,' said Tiger, and the Lead Stallion agreed. 'Too many cops here,' said Tiger, and the Lead Stallion agreed. 'Get down the beaches, maybe. Get mixing,' suggested Tiger and the Lead Stallion agreed. So they swaggered out on to the sea front. As they did so, each let slip, from sleeve into palm, various weapons of war.

'Oh! I left my bat on the bike!' said Mikey, aghast.

'Well, go and get it, then, nink. What d'you think we came here for? Catch us up.' So back he went—and found station officials busily sticking tickets on all the bikes:

... ILLEGALLY PARKED ON RAILWAY PROPERTY ...

Hastily mounting up, Mikey drove his Lambretta off the forecourt, wondering how he would find Tiger again among the heaving crowds.

Seashaw had prepared for the Bank Holiday invasion. There were police everywhere, squad cars parked on every street corner. But what could they do? Three thousand bikes and mopeds had growled into town, bent on war. The first window had been broken by ten, the first blood spilt by eleven.

Mikey saw some Mods throw a Rocker's bike off the sea wall, and gave them the thumbs up. If the tide had been in it would have been more spectacular, but the sand would wreck the engine anyway. He saw some Rockers throw a Mod off the harbour wall—could have killed him, the morons . . . But Mikey caught no glimpse of his friends.

The 'Rocker-Billies' gang overtook him by the Lido, swinging lengths of cycle chain. It felt like shrapnel hitting the back of his parka. When he saw them turn and start back towards him, chains swinging, he shot up a steep alley so narrow that one of his long-stemmed mirrors smashed on a drainpipe. Emerging at the top, he found himself in . . . a war zone.

Café tables, timber from deckchairs, shards of window glass, and stones gathered on the beach were all weapons now. A car was on fire—a lovely little Hillman—and a police van was being rocked so violently from side to side that its lamp had come adrift. A man was holding a reddening rag to his head. A blood-soaked boy wielding a car aerial and shouting '*We are the Mods! We are the Mods!*' was being slapped at by his girlfriend who was yelling, '*You've been knifed. Shu'up, can't you? I'm telling you, he knifed you! Look at yourself!*'

Somehow, Mikey wove a path through the melee and down a side street blocked by bollards, so that he had to drag his bike up and over. Then he was out on Marine Drive again and bowling along open tarmac, his heart jumping round his chest like a kangaroo. To the sound of breaking glass, all his thoughts shattered; he could not think, only ride and feel and shout and see, in crisp dazzling focus. Punches, kicks, weapons, burning litter bins, sea, shops, crowds, smudged mascara, broken shoe heels, police helmets, dogs. An overturned ice-cream van bled white blood; tram tracks showed like seams of silver in the black tarmac. Even the Rocker-Billies driving out of the sun were like something on a cinema screen. The gang had spotted him and were riding towards him again, swinging their lengths of chain.

He went straight over the roundabout—clear across its neat blue-and-white flowerbeds. (Alyssum. Mum liked alyssum; every year she planted alyssum.) Over the island and off the other side. He could imagine himself telling Tiger when they met up: *Great stunt! I drove straight over the roundabout, I did. James Dean or what!* (Was it all right to like James Dean? He wasn't a Rocker really—just an American. You could like James Dean, surely?) . . . *clear across the roundabout and away!* He turned in his seat and made a gesture at the Rocker-Billies with their stupid leathers and duck's arse hair . . .

That was when he saw the elephant. A strange enough sight to loom up from behind a bus shelter, a mechanical elephant, but this one was also swaying from side to side. Its trunk was not quite right somehow, detached from the head and hanging on by a single black cable. A gang of youths had set themselves the challenge of tilting it off its feet. They managed it just as Mikey went past—a slow-motion capsize on to a row of parked motorbikes, and then a spectacular shockwave of debris spilling out across the road. He swerved to avoid bits of elephant debris—a cheek—or was it an ear? That was when the front wheel of his scooter slipped into the tram track and wedged. The bike pecked, the back wheel rose into the air and Mikey went over the handlebars. His cricket bat—the one his dad had bought him—went skidding away and away . . .

Unhorsed, the Rider to the Sea was easy prey. Gravel embedded in both hands and one knee, he looked round to find leather jackets materializing like demons from every dazzle of sunlight. He fled the pavement for the beach, sliding down the sea wall on the seat of his tight white jeans. But then there was the impossibility of running in sand—like running in a nightmare—everything slowed down. Wished he'd gone out and bought a rounders bat now: that cricket bat was a Gray-Nicolls junior special edition. It had Ted Dexter's signature on it.

Legs like pieces of elastic—worn out elastic. Wonder why elastic loses its stretch. Does it get tired? Elastic's not a person. Throwing stones now. Someone could lose an eye. Mum always said that about boys throwing stones: someone could lose an eye. I'm only fifteen! But you can't say that. Babyish. Wouldn't listen anyway. Fainites! Pax! Only fifteen! *My Mikey's halfway to being a man, aren't you, son?*

The steps up from the beach—all much too high—tired knees can't lift. Why can't knees lift? And more Rockers at the top, more black demons.

Not really Ted Dexter's signature. Or did he sit down one day and sign lots of bats? A warehouse full of cricket bats? Fainites! Please! *No! Please!*

A police horse gallops by. Its hooves make a tremendous clatter on the tarmac. Horses are good. Silver and Trigger and . . . what was Tonto's horse called? Mounted policemen: Riders to the Sea, sort of. On hooves. Never saw a police horse gallop. At football matches they never gallop. Be all right now. Police won't let them kill anyone. *If ever you find yourself lost ask a policeman:* that's what Mum always said when he was little. *Or a lady with a child.* Horses never look that big on TV. Range Rider used to just jump into the saddle. Was Range Rider's horse really, really small, then? 'Find yourself lost.' Typical Mum, that.

And though the mounted policeman does not come to the rescue, there at last are Tiger and the others! If he can just make them see him. At school next week, the teachers will ask questions. *Got beaten up*, he'll say. No! On second thoughts: *Got in a fight, sir. Running battle, sir. Down Seashaw.* They'll be impressed. They'll pretend to be disgusted, but secretly they'll be impressed: Mikey Phipps the tearaway—from boy to man in one weekend.

They get him in an alley off Hawley Square—a snick off the alleyway, with dustbins in it and *Stage Door* written up on the wall. And they don't stop. Not even when he asks them to. Not even with Tiger pulling on the backs of their jackets and crying like a baby and telling them: *he's a kid, he's only a kid!*

Still they tower over him with their black leather bodies zitty with metal studs and he can see between their legs—between kicks—the words *Stage Door*, and remember waiting there for an autograph. On holiday. Matt Monro. Fantastic. Best holiday ever with Mummy. With Mummy. Mummy! and he thinks, *If I can just make it into the theatre. No one gets killed in a theatre. Do they, Mummy?*

❧

'And I did. Shot between their legs and ducked in here. Nothing to it,' said Mikey the Mod. He had got rather carried away in telling his story: could almost feel the pain, the bruises, the cuts all over again. He had got so carried away, in fact, that he could not quite remember what he had said, but hoped he had given them a suitably colourful and glorious account of his triumphant battle with the Rockers. No detail: just the everyday heroics performed by a true Rider to the Sea. 'So I shot between their legs and ducked in here. Nothing to it.'

Douglas Douglass's two hands turned his sou'wester round and round by its brim, round and round. 'No you didn't, sonny. You never made it. You died in the alley. Got the life kicked out of you by a bunch of yobs.' The others closed their eyes and winced, but they could not have found a kinder way of putting it.

Mikey kicked a red velvet seat. 'Shot between their legs and ducked in here. Nothing to it.'

Not until Frank Stuart climbed down from the stage and walked towards him did Mikey the Mod round his shoulders and cower down again with terror, tears leaking from eyes bruised and swollen afresh by the memories behind them. '*If Nellie got smashed,*

it was Rockers did it! Mods would never. They wouldn't! Rockers did it!
Rockers are the devil's spawn. Tiger says!'

Frank Stuart took hold of Mikey's arm, pulled him to his feet
and drew him away to the rear of the stalls. The others stood stock
still, as if the broken shards of Mikey's story were in their pockets
and would cut them if they moved.

Only the Oldest Inhabitant droned on ' . . . smashed everything in sight—elephants weren't the half of it . . . beginning of
the rot . . . never the same after . . . gave Seashaw a bad name . . .
gangs of hooligans . . . ' until Eugenius Birch said, 'Be silent. Please.'

At the back of the stalls Frank Stuart held little Mikey
close while the boy wept into his oily overalls; wept about
dying before he ever got started; about the loss of his friends, his
broken wing mirror, the torn seams in his velvet collared coat,
and what his mother must have felt. 'I'm sorry your elephant
got smashed. I never saw a mechanical elephant—not working,
I mean,' said Mikey at last, adding one more item to his list of
missed opportunities.

'None left to see, lad. Extinct. Like Mods and Rockers. Plenty
other gangs out there for those as want to be all the same as each
other. But no Mods or Rockers. Was a phase. Like bobby socks
and marcel waves.'

'So they're not . . . out there now? In the alley? Waiting?'
All these years he had feared it. It had wedged itself into his
head, like glass into the top of a wall, the idea that they were
still waiting for him outside the street doors; waiting to finish
him off.

Frank Stuart said that, as far as he knew, the lane outside
had been free of Rockers for fifty years, then steered the subject

round to cricket. His concentration was drifting, though. His eye had been caught by the growing crack in the ceiling above them, the sagging underside of the Dress Circle. When the two rejoined the others, the creator of Nellie the Mechanical Elephant was busy again with his own thoughts, shut up inside the garden shed of his own extraordinary brain.

Chapter Fourteen

NO WORRIES

'No worries. Not a problem,' said Mr Sapper, touring the auditorium with his peculiar rolling gait. He wore a suit and brand new trainers which his life-coach said would slim down his bottom. Fewer pies might have saved him the cost of the shoes, which made him walk like Donald Duck, but the walk added to his air of irrepressible cheeriness. He did not linger long to admire the golden stucco or the chandelier—'nice, nice'—he did not puzzle over the black mould, or count the number of seats that needed replacing—'new right through, total makeover'—but reeled and rolled around the stalls dispensing encouragement. 'Make a list. Anything you need. No worries.'

Gracie's mum and dad followed him, hypnotized by the rise and fall of his little head, the to and fro of his bulgy hips.

'Ideally we want to open in September to catch the Christmas trade, but that's uber-optimistic . . . ' said Will.

'Not a problem. Not a problem.'

'There'll be no Arts Council money until next financial year . . . I don't even have a staff yet.'

'No worries.'

'We want to build a programme to suit the locality—get a feel for what the community actually wants from us . . . '

'Pam Ayres. I like Pam Ayres. And blue comics. Bluer the better.' Sensing they had stopped in their tracks, Mr Sapper turned back. 'But don't take any note of me, right? You put on whatever you like. Seashaw needs this place. Been here centuries, right? Didn't ought to be shut. Man with money's got a duty to put that money to good use, got me?' And on he bounced, Willy Wonka forging a path towards a chocolate dreamland where everything could be paid for in chocolate buttons.

He had emerged from nowhere, this local benefactor, ready to fund the theatre, its performances, its staff, its advertising, its future.

'He will want to decide everything,' Will whispered to his wife. 'He will take it out of our hands.'

But Mr Sapper seemed to have no interest in running The Royal. He did not seem to care what they put on or who came to see it. He did not want to act in the plays, have an excuse to meet his favourite actresses. He did not want the theatre to be renamed The Sapper Theatre. It was as if he had woken up one morning and told his wife, 'Know what, flower? I think I shall give my wallet to that nice couple camping out in The Royal and make all their dreams come true.'

'So, I give you the money: you go ahead and buy the lease. No need to hang about waiting on the banks: I'll pay the first year cash-down! I trust you. I'm a good judge of people, me. I trust you. Let's keep everything in your name. Best insure the place, of course. Let's assume you've got the lease, right: next thing's to get the place insured, right. Can't be too careful. Many a slip twixt this'n' that, y' know? You got the ante? Thought not, I'll fix that up—though it has to be you signs the forms, of course, 'n' pays the premium. Look, I'll put five thousand in your bank tomorrow; bring the forms round for you to sign. But when it comes to the Council, leave me out of it. Everything in your name, right? Leave me out of it. Any questions?'

'Why?' was the only question that came to mind.

'Did you never hear the saying, "Do good by stealth"? I want to help out the town, is all. Town of my birth. Pam Ayres. Fan dancers. Blue comics. Good family larks!—Or Shakespeare, if that's your tipple.'

And he was gone, like an aeroplane dropping sacks of grain to the starving without ever touching down.

❧

'No! No! It's good! It's all good!' Gracie told the Residents. 'Mr Sapper is going to pay for everything, but he wants Mum and Dad to run the theatre!' Her happiness flared like a match and made all the ghosts blink.

They had tried to tell her they wanted the theatre to themselves, that all they wished for was peace and privacy. But like a ball in a skittle alley, she still hurtled through, knocking their plans askew.

In fact, with her own dreams about to come true, Gracie was determined that Mikey the Mod should tick off a few of the ambitions on his endless list.

For fifty years Mikey had lived in fear of Rockers waiting at the stage door for him, wanting his autograph written in blood. Now, when he stepped outside, all he found was a row of wheelie bins and a pizza box.

'I never ate a pizza,' he said.

So she took him to Mod Café where the walls were hung with pennants and tiger tails and photographs of gleaming mopeds. Fifty years before, the owner had been a Mod, like Mikey, and looked back on those days with joy. Suddenly, though, Mikey did not. He asked if they could leave the Mod Café, and Gracie was glad enough, because, despite Mr Sapper, she still did not have any pocket money to buy a pizza. She took him instead to the arcades, where shining stacks of pennies moved like glaciers towards the brink until, in reaching the rim, they loosed noisy cataracts of plashing cash into troughs at knee level. But not for Gracie or Mikey. Penny arcades demand pennies before they are willing to make you rich, and Gracie was out of pennies.

After that, they headed for the cricket ground where the great Fred Trueman had once played in an inter-county match. Mikey made sixty-four run-ups, planting his feet where the great man must have placed his, bowling googlies and leg-breaks and yorkers.

'Mind the donkeys, won't you?' Gracie called as Mikey bowled invisible balls at invisible wickets, but the unexpected donkeys in deep field did not seem much perturbed. (Whose *were* they? Gracie wondered.) In the blustering wind, the scoreboard rolled over to show six wickets down, all clean bowled. To Mikey's surprise, his innings was greeted with applause from the stands. Others of the Residents had decided to join Mikey on his first outing.

'We should go down Funland—ride the Big Dipper!' Mikey told them, his parka fish-tailing behind him as he pranced along ahead of them.

But, as Gracie had tried to warn him, Funland was now no more than a piece of waste ground strewn with cars and potholes. Gone were the Big Dipper, the chair-o-planes, the gallopers, the dodgems, the rocket rides. Gone were the steam organs and candyfloss stalls, the ducks with hooks in their backs, the goldfish in plastic bags, the gaudy nylon teddy bears, the rifle range.

'It's all coming back, though!' said Gracie. 'Honest! Honest it is!'

'So's Christmas,' said Mikey.

'No, no. Honest, it's going to come back! It truly, truly is! They've promised!'

It was certainly hard to imagine, as the wind blew litter up against the parked cars and stirred the petrol-stained puddles into greasy rainbows.

'My Hall stood here,' said Lord George, gradually getting his bearings from the railway lines.

'They took it down to build Funland,' said Frank Stuart.

'Then why, pray, did they take down Funland?' asked Sanger.

It was a sad, unanswerable question.

'The people just stopped coming. Stayed away. Went other places for their fun, I suppose,' said Frank.

'Why?' asked Gracie, her question as sad and unanswerable as the circus master's.

Across the empty wasteland, a neon sign flickered uneasily.

'The Kinema gone too?' said Mikey. His fish-tail parka tucked itself between his legs in the wind; he looked like a disconsolate puppy.

'Oh no. That's still open,' said Gracie. 'Why don't we go!'

❧

The cinema was enough like a theatre to feel comfortably familiar. Gracie found it surprisingly easy to slip inside—wondered if her friends, in surrounding her, somehow lent her their invisibility.

These days, the cinema had not one screen but six. Gracie could have opted for a rom-com, but she hated those. She could have chosen a war movie, but thought Maurice had seen enough of war. They could have watched a Polish movie with subtitles, but only Eugenius spoke a foreign language and it was not Polish. They could have gone for a horror movie, but the last thing Gracie wanted was to add to her friends' fear. That only left the X-rated movie, for which she was too young and the Victorians were far too old. So she chose the cartoon, even though it was the most crowded. They made themselves comfortable perching on the chairbacks of Row K, snuffing up that strange distinctive smell of cinemas.

'Is it pomade?' asked Roland Oliver sniffing the hair of the man in front of him.

'Is it delousing powder?' asked Maurice, sniffing nearby children.

'It's popcorn,' whispered Gracie. 'Should we sell it at The Royal?'

'Certainly not!' said Roland. 'I cannot act in such a smell! It would choke me!'

Afterwards, contemplating what went wrong, Gracie blamed the man who had given the cartoon a 'U' for 'Universal'. 'Universal' plainly did not include Victorians, Edwardians, or anyone who loved live theatre.

Peeping sideways during the advertisements, she saw her friends' astonishment at the noise that engulfed them, their alarm at the vast faces that pounced on their eyeballs, the motion sickness that came with the flashing and reeling images. When the cartoon began, Mikey was happy enough, but the theatricals grew more and more restless.

'Lantern slides. Simply lantern slides,' she heard Roland whisper soothingly to his wife, but she was not soothed. Where were the flesh-and-blood performers; the live actors and actresses? Where were the musicians playing the music? Where the back-stage hands to refuel the footlights and change the set? Where the genius of scenery built by such as Frank Stuart?

'What need do they have of . . . us?' she asked, clutching her husband's arm. 'We are become unnecessary!'

On the screen, surreal landscapes unfurled, and outlandish creatures hurtled about colliding with trees and each other, loud sound effects exaggerating the pain. An enchanted (live) audience ate their popcorn open-mouthed with pleasure. But Row K grew more and more restive. Queasy from the movement, headachy from the epileptic flickering, wall-eyed from the width of the screen, they perched on their seat-backs, a-flutter with complaints. Where was the beauty of expression? The poesie? Where were the *actors*?

And then they began to boo.

Gracie tried shushing them, but it was hopeless. Mikey joined in, remembering the pleasure of making trouble. PC Nixon roared at nearby children who were blowing sherbet out of long plastic tubes over the people in front. His anger had much the same effect as the booing.

An arctic chill laid hold on the auditorium. Bare, sun-tanned arms turned goosy with cold. Mothers slotted toddlers back into romper-suits, children into coats. Large rosettes of ice bloomed across the screen, blurring and then obliterating the picture. The audience called out but, in the fully automated Kinema, there was no projectionist or usherette to hear them. Finally seventy seats flipped up and Screen Three emptied, as ice fronds spread and merged, overgrew the gigantic screen and smothered the cartoon altogether.

The maintenance engineers could not understand what the fuss was about. By the time they arrived, the ice in Screen Three had all melted. All they could detect was a strange smell, which they tracked back to black spoors staining the seats in Row J.

As well as a mound of donkey manure in Row K.

❧

On the way back to the theatre, the expeditionaries paused outside a TV shop and stood watching the array of mute screens in the window.

'They're actors really,' said Gracie as the cast of *EastEnders* quarrelled and wept on seven silent TV screens. 'They just do it in boxes these days.'

'We have boxes at The Royal,' said Roland Oliver frostily. 'We put members of the audience in them, *not* the actors.'

Only Mikey hankered to know how the cartoon would have ended.

'I never seen that film,' he said.

Chapter Fifteen

DANGEROUS ENLIGHTENMENT

On the Sunday, Shadrach and Maurice went off to hear the brass band up at the Fort; Gracie climbed into the orchestra pit and sat down at the broken piano to see if she could coax a plink out of it. She could not. The keys would not sound.

Propped up around the walls of the pit were dozens of paintings—sunsets, sea battles, rushing trains, cliffs and moors. Strange that she had never noticed them before. She said as much to the gloomy figure in the corner, but the artist-in-residence—'Mr William'—turned his back on her. She noticed how rusty old pins held the ragged strip of cloth to the brim of his hat.

'Why do you wear your hat indoors?' she asked, because whenever Gracie was at a loss, it was her way to ask a question. He ignored her utterly.

'I hate painting at school. It never turns out like it starts off in your head.'

'Quite so,' the old man conceded.

'Though I suppose it does for you, because you're an artist and everything and you know what you're doing. And sugar paper's rubbish anyway. I bet you'd be not so good on school sugar paper.'

This too the artist conceded.

'So why did you choose . . .'

The whole black bulk of the man shuddered with irritation. 'Nay, nay! You may rattle at my latch but I do not choose to open. What of your story, Miss Grace?'

'It's Gracie, not Grace—oh you know,' she said with a shrug. 'Lots of schools. Lots of theatres. Coming here to Seashaw every summer. I had a dog once, but it was next-doors's: I only walked it. We wrote off the car a while back. Spectacular. That about covers the highlights.'

'But you had some gallant and cherished dream, I imagine?' He made little effort to keep the contempt out of his voice.

'To open up our theatre, of course, and live here for ever and ever and ever.'

'And be an ack-tor-ess, naturally.'

'Oh no,' said Gracie with some surprise. 'Lighting, me. I want to be a lighting director and do the lamps. You can do anything with lamps: firelight, moonlight, twilight, sunshine, lightning. You can do without scenery but you can't do without light.' At which Mr William swivelled round and looked at her—really looked at her—for the very first time. The cloth round his hat cast his face into permanent shadow, but she could make out a pair of eyes milky with age.

'To answer your impertinent question, I came here as a boy, to attend school. It was a great rift to leave London—more so to leave the little sums of money I earned as a colourist there. In search of funds, I enquired after work here at The Royal, and was set to painting a backcloth for some drama that was in rehearsal. A stormy sea, as I recall, to back some tempestuous drama—though I never saw it myself: my tutor did not care for theatre. The theatre did not care greatly for the backcloth either. I seem to recall it was later used to mend a roof.

'My backcloth was a daub—what else could it be?—there is no light in here and at thirteen I had little skill. But it bought me those pleasures a boy of thirteen dotes on—shellfish, porter, badger-hair paintbrushes . . . I missed London and my father. But Seashaw brought its own rewards. This place—this coast—it has the loveliest skies of any space on earth. Did you know that? Do you ever *consider such matters*? How I craved to capture the sky—to trap it within a square of canvas. Huh! A man might as soon look at the sea and think to carry it home in a beer mug. The light, child! The light! The whole round world is sleeved up in it, and I set myself to the labour of caging it! Later in life, I returned here—again and again. Took lodgings in Cold Harbour, being in thrall to the light. Each summer brought me here with easel and oils. Still the skies showed me the rarest concatenation of wonders. I travelled the world. I painted mountains and cathedrals and forests. But nowhere saw I a sky that surpassed that of Seashaw and the Estuary!

'Like a fencer's foil, the sunbeams pierced my eyes. Like pokers in a fire, they raked at my pate and said *Paint me! Paint me!* And as my strength failed, so I cast my eyes about me and saw there more and yet more! Beauty assailed me on every side. *Paint me! Paint me!* It asked too much! I had neither the time nor the vigour to obey—nor the canvas neither. This way, that way: the sun drowning in the river; the breath of a mouth condensing on a window pane; the glow of a workman's brazier. Dawn gilding all the windows in a house. The brass instruments upon a bandstand catching the sunbeams. Hansom cabs on a rainy night, and all their lamps lit. The moon ringed round with gossamer. The dew steaming off lawns. It beset me. *Do you even begin to comprehend me, brutish child?*

'. . . Worst of all was the sky, in her vanity, changing her clothes fifty times a day—feathered hat of cloud, fichu of rainbow—powdering herself with snow like a wanton! What is one man to do, bewitched by such sirens? *Paint me! Paint me! Paint me!*'

Such distress shook the old man that his hat slid to the floor, laying bare a wildness of dirty grey hair. Above them, the other Residents had gathered on the brink of the pit like people watching goldfish in a pond—cautious—not wanting to startle the fish into hiding. Gracie picked up the hat. She said nothing. She had the wit to know that some people tell more when they are not asked.

'While my adoring public cheered my every picture, the gods jeered at me for my so few achievements. "*Too slow! Too tardy!*" they railed. "*A lifetime and but two hundred canvases painted? You must needs live a million years to net all the butterfly beauty in the world! Despair, you fool! Each day thrusts forth a million more!*"

'Small wonder that my eyes rebelled at last and would not serve me. They let in too much; they let in too little. Dazzle pained me and darkness blinded me. It was not to be endured. Seeing one day a hackney horse blinkered, I resolved to blinker myself against the great onslaught of Beauty.'

'The light hurt your eyes?' said Gracie, trying on the hat. The crumpled crêpe formed a curtain round her head, leaving an opening only for her face.

The painter made a wild gesture of impatience which sent red oil paint spraying up the wall of the orchestra pit like music notes. 'The light hurt my *heart*, you little fool!' he raged. 'The light persecuted my soul. Take that off.'

They sat in silence for fully a minute. Questions and quibbles still filled Gracie to the brim, but she found she could not phrase any of them because her mouth was full of pins.

'Why did I come here in death?' the artist said, attempting to govern his temper. 'I came here for the dark. I remembered from boyhood its restful gloom. I found—how very appropriate—that I could paint rather well by the light of the ghost lamp.' And he nodded towards the light-bulb which glimmered over the stage.

'And dark places are good for moping in, aren't they,' said Gracie brightly, lining up a row of rusty pins on the lid of the piano.

The old man scowled at her and thought what heartless, super-ficial brats children were and how wise he was to have shunned fatherhood. He felt a strong desire to break the child's spirit utterly. He thrust his latest canvas towards her, in doing so larding the heels of his hands with scarlet paint. 'What do you see?'

'*William!*' The interruption came from above: a voice carry-ing a sharp warning.

The picture was of a beach lit by sunset: a gap in the cliffs, a long boat battling the surf. 'I don't . . . ' Gracie began.

'Come, come, child. You are acquainted with the area. Seek the story within the landscape. Look!'

'*Mister Turner!*' The toecaps of Eugenius Birch's well-shined shoes lipped over the edge of the pit. His eyes were fixed so firmly on the artist that they might have been sinking the piles of a pier into the seabed. 'What is once said, can never be unsaid. And *you* are not the man to say it.' William returned his canvas to the easel and snatched back his hat, cramming it down the better to sulk. 'You forget yourself, Mr Turner, such is your fear of being forgotten.' Eugenius was angry, no doubt about it. But Gracie interrupted him, jumping up excitedly and pointing at the artist.

'Oh! Are you—? Yes you are! I know you! You're the steam-and-smoke man! We did you at school!'

The artist pushed up the brim just enough to scowl. 'Did me? I am not sure I care to be *done*. In what regard *did* me?'

'Oh, everybody does *you*!' said Gracie sweepingly. 'You're the steam-and-smoke man! Get that paint off your hands: you have to go out now so you have to look respectable.' She screwed up the length of frayed, grubby crêpe she had detached and shoved it down inside the broken piano. 'You've got to see somewhere. Everybody has to!'

They all protested. They all cited reasons why they could not come—William more than any. But they were all secretly intrigued as to why the patchwork child should know of the taciturn painter in the pit, and Gracie would not explain—'You'll see! You'll see!' Grudgingly, fearfully, another expeditionary party mustered in the alleyway.

Only the donkeys fell willingly into line.

Chapter Sixteen

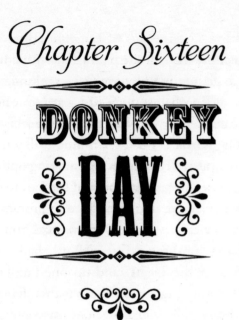

DONKEY DAY

'So,' said Gracie. 'The donkeys. How long?'

The Residents looked at one another, made calculations on their finger ends, but could not agree. Beach donkeys had been in Seashaw for two centuries, but these particular donkeys had only been turning up at The Royal for a few decades.

'I reckon these beasts are Victorian,' said Douglas. 'You could ask them, but they won't tell you. On account they're donkeys, see.'

'Why do you say Victorian?' asked Bodkins who knew horses inside out, but had no insights into donkeys.

'Well do they not look Victorian to you, man?'

'All donkeys look Victorian to me. Bein' as I am Victorian.'

'When I was a child,' said Lily, 'the beach donkeys were housed overnight in an assinarium yonder.'

'A what?'

'An assinarium—like an aquarium, but with donkeys.' (Gracie pictured a huge glass tank with donkeys swimming up and down, but decided it was probably more like a stable really.) 'I surmise, when it was knocked down, the poor homeless animals found their way to The Royal.'

A long crocodile of Residents was walking up Marine Parade towards the large white building behind the harbour. William had his hands raised to either side of his face to protect his eyes from the light. Or the views. Almost everyone had quit their mouldy sanctuary for the sunshine. Miss Melluish had said she would 'stay and look after the Twins', and no one had challenged her. Eugenius forbade any suggestion she was too afraid to come.

But the donkeys following on behind were a surprise to everyone. As Gracie's expeditionary force set off, they had simply attached themselves to the end of the procession.

'They fancy a day on the beach, maybe,' said Mikey.

'I hope they have a sixth sense for landmines,' said Douglas gloomily.

'The mines are long gone, Doug,' said Frank Stuart. 'The beaches were cleared sixty years back.'

But the phantom donkeys did not turn aside at the beach steps to visit their old stamping grounds. They trotted on along the unforgiving pavement, flinching from passing cars, but obstinately tagging along.

'Plainly they want nothing to do with the scene of their *criminal activities*,' said PC Nixon. His cheeks were bright red with pent-up indignation and a dab of shame. 'Am I alone in recognizing the beasts as took part in the Great Night of Disorder?'

Bodkins turned on his friend with a look of astonishment. 'You knew of it all along! You are a dark horse, Arfur Nixon!'

'Tell the Quilt what you know,' said Roland Oliver, looking pained. 'Else she will only ask.'

❧

The toffee apples started it. They drew wasps, and the wasps set about pestering the donkeys. If there had been fewer toffee-apples or more children to eat them, the whole thing might never have happened.

The donkeys—Josephine and Penny, Buttercup and the rest—were enjoying their day even less than usual. It is work of stultifying boredom, walking fifty yards along the same piece of sand and then fifty yards back again. The schools were not yet on holiday, so the only riders were infants and toddlers who had to be held in place, and cried as often as not. The wasps and the crying filled the creatures' velvety ears like sand on a windy day. They were sluggish and sulky. The donkey-boys were in much the same mood.

'Be better off with a tortoise, you,' said Jack. 'Cheaper to feed. Get yourself a tortoise, you should.'

'My Josephine looks like a greyhound 'longside of yours,' said Ned.

'There's a statue of a n'orse in the park would look lively 'longside your Barbara!' said Patch.

There were always flurries of rivalry between the donkey-boys. What else is there to do, standing on a beach in all weathers, day after day? They also competed for customers, praising the merits of their animals to passing families:

135

—'Gentle as a pussy cat, ma'am.'

—'Sweet as the Queen's cocoa and only half as lumpy!'

—'Look, she's winking an eye at you, Miss! Likes you already.'

But the new toffee-apple stall was making for wasps, and wasps are almost as vexing to donkey-boys as they are to donkeys. They were keeping the customers away, too.

'Got a milking stool at home got more legs than your Marigold.'

'What you keeping Buttercup for, then? Flea farming?'

Josephine, Marigold, Primrose and the rest looked at one another and shook their heads, edging away from the toffee-apple stall.

Then Primrose got stung and broke into a trot and knocked over a child, and the mother was just saying how Primrose was a dangerous animal and ought to be shot when she was knocked over by the other donkeys who thought Primrose was leading them to safer ground. The mother changed her opinion and said all donkeys were killers and ought to be shot.

Now the donkey-boys might insult each other's animals, but woe betide the outsider who did the same. Josephine might be missing an eye; Buttercup might cast shoes quicker than the blacksmith could fit them; Primrose might (on occasion) bite, and Marigold might kick a man and break his knee caps. But woe betide the tripper who found fault or the child who threw sand.

'You should enter your Barbara for the Derby,' said Patch.

'Nah, the National,' said Jim. 'She prefers steeplechase to the flat.' And the donkey-boys laughed and moved to the other end of the beach.

The donkey-boys did not return to the toffee-apple stall till after dark and by that time an idea had taken shape in Jack's head. As the four boys tipped the stall on its side and set about burying it deep in the sand, he returned to the subject of speeding donkeys. 'A donkey can raise a gallop if she sets her mind to it, right?' said Jack.

'You think?'

'Yer. Racing is a state of mind.' Jack had decided to become a philosopher ever since sitting next to one on a bus and discovering the astounding fact that philosophy began with a P.

'How d'you make out that?'

'Well, a donkey wakes up, she thinks *What did I do yesterday? I walked. Ergo, donkeys walk. Ergo, I'll walk today.*'

'What's "ergo"?'

'Ergo. So. It's foreign for "so".'

'So's shorter. Why have a same word that's bigger?'

'Never mind that. Now s'posing that donkey meets a n'orse . . .' Jack persevered. 'And the donkey thinks 'eyup—I am like to a n'orse and 'orses gallop. Ergo, tomorrow I fancy I'll gallop like a n'orse.'

'I don't know what's wrong with "so".'

'Stow it, Bill. I'm talking races.'

This came as a surprise to the others who had thought Jack was talking philosophy with a P so had not been listening.

'I say we should race ours. Give 'em the notion of being fleet of foot.'

'Fleet—?'

'Don't start. Quick. Gallopy. We should race 'em, that's what I say. And not just ours—all the beach donkeys. Run a tote. Get a bookie along. Cash prizes.'

'Cash?!!'

'Old Nickers would never let us,' said Dan.

'Nickers shan't know. We shall run the races at night, when the beach is empty. And we shall pick a night when Nickers in't on duty.'

'Would there be a cup?' asked Sammy who was still too young to know that money is everything in life.

'I'll make sure there's a cup, Sammy,' said Jack who was Sammy's older brother.

Jack's way of making sure was to unscrew the headlamp from an Oldsmobile parked outside the Grand Hotel. He left the bulb hanging down like a displaced eyeball and carried away the shiny silver socket. Once the donkey-boys had seen this goblet of gleaming chrome, every one of them craved to win the Seashaw Silver Stakes himself. Ergo, what started out as a money-earner ended as a noble sporting endeavour.

❧

Tacky-Tick the bookie had his doubts. 'Six donkeys do not a Derby make, boys. Well known saying.'

'There's four teams use the assinarium. There's another one up Bankville,' said Jack. 'Then there'll be the Sheepsgate boys and a few from Easterbarn.'

His friends stared at him. They too had been picturing a handful of donkeys. But as Jack had knelt in the gutter in front of that Oldsmobile, seeing his face reflected back sixteen times over in the headlamp, his plans too had multiplied. The whole county would compete for the Seashaw Silver Cup. Also, there would be a goat-cart derby, a dog dig, walking races, bathing machine competitions and finally a Donkey National with entries from all over.

'When?' said Tacky-Tick.

'Next time Nickers is off duty,' said Jack like a flash.

In fact it took a full month to organize, what with the secret messages to be passed, the rules to be finalized, the race tracks to be planned, the tide tables to be consulted. (You cannot hold a race meeting and have the sea turn up unexpectedly in mid-race.) Further delays were caused by trips to the police station to answer questions about the disappearance of the toffee-apple stall: Sergeant Nixon could pin nothing on any of them but it did not stop him trying.

The town was a-buzz with rumour, of course, but if the Sea-shaw Constabulary of Police got wind of Race Day, they did not cordon off the beach. This probably had something to do with them all being keen race-walkers. Every one of them regularly competed in the Annual Inter-Church Walking Championships. Unknown to the rest, every officer asked his wife to wash his shorts and singlet and not to ask any questions.

On the day itself, a strange mood pervaded the town. Dogs multiplied. Dog-owners could be seen walking to and fro along the Sea Terrace, hoping to glimpse clues that would give them an unfair advantage.

But not until the innocent, ignorant holiday-makers packed up their buckets and spades and children and herded off to their boarding houses; not until the deckchair men had stacked their chairs away; not until the seafood booth had stopped trading and the band was gone from the bandstand did Jack and the donkey-boys work their magic on Seashaw beach.

There were slaloms for the goat-carts, bones buried in the sand for the dogs to find, a winning line for the walkers, and a race track for the donkeys, including four kinds of jump. All afternoon donkeys kept arriving, some exhausted from a ten mile walk, some wobbly from riding on the backs of carts. One even came by rail from Bankville, the journey almost over before the conductor mastered his surprise enough to turn the beast off the train.

It was a still, sweet night with a half moon. Tacky-Tick the Bookie was overjoyed to see an even bigger crowd than at the Apprentice Stakes in Dover. He did most of his business at illegal dog-fights in farm outbuildings, selling betting slips by the light of a storm lantern. It put a spring in his step to mount the band-stand for a change, and set up for trade there. He took enough money before the first race to fill his large suitcase.

He made a killing on the Dog Dig. Who would have thought a dalmatian would unearth seventeen bones in ten minutes? The labrador only managed six, and the terrier got side-tracked catch-ing crabs. The rest of the pack started fighting or mating and had to be dowsed with buckets of water fetched from a distant sea.

The goat-traps bowled elegantly over the hard, damp strip of lower beach. The walkers were less elegant, sinking into the soft, dry sand of the upper beach, reeling and rolling with the effort, getting cramp and losing their plimsolls but ploughing on, cheered by wives, children, and locals all clutching betting slips.

Even up at the Royal Theatre, where the divine Ellen Terry was playing Guinevere, the sound of cheering could faintly be heard during the quieter sections. Sergeant Nixon stirred in his seat, consulted his pocket watch and wondered once again why his friend Bodkins had not met him as arranged. Instinct whis-pered in his ear, of mischief and mayhem, but how often in his life would he have the chance to see Ellen Terry on stage? Sergeant Nixon turned a deaf ear to instinct.

Bodkins was, at that very moment, overtaking bathing machine 28 and stealing second place in the Bathing Machine Challenge. 'Good girl, Rosie! Bucketsa carrots, Rosie!'

At nine o'clock the donkeys were lined up, as for a cavalry charge, their pink-lined ears serried, like the blades of spears. The half moon hung reflected in forty pairs of blue-brown eyes. The beasts had been stripped down to basics—no saddles, no bridles, just bare untrammelled donkey but for brow-bands carrying paper numbers. Names were useless: beach donkeys share a very small assortment of names. So they were numbered 1 to 40.

The incoming donkey-boys complained their animals needed a head start because they did not know the beach. The Seashaw donkey-boys said, 'Your hard luck.'

'Under starter's orders!'

The moon glinted on a dozen brands of cheating: glass jars containing wasps, riding crops, tin tacks, Lucifer matches . . . The spectators complained that, in the dark, they could not tell which of the donkeys they had bet on. Tacky-Tick the Bookie counted his money by the light of his cigarette.

❧

It was not the clatter of the starter's rattle that shot Sergeant Nixon out of his theatre seat and set him clambering over the knees of those in the same row. It was instinct. All day his brain had been unconsciously piecing together clues and slight alterations to the town's routine. He was suddenly convinced that a major crime

141

was being committed, under cover of Ellen Terry—in his town, behind his back.

❦

Some of the donkeys ran five steps and stopped. Some set off at a walk. Some turned round to reproach their owners for a tin-tack or a match-burn. Some went on thinking whatever it is beach donkeys think to pass the tedious time. But some trotted smartly away and plunged into the trench which was the first obstacle on the race course. The donkey-boys pelted down to the other end of the beach and began to rattle buckets and shout encouragement. The crowd too bawled at the dim shapes of donkeys, threatening, cajoling or just gargling with frustrated rage.

'*Don't just stand there! Move!*'

'*Run! Run! No not that way, you—*'

Seashaw's donkey-boys had had their beasts in training. Josephine, Janice, Barbara and Primrose all picked themselves up out of the trench, clambered over the sandy hillock and trotted on towards the deckchair barricade. Once or twice (during training) they had tackled this wicked wooden 'jump' and felt the collapsing deckchairs snap at their ears or snare their feet. They did not like it. Still, there were the carrots to be considered at the finishing line. Being sensible beasts, they turned right and, to the apoplexy of the spectators, trotted *round* the jump, wading through the surf to do it.

'*Is that allowed? Is it? Is it?*'

'*Disqualify them!*'

'*Cheat!*. . . Wait, what numbers are they?'

More donkeys pulled themselves out of the sand trench. Homesick, visiting donkeys sauntered off in the direction of Bankville or Sheepsgate. (Donkeys have a marvellous sense of direction.) A general welter of donkeyness spread across the beach. Spectators sent their children down the steps to check the numbers of the brow-bands.

'*Son! Son! If you see number eighteen give him a kick up the backside!*'
Then the moon went in.

Donkeys have good night vision, too—their eyes are full of liquid darkness—whereas humans can see very little once sand and stone and steps are all coloured black. It was suddenly very dark.

The Seashaw Constabulary might have helped, but they had all gone home to get the sand out of their shorts and vests. The crowd might have helped, but as soon as it was discovered that Tacky-Tick the Bookie had skedaddled with the takings, they set off to hunt him down and kill him.

In Jack's opinion, Marigold, Primrose, Barbara and the rest had been planning the thing right from the start—awaiting their chance . . .

Because they melted into the night.

While visiting donkeys from Sheepsgate and Bankville toiled up the steps and explored the alleyways and inn yards in search of hay, the local animals clambered over the rocks and found new plains of sand, new alcoves of rock, new coves empty of children and wasps. They found pirate caves leading to private passageways, that in turn led to secret cellars and winding stairs . . .

Or just maybe the incoming tide cut them off and drowned them.

Because they disappeared without trace.

To stop Sammy crying, Jack told him Buttercup, Molly, Josephine and the rest had turned nocturnal, like foxes, and gone to earth.

❧

When Sergeant Nixon appeared on the scene, there were tired children crying, mothers slapping at their husbands, men mustering weapons and splitting into packs to hunt down Tacky-Tick. The bathing machines were all out of position, and deckchairs were washing about on the incoming tide. He knew he ought to restore order. If he had just come mounted on his trusty police horse Reg; if he had been dressed in uniform instead of his best suit; if the divine Ellen Terry had not been playing Guinevere at The Royal (music by Arthur Sullivan, no less) he might have tried harder . . .

As it was, he turned on his heel and ran back as fast as he could, hoping to catch Act III. He encountered several donkeys on the way, which was strange, unnerving, and probably contrary to by-laws. But how often does a man get the chance to see the greatest actress of the day? And he had missed so much already! The tug of Art was just too strong for Sergeant Nixon. He clambered back into his theatre seat.

❧

The ghosts of Josephine, Marigold, Barbara and the rest refused to be left in the car park. Maurice and Shadrach offered to take them up to the Fort to hear the band. But the donkeys had opted for art rather than music, and there is no arguing with a donkey once it has made up its mind. Now Buttercup, Primrose, Molly and the rest stood in the art gallery and looked at the work of Mr William T, but passed no comment. Donkeys are colour blind, so they probably saw less to admire than the Residents did when they studied the crimson sunsets shrouded in storm clouds or the fiery conflagrations of dawn over Seashaw beach.

Their little donkey feet made no clatter on the white marble flooring. Their manure made no stain—only a faintly familiar smell of childhood days on a beach. The museum visitors sniffed and smiled and wondered if the gallery had got the smell in specially, for the sake of atmosphere.

Engrossed in the paintings, each Resident rested a hand down on coarsely fluffy shoulders: donkeys are a very convenient, dining-table sort of height for leaning on. And insofar as a donkey can look happy, these six appeared to be blissfully content.

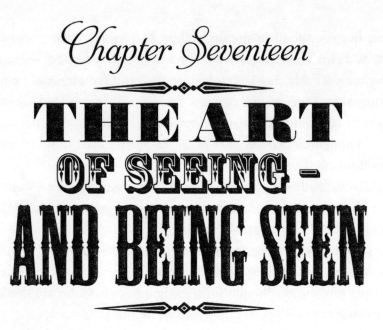

Chapter Seventeen

THE ART OF SEEING – AND BEING SEEN

'It was in the papers,' said Gracie.

But the Residents of The Royal did not have ready access to the *Seashaw Star*. So William T had not read the endless articles about Seashaw's new art gallery. The town had built—like a temple to a favourite god—a multi-million-pound gallery, and named it after him. It stood on the seafront by the old harbour, as white and stark as a vast refrigerator. Like a fridge, it was full of lots of old stuff and an assortment of lovely, tempting things.

And some of the things were his.

He walked to the gallery with his hat brim pulled down and both hands shielding his eyes from a century he had never intended to see. He entered the gallery leaning heavily on his walking cane, still questioning the need to venture so far from the theatre, still complaining bitterly that Gracie had vandalized his hat. Two rooms in, and he was no longer in need of his stick. His back was erect, his shoulders square and his hair had turned from white to iron grey. Around the plain white walls, lit by level laths of light sliding through slits in the plain, white walls, were *his paintings*: objects of such precious worth that they had been hung up like holy relics.

To William, each wall was a page in a picture album, reminding him of his youth, of his travels, of his father who had mixed his paints, of his glory days. The hair in the nape of his neck darkened and curled spontaneously. When he had finished studying the pictures, he turned and looked around at the faces of the people moving reverently through the gallery, like worshippers in a church.

'They love my work. They *know* my work! I was famed in my time, yes ... but that time was so very long ago! I had imagined ... ' His cheeks—growing younger by the minute—were flushed with happiness. 'The town named this place for me? Why? They thought nothing of me when I was living here. At twelve I was a boy—and who likes boys? At sixty I was ... ' He glanced sideways at Gracie. 'Let us say the town talked of me behind their hands.'

'But you liked the town, I suppose, so the town likes you,' said Gracie.

'I thought *nothing* of the town!' he insisted. 'I thought only of the ... ' He broke off in sudden alarm and fairly ran to the stairs and on up to the second landing.

When Gracie caught him up, he was leaning his palms against the plate glass window and staring out, eyes creased against the light. 'All's well,' he said, laughing at his own panic.

The landing looked out over the sea. 'I feared, with so much changed in the world, the sea-sky might be altered also. But it is as it was. Did I not tell you that the finest skies in all Europe hang over Seashaw? I travelled Europe and nowhere altered my opinion. The sky over Seashaw is all a sky can be. Majestic in size. Infinite in its splendour!' His hat was in his hands, his face wreathed with smiles. His varying age levelled off at about forty. 'I have no need to capture it! I need not stain canvas to save it from extinction! It is still here for everyone to see!' As he took it all in—the seagulls wheeling, the clouds morphing, the sea dancing at the wind's behest—he rested a hand on Gracie as if she were a donkey that had carried him down a long and stony road. 'I never before thought to rejoice in any death, but I must needs say . . . '

'*Mister Turner?*' called Eugenius Birch sharply from the bottom of the stairs. His earlier temper did not seem to have been soothed by smoky skies, sunny beaches, and lush landscapes. 'I regret to interrupt, but something has occurred.'

He did not need to go on. Shadrach, dashing from room to room, was still breaking the dreadful news to whomever he found. Now he appeared on the landing above and leaned over the stair-rail. 'It's Maurice!' he called down. '*I have lost Maurice!*'

❧

The temperature rose several degrees as the Residents streamed out of the gallery followed by a string of donkeys. The curator checked the thermometer: a regulated temperature is very important in an art gallery.

'Nice touch, that,' remarked a tourist.

'What is?' said the curator.

'The Turner look-alike on the stairs. Very lifelike. Nice touch.'

'The what?'

Frank Stuart, last of the Residents to leave, took out a notepad and wrote in it. He returned to the second floor landing and also took note of the two red palm prints on the window glass.

❧

Shadrach and Maurice had been coming back from the brass band concert, exchanging delight like a rally in tennis—

'Wonderful!'

        'Extraordinary!'

'The tone!'

        'Better mouthpieces.'

'Short on banjos.'

        'Not brass enough, I suppose, banjos.'

When the traffic lights on the Bankville Road changed to red, a big open-topped sports car halted beside them, engines throbbing. Its radio throbbed too: Miles Davis playing 'Kind of Blue'. Maurice stepped over the door and slid down into the passenger seat, the music enveloping him in happiness.

The driver—hair like loose tobacco, and wearing a chunky gold necklace—felt suddenly cold and pressed the button to bring up the car's roof. Shadrach saw it coming, saw too that the traffic lights were changing. 'Get out, lad. Quick!'

But the driver was not one to wait beyond amber. He set off with a shriek of burning rubber and sped away, carrying the music and Maurice with him.

❧

'He will find his way home,' said Lily Oliver soothingly. 'Like Bo Peep's sheep.'

'But the town is so altered!' Shadrach, on his first trip out of the theatre for a hundred and twenty years, had been frightened by the number of changes. 'How *can* he find his way when everywhere looks so different!'

'The sea is as it was, man,' said Eugenius Birch. 'Maurice has only to follow the coast back to the clock tower. From there he can assuredly find the theatre.'

But everyone was shaken by the thought of Maurice being snatched, as mail was once snatched from railway platforms by the night mail train. What if the car was heading for Dover— or London—or some distant destination from which Maurice would never find his way back?

'Longing brought him home from France to Seashaw,' said soft-spoken Frank Stuart. 'I wouldn't worry. Longing is a pretty good compass.'

William T tried, but failed, to be sad about the loss of Maurice. If the boy did not turn up, he personally would be glad not to have to look at the black greasepaint any more. It stole the features from a face, and he liked faces, as well as seascapes, smoke, and fog. Besides, he could not help being happy. Delight surged through him whenever he turned his head. There were pictures in the gallery (never mind his own) that shook up his every thought about Art and what it could do. Outside on the street, graffiti spattered the buildings with ugliness, as if Art had been murdered and its blood left on the walls. William was unsettled and excited by it all. Images poured into his head through his eyes, ears, and open mouth . . . He could almost taste the colours! An anarchy of happiness was running riot through him. Passing a shop window, he paused to look at himself in the glass and rather liked what he saw.

Chapter Eighteen

MAURICE MEANWHILE

Maurice, never having ridden in a car before, did not question the quality of the driving. The magnificence of the music strapped him to his seat like a safety belt and the novelty of moving at ninety miles an hour left him merely intrigued. It was not that he had lost the knack of being scared but, not knowing any better, he assumed that twenty-first-century transport always felt like riding inside a football as it bounces down Everest.

The driver tripped three speed cameras and scraped two parked vehicles before skidding to a halt outside a scrapyard in the middle of nowhere. He bailed out of the car like a greyhound out of a trap, and sprinted into the site office. His distress leaked out of its aluminium windows:

'. . . *someone in my car!* . . . *looked in the mirror* . . . *phone the police!*'

Maurice, meanwhile, began to wonder how far he had come and how he would find his way back to the theatre. The sea was nowhere in sight and they had driven many miles. It was not a happy thought. There was no music on the radio now, to cheer him.

A man in a vest and combat trousers lumbered out of the office and came to peer in at the windows. Maurice smiled pleasantly and started to explain about the lure of Winton Marsalis. 'No one there,' said the man in the vest. 'There's no one. Look for yourself!'

The driver emerged and dared a step or two towards the car then, seeing no one inside, pounced on the boot handle and threw open the boot. Empty. He was not stupid, he asserted. He knew when there was a man in the back of his car. 'Black, with white circles round his eyes.'

'Circles?'

'And mouth.'

'What, like the *Black-and-White Minstrel Show?*' The scrap merchant sniggered.

'Disguise, man! Disguise!'

'So he didn't sing, then?'

'Well yes, he sang. I definitely heard singing too. Don't laugh, you moron! Why are you laughing?'

They went back into the office. Maurice decided to climb to the top of the crane which stood hunched over the scrapyard. From up there he would surely be able to glimpse the sea and get his bearings. As he climbed, he thought over the implications of Being Seen. Clearly theatricals were not the only ones able to glimpse spirits. So what had Maurice done that had briefly rendered him visible? And why had it worn off?

A flat expanse of fields, roads, and housing developments stretched out on all sides of the crane. So very many roads. So few hedges. But not the sea. Try as he might, he could not catch a glimpse of the blessed sea that ought to steer him home. The air thrummed with the drone of aeroplanes, and all of them *so* much higher up than the Gotha biplane when it dropped its bomb on Windsor Avenue. Maurice climbed back down the crane and went into the site office. The driver was diluting his coffee with vodka. His hand shook as he poured. But he did not see Maurice standing in the doorway. Not a hair of him. Baffling.

Maurice did the only thing he could, and stayed close to the driver of the car. Perhaps the man would head back to Seashaw after his business meeting. Maurice got back into the BMW. When the driver re-emerged he scoured it for signs of a stowaway, checked his driving mirror repeatedly but, seeing no one, started up the motor. True, he felt the need to turn the heating up, and to button his jacket across his paunch, but he had drunk enough vodka to persuade himself he had imagined the greasepaint minstrel. When the radio was switched on again, Maurice put his fingers in his ears so as not to sing inadvertently and cause a car crash.

Sadly, the man did not drive back to Seashaw but went home, to a farmhouse surrounded by several acres of paddock. Giant garden ornaments lined the driveway—giraffes and rearing horses, King George III, a scale model of the Eiffel Tower and, on either side of the front steps, lacquer lions—the kind Chinese restaurants put by their doors to bring them good luck and scare off small children.

The living room was ornate, too, with a glass coffee table held up by a model tiger, a mirrored bar and an aquarium with coloured lights. The fish in the aquarium were disturbed by Maurice tapping on the glass; their owner was disturbed by the sight of his fish hurtling about the aquarium in a way he had never seen before.

The first thing he did was to kick off his fat trainers and walk about in his socks, stiff legged, flat-footed. It added to his air of discontent. He turned on the fifty-inch television while he checked his email, checked his answer-phone, poured himself several more vodkas and heated his dinner. Maurice followed him about, admiring the mirror-fronted wardrobes, the upside-down bottles hung above the bar, the cunning of the microwave.

The man took his temperature, ran himself a bath, checked his blood pressure with a lumpy wristwatch device he strapped to one arm. And all the while Maurice followed him about, intrigued by every gadget, from the stick-on forehead thermometer to the TV remote control and the movement sensor that flushed the toilet at a wave of a hand. Maurice was delighted by the lamps which turned themselves on without need of a switch.

'If Mr Eugenius Birch could see this!'

Shivering convulsively, the owner turned on the CD player in the bedroom, the radio in the bathroom and docked his iPod in the kitchen. A single man alone in a big house, he made sure he was never without noise. Maurice, meanwhile, discovered a collection of framed, vintage, rude seaside postcards. He could remember his mother smacking him for looking at similar cards outside the newsagent's. As his host sat opening mail with a crystal paperknife, Maurice leaned over his shoulder and read the post.

That was how he found out. By sheer chance, he had invited himself home to the house of Gracie's Mr Sapper: financial saviour of The Royal.

The names of the theatre and Gracie's parents were all there, snagged in brambles of legal jargon; there were bank forms, solicitor's documents and insurance policies. Not that Maurice knew a thing about legal matters, but he was eager for any news about The Royal, so he leaned in closer to read the small print.

Mr Sapper buttoned the collar of his pyjamas, drew his dressing gown closer around him. 'I'm not well,' he told the telephone.

For despite the CD, the TV, the computer, and the answerphone, Mr Sapper needed the companionship of a human voice. Throughout dinner, in the toilet, at the bar, even in bed, he was on the telephone to one business associate or another, checking on progress, arranging a meeting, asking for confirmation, instructing his secretary. 'I'm not well,' he told her piteously. But his secretary only suggested making him a doctor's appointment. His office manager did not offer to call round either.

Maurice would have liked to help: Mr Sapper might be noisy, foul-mouthed, drunk, and partial to dirty postcards, but The Royal needed him.

Sapper jabbed another telephone number at random. 'The fish've gone mad! The heating's on the blink! I'm not well,' he complained to an auntie he had not called for years. 'And someone's been in my house, I'm effing sure of it.' But his aunt, who was in Scotland, told him she was not going to set off and drive through the night to rescue a man from his indoor fish.

Sapper turned round suddenly, in the hope (or fear?) of catching sight of a face at the window, a burglar under the couch. 'There's someone here! I can feel it!' he told his accountant who advised him to call the police but did not see what else he could

do to help. Sapper threw a cushion at the curtain, for fear someone was hiding behind it, and dialled another number.

'I've got business to discuss—No, not on the phone. Get
yourself over here. There's money in it,' he wheedled, but the
voice at the other end could only manage to meet him at breakfast time in Seashaw.

So Mr Sapper got dressed again and went in search of a hotel:
somewhere safe and warm to spend the night. Naturally Maurice tucked himself in alongside the driver: Mr Sapper needed
company and did not seem in any fit state to drive, especially in
bedroom slippers. At the Premier Inn, Maurice got sidetracked by
the lift music and spent some time riding up and down memoriz-
ing the tune. But remembering his duty to look after the theatre's
saviour, he searched the hotel until he found Mr Sapper watching
TV in bed and eating peanuts from the minibar. Maurice slid into
bed beside him. There was plenty of room. It was the biggest bed
Maurice had ever seen—quite the size of Kent—and the minstrel
took up precisely no space at all.

Now and then he did reach out and lay a hand to Sapper's
brow, but found no sign of fever and was glad. In fact, knowing Mr
Sapper was not dying and was intending to revisit Seashaw in the
morning, restored Maurice to happiness. When a concert turned
up on the TV, live from the Proms, he was more than happy.

'If only Mr Shadrach was here!' he observed, joyfully sniffing
the spotless sheets.

'Who?' said Sapper sleepily. A second later, he was sitting bolt
upright, texting his personal coach to say there was someone
in his bed who was trying to steal his ears. His personal coach
doubted his word. When Sapper called his secretary to tell her

there was a black-and-white minstrel in his bed, she called him a smack-head, resigned and put the phone down.

Briefly, thanks to drinking everything in the minibar, Mr Sapper did finally get to sleep. But that was worse. Much worse. He dreamed a dream stranded with barbed wire, in which he was up to his thighs in mud, shells bursting around him, men screaming, horses writhing on their backs till their girth's burst, a night sky bright as day with sodium flares, and machine gun bullets peck-peck-pecking their way towards him through the mud.

And there was nowhere to hide.

Chapter Nineteen

LOST

When Maurice did not return, the Residents went out and searched for him, but it was futile. They rode in the miniature train that plied the promenade, and they scanned the beaches, peered up side streets and in at the doors of the penny arcades. But Seashaw is a big town. It stretches inland almost far enough to rub flanks with Sheepsgate, so far along the coast that it touches fingers with Easterbarn.

They passed two donkeys eating the alyssum in the flower beds on the roundabout. They saw three more standing at the end of the harbour wall. But there was no sign of Maurice.

They passed the ranks of charioteers drawn up in the supermarket car park, trolleys at the ready, waiting for the off.

'They're the Eco Warriors,' Gracie explained.

'*I see them stand like greyhounds in the slip,*' said Roland. 'What war are they waging?'

'They're waiting for the sell-bys to be put out.'

The Bin Raiders were a motley alliance—students, pensioners, housewives—whose friendship made every trip to Grosser's Supastore a social event. Today's conversation was even more animated than usual.

'Really? In Aldi?'

'That's what I heard.'

'And rolling on the grass up by the Castle Arms.'

'Same ones, I suppose. Wandering.'

'No no! There were two more grazing in the churchyard and they were grey not brown!'

'Weird.'

'What, saddles? The lot?'

At the end of the day, food past its sell-by date was consigned to the big green wheelie-bins, still wrapped, still wholesome. The shelf-stackers put food into the bins; the Eco Warriors took it out again—to save the planet, to make ends meet, to feed hungry mouths . . . It was illegal, and now and then the store prosecuted somebody and the charioteers melted away. But their ranks always reformed under the leadership of Boudicca who had taken a sacred oath to rescue loaves and lamb-chops from landfill, and to make the world's food go further.

'It's not that they're poor necessarily,' said Gracie. 'They just don't like good food going to waste. I'll take something home for Ma. Every penny counts.' And she set off to join the ranks of the Eco Warriors, thinking of the thanks she might win by it when she got home.

'No, Gracie.' said Shadrach sharply.

'It's all right! There's nothing wrong with the food, honest! It's all wrapped up.'

'No, Gracie,' said Lily.

'But I could ask Boudicca if she's seen Maurice. We're friends. She's not a theatrical, but she's dead arty. Does screen-printing and hypnotizes herself so as not to get shingles.'

'Do not, Gracie,' said Roland.

'Really, it's all right! They do kosher and everything. Should I . . .'

'Gracie. *NO.*' And when Eugenius Birch added his formidable voice to the others, she felt outnumbered, without understanding why. Did they not want her talking about them to strangers?

'If I promise not to say a word about . . .'

'*NO, GRACIE,*' they said in one voice, their eyes all on her, their arms held wide to block her path to the giant wheelie-bins. For some reason her hair stood on end, and her breath wedged in her throat. They walked back to the theatre in silence.

❧

That night, the Residents dispersed throughout The Royal, some to Frank Stuart's scenery loft, some to the costume cupboard and the understage, some to the alleyway outside. Even the Twins were nowhere to be seen when Eugenius invited Gracie to sit with him in the Dress Circle. Her heart squirmed at the thought he was going to tell her some news about Maurice that she did not want to hear.

'Pray, do not let us sit in the centre, but keep close to the edge. The ends of rows are well supported. Foolish, I know, when my weight is . . . negligible, but I find I still fear to walk over an unsound structure.'

Unsound? Was that it, then? Was that the bad news Eugenius had been hinting at all day? Ever since the car park—no, before that—he had been looking at her like the doctors do in *Casualty* when the X-rays come back looking grim. 'What, is the Circle falling down or something?'

'Oh.' Eugenius faltered. (He had forgotten momentarily that she did not know of the danger.) 'Oh. Yes. At least, it is sagging. Cracks are opening in its underside. Something of a sorrow for your excellent parents.'

It certainly was. A sick feeling griped at Gracie's stomach. 'I'll tell them. Mr Sapper will pay for it to be mended.' But still the nausea plucked at her insides. She ought to have something to eat: she could not remember the last time she had sat down to a proper meal. Gracie did not care for Eugenius's manner—it reminded her of Frank Stuart escorting Mikey to the back of the stalls for a dose of the truth.

'There is another matter . . .' began Eugenius, as they perched on seats A2 and A3 in the Dress Circle. On stage the ghost-light glimmered, dimly illuminating an empty stage. No Songbird. No Roland Oliver or Lord George. And still Eugenius Birch did not get round to mentioning this 'other matter' of his.

Gracie said, 'Did you have *Fiddler on the Roof* in your . . . when you were . . . Would Mr Oliver know *Fiddler on the Roof*? I don't know how old it is. He'd like *Fiddler on the Roof*. It's great. Singing and everything . . . Is there going to be a show tonight?'

'It has passed two of the morning.'

'So?'

'Not a show, no. Yes, a show. Possibly. Most nights . . .' said Eugenius confusingly. 'Tell me, Miss Grace—'

'Gracie. I'm not Grace. It's not a diminuendo.'

'Miss Gracie . . . Why do you not attend school?'

That was easy. 'Too late in the term to sign up. I'll go next term.'

'Say, then, why do you pass your every day with us . . .'

That was even easier. 'Well, how often does someone get to hang out with . . .'

' . . . and not with your parents . . . '

Ridiculous! Such easy questions! 'Oh, they're up to their eyes, what with . . . '

' . . . parents who allow you to come and go as you please, and ask nothing of your whereabouts and take no note of your absence, nor chastise you for it.'

Gracie pressed her lips tight shut.

'Nor wash your clothes, nor make up a bed for you.'

She had a sudden mental picture of Miss Melluish cornered by questions, badgered to speak of things she did not care to remember.

'Am I grubby? Do I smell? Is that what you're saying?'

'Not at all. You are as you were the day we met you. Not one jot altered. Except perhaps for your eyes. Pray, when is the last time your parents spoke to you? Or gave you nursery tea, or a pair of pennies to spend at the shops?'

'Be quiet. Shut up! Mind your own business!'

Beneath them, the doors of the auditorium click-clacked as someone came in from the foyer. Gracie flinched and saw the flinch mirrored in Eugenius's face, saw his eyes dart sideways in dread.

It was Gracie's mother.

What to do? If Gracie was spotted, she would be in trouble for not being in bed. She wriggled down behind the balcony wall, kneeling up just high enough to see over. Her mother was wearing dance shoes and her husband's shirt which billowed around her slight frame. She carried no bucket and knife for scraping mould; no clipboard to note down measurements or which seats were broken. Instead she went straight to the stage—and began to dance.

It was tentative, awkward, half-hearted at first, as if she should be doing other things, putting her time to better use. But little by little she forgot herself, forgot where she was, forgot the laws of gravity, the limitations of the stage, the frailties of the human body, as she flung herself about in the silvery ghost-light. She was a cranefly buffeting a lamp in ecstasies of desire. Gracie watched open-mouthed. She had seen her mother dance before—of course!—countless times—sometimes just for Gracie's benefit. But never like this.

The dancer fell, picked herself up again and went on dancing, answerable only to some music playing inside her head. The only sounds in the cavernous theatre were the whisper and thud of her dance shoes and the sobbing of her breath as she pushed herself on and on, wrestled through thorn groves of weariness and pain. She did not hear the door click-clack, nor the first five times her husband shouted at her to stop, begged her to stop. She had her eyes shut now. He had to mount the stage and place himself in her path and suffer her to collide with him sooner than pitch down into the orchestra pit on top of the derelict piano.

And then he held on to her. And Gracie, up in the Dress Circle, had to close her eyes, because everyone knows it was written down at the beginning of the world that a girl should not see her parents cry.

'I expect Mr Sapper has pulled out,' she whispered, in case Eugenius Birch needed an explanation. The builder-of-piers did not reply.

Her mother was saying, 'I keep thinking, *If I turn round now, she'll be there.*' The beautiful acoustics of the theatre delivered her words clearly to the Dress Circle. 'I keep thinking, any moment she'll come through the door and start on with the questions and the chat—who she met on the bus; who she buttonholed in the shops; who she dragooned into playing h-h-hangman. Oh, Will! I keep looking—I keep thinking I'll spot her in the street and it's all been a mistake and she's just mislaid—just a bit . . .'

'*Lost,*' said Gracie, but theatre acoustics do not work in reverse.

'*What are we doing here, Will? Why did we come? What did we think it would achieve? Stinking, mouldy place. What are we doing here? What does it matter? Any of it? Without our girl?*'

Her husband had corralled her in his arms, imprisoning her—or shielding her from the dark. 'It's her theatre, Ellie. Her favourite place. That's why we came, isn't it? Remember? It was always, "*When we live in Seashaw . . . When you're working The Royal . . .*" Remember?' He pleaded the Theatre's cause to his wife, just as he had pleaded its cause to town planners and English Heritage, to the Arts Council and the Town Council and the sanitation department. He offered it now like a cake through the bars of a bear's cage—small comfort, but the best he had to offer. 'We came here to make it happen for Gracie. Wish-granting for Gracie. When everything comes to nothing what can you do? Make something out of nothing. We can't bring her back, but we can bring back this place—the place she loved best.'

The woman in shirt and dance shoes looked into the dark of the big auditorium and saw no glimmer of comfort there. 'Work. That's the thing,' she said. 'It fills up the being-awake, doesn't it?'

'So sleep. Don't dance at night. There isn't enough light.'

'She liked me dancing.'

'I know, Ellie.'

'I was dancing for her.'

'I know, Ellie . . . but she would hate for you to fall into the orchestra pit.'

And finally, gently, he coaxed her off the stage and back to the dressing rooms where they had nested amid their few belongings, like squirrels in a drey.

And no amount of shouting, no waving of arms or kicking at the balcony wall or calling out of names could make them look up and see Gracie leaning over the rail of the Dress Circle, begging to be seen.

Chapter Twenty
Smoke AND MIRRORS

From their various roosts around the theatre, the Residents heard their cue to return and drifted back into the auditorium.

'No. No! That's not right! You're wrong! Don't! Stop it! Don't stand there looking at me! You're wrong! Take your faces away! Stop looking at me!' When Gracie had been little—littler—and running a temperature, the fever had brought a host of faces to gaze down at her in her cot—shapeless faces, features all mixed up; fierce faces with piercing eyes; soft faces that turned inside out and melted in the heat. Now the Residents of The Royal surrounded her with their pitying, peering, pallid faces, telling her she was dead, telling her she was one of them.

'Are you stupid, or what?' she shouted at them. 'What about Tamburlaine? What about Tintin? What about the stepladder man with the pliers? Huh? Huh?' she huffed triumphantly at them as

confusion crumpled up those horrible faces and everything written on them.

Frank Stuart took out his notebook and opened and closed
it several times before putting it back in his pocket. He was very
measured in his explanation. Miss Melluish was dabbing at her
eyes with a handkerchief, Lily and Roland sat praying in Row
C, keeping Kaddish for the soul of Gracie Walter; Mikey was
roaming the theatre kicking the seats, but Frank Stuart's voice
was as even as the Shipping Forecast on the radio. 'You spoke of
a car accident. Writing off a car? Not very long ago. You cannot
operate your music machine or your telephone. You got into the
cinema and gallery unseen, without paying.'

'*Be quiet. Shut up.*'

'You hold no converse with your parents,' said Eugenius.
'There are no expeditions to the beach. No third place is set at
mealtimes.'

'*Shut up! Shut up! Shut up!*'

'You feel our touch,' Frank went on. 'You see William's paintings. You are done with bedtimes and sleeping. You don't fold
down a seat.'

Gracie looked down at the seatback she was perched on like
a robin on a tombstone.

'Tamburlaine! Tintin!' she jeered at him. 'You ask them.'

The Residents sat up a little straighter. Some nodded as if
they were siding with the patchwork child. There *was* Tamburlaine to be considered. There *was* Bob the Yes-We-Can-Man, and
the electrician on his ladder. They had all seen Gracie.

'But not your parents, whose brains are too full of the truth
to be deceived.'

Eugenius Birch allied himself with the inventor. 'Mr Stuart and I have been discussing this. It greatly confused us when you arrived. For a week at least we rested convinced that you were a living soul. But Mr Stuart here is of the mind—and I concur—that the kinetic energy of . . . well . . . *happiness*, excites the molecular structure of the aether sufficiently to allow . . .'

'*Blurgh!*' said Gracie. '*Blurgh-di-blah-blah.*'

George the Circus Master approached, as once he had approached his wife's lions: soft-footed, cautiously, making no sudden movement. He took Gracie's face between his hands—she could feel the dryness of his palms, smell the pomade he wore.

'You were so very *alive*, child, so happy that you dented the air still, as you dented it in life.'

'Oh, so *very* much alive,' said Lily rising to her feet.

'Too piggin' full-on to take deadness,' said Mikey.

'Unquenchable,' said Miss Melluish.

'Incandescent,' said Shadrach in his pit.

Gracie snarled at them all, incandescent only with anger and fright.

'Look at it this way,' said Eugenius Birch. 'There is a meniscus layer on the surface of water, like a skin, yes? It allows insects to stand upon the water without sinking through.'

'Like Saint Matthew,' said Miss Melluish confusingly. 'He too walked on water while he believed he could do it.' She took hold of Gracie's hand and led her away to the privacy of the Royal Box, shooing the Twins out first. And there she sat the girl down, holding Gracie's hands in her own lap. 'We are the People Below, child. The cause of our death—whether by fire, or tempest, or bullet—somehow plunged us into this gloomy Elsewhere. For what purpose is not yet clear to us, but here we wait. Here we were waiting. Suddenly a mayfly! A mayfly plunged into our quiet pond. Caped in silvery air, she clambered down amongst us—in amongst us—looking about her with large and shining eyes. To us she was a thing of wonder, an intruder from the sunshine above: out-of-place. She was fearless—of course she was—for that she thought she had only to let go and she would rise back to the surface. And yet . . . and yet . . . Her silvery cape was no more than the happy sunlight that clung to her as she fell through the surface. In no time, it dissolved away. Gracie, you came to us so swaddled in happiness that even we mistook you for a living child. But now there can be no more mistaking.'

Then Miss Melluish wept and the Twins (who had not understood a word) also wept, while below them William painted black smoke, and Shadrach played 'Eurydice' on the piano in a minor key no one could hear.

But Gracie was having none of it. She snatched back her hands, slammed her way out of the box, out of the auditorium and through the shabby bar to find the shabby Stalls toilets. It took her a while to locate them: for some reason she had never felt the need of a toilet since moving into The Royal—did not feel it now. She was only in search of a mirror.

Leaning her hands on the sink edge, she looked into the speckled glass. Looked and looked and looked and looked and looked and looked. No eyes looked back at her. No patchwork dungarees. No face. The only movement she saw there, as the horror and sadness sobbed out of her, were tendrils of black mould spreading across the glass until their reflection of the empty Ladies was all but scribbled out.

❧

When she returned to the Stalls, the pall of regret and pity had been replaced by shock. The Residents were a-jitter with nerves. They were not accustomed to suddenness. Apart from Gracie, nothing sudden had happened to them for several decades. In a single day, triumph, tragedy, and disaster had disrupted their quiet routine. And now, with the suddenness of an explosion, but no sound at all, Maurice had come home.

He was leaning on his knees, centre-stage, as if back from some marathon run—and he was about to drop a bombshell bigger than the Gotha biplane had dropped on Windsor Avenue. Catching sight of Gracie as she re-entered, he pointed a wagging finger at her.

'Sapper! Your man Sapper? Was that his name?' Gracie nodded dumbly. 'Well, the Council do not care for him—think he smells wrong—kipper kept by too long. Has a reputation. For double dealing. Not on the level. The Council will not deal with him. That's why he needed your ma and pa. Now he has what he wanted, without ever putting his name to a paper.'

'Wait! Stop! Why? What *does* he want?' they yelped at him.

'Well, to have the ground and not the bricks!' Maurice's outstretched hands implored them to grasp the full horror of the situation. 'I was with him this morning when he met with his confederate!'

In their various lines of business, Eugenius the architect, Bodkins the barrow boy, Lord George the ringmaster, and PC Nixon had seen villainy and dirty dealing many, many times. These men grasped at once what Maurice was saying. Poetical Miss Melluish, ignorant Mikey, God-fearing Lily and Roland, eleven-year-old Gracie—these needed it spelled out more plainly.

Maurice threw down his straw boater and jumped on it, such was his rage and frustration. 'Do you not understand me? *Sapper means to burn down The Royal!*'

Chapter Twenty-One

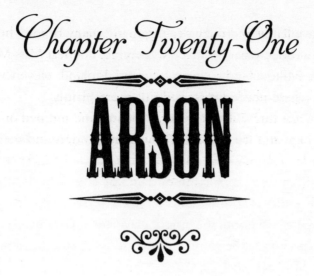

ARSON

If The Royal burned, there would be no reason for the 'London theatricals' to stay, no theatre for them to run. All that remained would be a half acre of prime building land on the corner of Hawley Square, ripe for redevelopment. And, to the town's disgust and astonishment, it would prove to belong to the couple's 'business partner', Herbert Sapper. He would make of it something useful, something valuable, something with a future. A shopping arcade for instance. Or offices.

Gracie's temper was slow to kindle. Over and over again she asked Eugenius Birch to explain it to her—how a pile of ruins could be more valuable than a beautiful 800-seater theatre, white and gold, with a chandelier, balconies with little lamps, hand-painted back-cloths, and all those costumes below stage. Patiently he explained it. Patiently she listened, then she asked him to tell her again.

'I have to get it straight, so I can tell Dad,' she said, frowning with concentration.

The Residents looked at one another.

'Pray do not attempt it, child,' said Eugenius.

'You cannot,' said the artist.

'Oh, I won't say I heard it from you people. I'm not stupid,' said Gracie. 'I can say I overheard it at Ye Olde Launderette. I can say Boudicca told me. Or Tamburlaine or one of his brothers . . .'

'The child is foolish,' said William tersely, and had Gracie been paying attention she might have seen Eugenius push the man sharply so that he stumbled against his easel and got yet more paint on his frock coat.

'We should mount guard, and defend our home from fire and fiend!' declared Lord George.

Mikey was game. 'Let's hunt him down and kill him!'

Gracie simply gathered up her gel pens which (annoyingly) had all dried up, wound up the wire of her iPod (which still refused to work) and clambered out of her broken seat. It was late, she said: she must tell her parents about Sapper before they went to bed. She ignored absolutely the glance that passed between the Residents.

'He'll come at night,' said Frank Stuart quietly. 'We should mount watch.'

Douglas Douglass agreed. 'I did fire-watching here, during the war.'

'My war?' said Maurice.

'Mine, you ninny. The Second one. You with your one bomb. We had thousands—incendiaries a lot of them. So folk volunteered to sit up on roofs, watching for fires breaking out. Arson's

174

not the same quite, but the principle is. Best done in pairs: one can fall asleep. Pair up with me, will you, Gracie?' He said it just as she was about to leave. Gracie looked round, feeling faintly ambushed.

'Doug's right. The arsonist could come tonight,' said Frank Stuart.

'There is not a moment to lose. Possibly,' said Eugenius Birch.

'That's why I have to warn Mum and Dad,' said Gracie levelly and pressed on, dodging the hands that reached out to comfort her, pushing a donkey aside, through the little door that led, by a whorl of corridors, to the dressing rooms.

Her parents lay asleep in each other's arms. Her mother must have fallen asleep crying and before taking off her eye make-up. There were dirty marks on her husband's chest. Gracie pawed and pulled at their clothes. She shouted and slapped at them. She tugged at the bedding and sank her fingers in their hair. But though their eyelids quivered with dreams, and fresh tears oozed from between their lids, there was no waking them. They might as well have been . . .

'Dead,' said Gracie to herself. They might as well have been dead. 'Might as well be dead.' She was saying it all the way back to the auditorium, hysteria making her dizzy and unsteady on her feet. She would say it to the Residents. They would think it was funny . . . 'I tried to wake them, but they might as well be . . .' She took the stairs that led to the Dress Circle, the better to shout it from there. 'Might as well be . . .'

. . . except that the Residents were no longer sitting in the Stalls or along the stage edge or the rails of the orchestra pit. They had drawn back against the walls, aghast, helpless, pale with impotent rage. With a torch in one hand and a metal can in the other, up one aisle, down the next, the man from the building site—Sapper's arsonist, Demolition Des—was roaming the auditorium looking for somewhere to start his fire.

❧

'I arrest you in the name of the law!' said PC Nixon, lunging at the arsonist, laying a stern hand on his collar. The man walked clean through him.

'If I had my lions by me now . . . ' boomed Lord George, 'by God I would set them on you, sir!' But the man from the builder's yard was unmoved, following an electrical cable back to its junction box at the foot of the stage. Crossing the stage, he found the staircase and descended to the cellars understage uttering a sigh of satisfaction. A vivarium of cables coiled in every corner and he set about pulling them into a single tangled heap. Delicate as any French chef, he poured a long, thin stream of petrol from the can of olive oil over the spaghetti of cables and unions and plugs. Going in search of tinder, he found the costume cupboard and threw the dresses into a pile nearby—not so carefully as to suggest a deliberate fuse, but as if the theatre properties had simply been left lying hugger-mugger, any old how.

'I would have you know, that dress was worn last in *Rosmersholm*' Lily informed him, as if such an affront to classical theatre was one step too far along the road to damnation. 'You try our patience, you vandal!'

The Residents threw both fists and insults at Demolition Des. They threw themselves headlong in his path. They wrestled with him. They cursed him, his forebears and his offspring. And

176

all it brought them was proof: they were powerless, ineffectual nobodies. No-Bodies. All they managed to raise were the fine hairs on his arms and a slight shiver in the nape of his neck.

Demolition Des retreated to the foot of the wooden stairs and looked around the cellar with satisfaction. Every arsonist takes pleasure in setting a fire. It was not the first time he had, at Sapper's bidding, put a match to some Seashaw landmark—for the sake of the insurance or to be rid of some protected building—but this would be his biggest and best. This one would rate a spot on the regional TV news—a reporter standing in front of the smouldering ruins talking of tragedy and heartbreak and the cost. An electrical fault would be blamed . . . flammable costumes and centuries of cobwebs; a wooden stage, oily backcloths, paint cans . . .

As a schoolboy Demolition Des had been dragged along to The Royal to watch improving plays by Shakespeare and the like. He had been bored rigid. The only good part he could remember was Julius Caesar's ghost rising up out of the ground. Looked at one way, he was saving another generation of schoolchildren from having to watch boring old Shakespeare.

Halfway up the wooden staircase, he put a cigarette lighter to one of the ratty wigs from the costume cupboard and threw it in among the makings of his bonfire; also (unknowingly) among a dozen panic-stricken ghosts. There was a *whoompf* of ignition, but he had left himself plenty of time to climb the rest of the stairs.

The fear of death by fire goes so deep that even the Dead feel it. The ladies dragged in their skirts and screamed; the men

177

recoiled. As the flames sprang up, so did thoughts of blistering skin, of hair set alight, of incandescent pain. Perhaps, after all, ghosts could be purged as easily as cobwebs or old costumes.

Exorcism by fire.

The Twins (who had never cottoned on to being dead) gaped with ignorant excitement at the flames . . . but were terrified by the black smoke that might enter their damaged lungs and set them coughing. Miss Melluish drew them to her breast.

Gracie, still perfectly sure she was alive, headed for safety the quickest way she could, leaping across the smouldering, writhing cables. She cleared them easily . . . but landed on the arsonist's discarded can of petrol. At that very moment, the fumes escaping the can reached the bonfire, and an arc of flame flashed between the two. Like an egg hatching, the can crazed, shattered, and plumed.

Gracie was suddenly enveloped in a caul of flame. She stood for age-long seconds, like the wick of a candle, her hair orange-tinted by the fire, her lips mouthing terror.

A fine place for truth to dawn.

When she stepped clear of the flames there was only one thought left in her mind: all the rest had burned away. *'Mum! Dad! The theatre's on fire!* **Wake up! FIRE!***'*

It was Shadrach who brought everyone to their senses—Shadrach, whose death had been a fiery one amid the tumbling masonry of the Assembly Rooms. 'Death hath no dominion over us, my friends,' he said levelly. 'Not so with the theatre. We must save The Royal.'

'Never mind The Royal! My mum and dad are asleep upstairs!'

The photographer began to beat at the flames with his black cloth. Bodkins stamped on a burning cable. Lord George tried to drag the bonfire apart with his circus whip. It did no good, of course, but they had to try.

Not for decades had the Residents put themselves to the humiliation of attempting the impossible. Today they tried. Leaping up the staircase, Mikey struggled to trigger the fire alarm. He thumped at it with an elbow, then the heel of his hand—took off a pointed suede shoe and beat that against the fragile panel of glass. '*Break! Break, damn you!*' he yelled. For half a century he had existed with the memory of shattering glass, of vandalism, of wanton breakages. His wing mirror had broken easily enough, hadn't it? Now this one tiny circle of wafer-thin glass defied him: the round eye in its red box—

stared insolently back at him.

'*Drop the iron! For God's sake, drop the iron and open the lanterns!*' yelled Roland, and in the wings Frank Stuart hurled his body against the lever that ought to release the safety curtain. Over and over again the lever carved through his insubstantial body . . . but it did not shift one hair's-breadth.

Maurice and Shadrach tried to pull the fire axe from its bracket so as to cut the ropes that would open the roof lanterns. A fire starting backstage need not take the whole building down to its foundations, if it can just be trapped behind the safety curtain and the smoke drawn up and out of the roof: a flue funnelling the smoke and heat into the sky. They fumbled at the axe, they snatched at the rope, but they could no more grasp either than they could grasp running water.

Emerging on to the stage, Demolition Des felt quite as all-conquering as Julius Caesar. Part in love with fire (as all pyromaniacs are) he paused on the top step and contemplated the huge stage. A glow of orange light was starting to leak between its planks—a beautiful tessellation of flickering gold. It even picked out the square of the trapdoor where Julius Caesar had risen from the grave all those years back.

The tall, narrow curtains hanging to either side of the stage fluttered towards Des as the fire breathed in. Beautiful, the way fires breathe. Like dragons. Soon those curtains would be twisting columns of fire, tall as trees, shedding leaves of flame into the auditorium, one leaf fluttering down on to each of the red velvet seats. Lovely.

It was in this poetical frame of mind that Des turned to go. So he was rather taken aback to be greeted by the rear end of a donkey.

'What the—'

Jennifer's heels hit him in the head and he slid back down the wooden stairs on his stomach, nose scraping each step in turn.

To the Residents down below, it seemed simply that he had tripped and fallen back into the arms of his own fire. A couple of the men even cheered the justice of it.

'No, no!' Miss Melluish upbraided them. 'We do not wish him dead!'

'Good riddance to bad rubbish,' snarled the lifeboatman.

'No, Mr Douglass! You fail to grasp my point! If the horrid man dies, we shall be burdened with his company for ever! Conceive! A fire-raiser living among us, lighting the fires of loathing every time we look at him!'

The fire had risen and spread its wings, phoenix-like, above the costumes now. Fiery feathers were licking the planks of the stage overhead.

'*Mum! Dad! Fire!*' screamed Gracie.

'Boo!' said Mikey, and Douglas Douglass slapped him with his sou'wester and called him a facetious noddle. 'No, I mean it! *Boo!*' said Mikey. 'Like in the cinema!' And he set his face towards the arsonist, and booed as if the pantomime villain had just entered stage-left. Lily Oliver was quicker on the uptake than Douglas. She too began to boo.

'Are we improvising?' enquired her husband with distaste, but he too began to boo without the smallest idea why he was doing it. Eugenius, who had started down the stairs to fetch his friends out of the blaze, was soon leaning over the banister rail, red in the face, booing at the arsonist.

No! not at Demolition Des, but at the fire he had set: at the tongues of flame licking round the hat basket, blackening the faded playbills. The understage emptied of air. The fire had eaten it all.

At the foot of the steps, the arsonist coughed, stirred, and rose woozily to his hands and knees, his nose dripping blood. They booed him too, booed his smoking army-surplus jacket, his low-rise jeans, steel-capped boots, and fingerless gloves. As Demolition Des woke to the realization that he had fallen into his own fire, he screamed at the thought of burning to death, and lurched upright. But he found he could not grasp the handrail of the stairs: his hands were too cold.

The roasting heat subsided. The deep roar of conflagration, then the flames themselves sank down. Crystals of frost formed on the ceiling of the understage and turned instantly to melt-water. The arsonist, whose hair and clothes had begun to smoke, felt both turn brittle with ice. The charred oak props supporting the stage did not burn. The costumes stopped flailing their sleeves, and the cables, though welded into a mat, stopped throwing off sparks. And still the Residents went on booing. By the time they allowed themselves to open their eyes, the whole understage had been transformed into an ice cave, a Santa's grotto hung with icicles and plush with furry frost. The fire was out.

From the smoke-smutted flies, where rolled, inflammable backcloths were racked up like rolls of carpet in a carpet store, Frank Stuart watched the cheerful donkey trotting up the aisle towards the Stalls Bar, and wrote a few words in his inventor's notebook.

❧

Waking to the smell of smoke, Will Walter opened the auditorium doors to be met by a choking stench of burned rubber, wood, and nylon, as well as a trace of donkey. Instead of calling the fire brigade, as he should have done, he went looking for the fire himself and traced it to the understage. His wife found him there, squatting among the heaped ashes of costumes, the knot of cables, cradling an olive oil can in his lap. She fetched out her mobile phone and started to dial.

'Leave it,' said Will.

A fearful enlightenment had hit him (rather like the one that had hit Gracie the night before). 'This fire was set,' he said.

'So? It could still be smouldering! We have to call the . . .'

'We just insured the place,' said Will. In his wife's hand the mobile asked which emergency service they required. 'They will say we set it ourselves. For the insurance money.'

Ellie switched off the phone. 'Whereas Sapper did that?'

'Whereas our wonderful benefactor, the delightful Mr Sapper did that.'

Chapter Twenty-Two

KINETIC HAPPINESS

'Then this donkey kicked me in the head,' said Demolition Des, 'Thought I was done for.' He was surprised to get so little sympathy from his employer. After all, he had almost died in the cause of Mr Sapper's plot.

'And this is how you contracted pneumonia?' hissed the property developer, his rage reined in only because he was sitting in a public ward of Seashaw General Hospital.

Des shrugged, which hurt his chest. 'Came round: place was like an icebox. Dry ice, that's what I'm saying. They must've installed one of those extinguisher systems like they have on aeroplanes. Dry ice.'

'What, and got donkeys in, instead of guard dogs? Yeah.'

Desmond would have done better to miss the donkey out of his account, but he was still breathing oxygen through a mask and had only enough energy to tell the truth. True, he could not explain what a donkey had been *doing* on the stage of the Royal Theatre in the first place, but it was not the kind of thing a man made up, and he took it hard that Sapper doubted his word. 'Had a really nice fire going, too,' he complained, like a man who has had his barbecue washed out by rain.

Then a sudden, vivid recollection—of lying helpless, at the mercy of his own fire—sent such a jolt of fear through him that his heart-monitor bleeped in alarm. Des knew he had lit his last bonfire. Then and there, he shut his heart entirely to the joy of arson.

❧

The Residents of the Royal Theatre rejoiced in their triumph over the powers of evil. After fifty years of being a mere nuisance, Mikey the Mod found himself a respected member of the community, congratulated for his quick thinking, admired for his cleverness in suggesting they boo. There was no thanking the donkey for her part. The Royal donkeys came and went at their own sweet will and were anyway, as Frank pointed out, only donkeys.

The cheerfulness was short-lived, though. Gracie made sure of that. Her face was sour, her lips tightly puckered. She was making one last attempt to deny the Truth. She stood up. 'There are still grants. It will be fine. I just have to tell Mum and Dad not to trust Mr Sapper.'

The others began trying to dissuade her all over again, but Eugenius Birch held up a hand. 'Can we teach the moth not to beat itself against the lamp?' he asked them quietly. 'Let the moth learn by experience.'

185

At the door, Gracie paused without looking round. 'By the way. I won't come here any more. Sorry. But you're all useless and you tell lies.'

Eugenius allowed time for an apology. When it did not come, he said, 'Adieu, then, child. But when you do warn your parents against the odious Sapper, warn them also of the crack beneath the Dress Circle.'

The girl in the patchwork dungarees at last turned back and looked at him.

'Sapper may not have made wreck of The Royal, but Time has done the job for him. Any day now, the Circle will come tumbling down, and, I fear, the building with it.'

❧

Whatever its effect on Gracie, his remark threw the Residents into uproar. They clamoured round Eugenius asking was it true? What was to be done? How could they help? Where would they *go* if, like a wedding cake, The Royal collapsed layer upon layer? The builder-of-piers concentrated all his attention on winding a fob watch which had not ticked for a hundred years. Lord George sat down beside him.

'Come, man, you of anyone here knows how a building may be kept from falling down. A man who can build sure-footed in the sea itself can surely make safe a mere theatre!'

'Yes, yes, Mr Birch!' chirruped Miss Melluish. 'You are so *very* clever!'

Eugenius frowned at his watch. He confessed that yes, he had thought long and hard about a means of propping up the ceiling, but that there were problems, complications—most of them relating to being dead.

Shadrach produced a page of sheet music and slapped it face down in front of him. 'Try anyway, man.'

Finally, tentatively, Eugenius began to draw. He drew a cartoon of an arch. The onlookers exclaimed at the beauty of the pencil-work and his ability to draw a straight line without aid of a ruler.

Frank Stuart, though, swept everybody off the stage and summoned William up from his pit with as many paint cans as he could muster. 'An RSJ is easy come by, 'Genius. Go on.' He thrust a scene-painter's brush into William's paw. 'Show us in large scale, man.'

After a quick downward glance at the cartoon, William T daubed an arch as high as he could reach, across the full width of the stage.

The Residents speculated on what an RSJ might be.

'Roman-style Joinery?' said Douglas.

'Royal Shakespearean Joints,' said Lily.

'Really Sticky Jam,' suggested the Twins.

'Rigid Stacked Jardinières,' said Miss Melluish. 'They could be planted to very good effect with aspidistras and trailing fuschias.'

Eugenius dismissed his own efforts with a flick of the hand. 'But the cracking is caused by the walls of the building dropping on either side. Tree roots from the square have undermined them. They may drop further yet. This structure will not flex if the stresses alter.'

To which Frank said, 'Acrows! Adjustable. Screws here . . .' He went down on his knees beside Eugenius and borrowed the pencil. 'Not a thing of beauty, an acrow, but you can dress it up—wrap your fancy Corinthians around it: pillar on the outside, acrow on the in. Then if the walls drop any more, you just adjust the height of each acrow . . . ' Frank added annotations in the margins, in the same beautiful handwriting that had first made his wife contemplate marrying him. 'Besides, you can always under-fill the walls with float concrete.'

'I have not yet added the radials and finials,' said Eugenius, snatching back the pencil.

The Residents, perching themselves along the front row of the Stalls, speculated on the meaning of acrows and finials. The Twins (who had learned a whole lot from Gracie) said they were probably kinds of grant, because there's a grant for everything.

Meanwhile, William T, snatching glimpses of the diagram between the men's shoulders, rendered his version in scenery paint, getting smears on his waistcoat as he reached up. His canvas, which had last been a backdrop for *Oliver!* three years before, disappeared under lines and arcs, catenaries and measurements, which Lord George shouted out from the back of the Stalls. He was measuring the space beneath the Dress Circle using his walking cane, calling out heights and widths in cane-lengths.

'You shall lose four seats,' he called, 'but that is a small price to pay to save the evening suits and fur stoles from crashing into the Stalls!' They were truly happy; men-friends working together to solve a problem.

Some small part of Gracie was appalled, though she could not care enough to protest. What did it matter if one old backcloth was painted over? What did it matter if the theatre stood or fell? She was just someone who no longer existed: not really.

The designers produced a blueprint. The artist behind them produced a blue-green-ochre-and-red impression of what the arch might look like once it was in place. Fronded with leafy curlicues of wrought-iron, it had the look of an exotic temple overrun by jungle. The Twentieth Century had collaborated with the Nineteenth to heal a rift in the Dress Circle.

The only trouble was, no one would be able to see it.

Eugenius Birch flung himself down in a broken seat and raked his fingers through his hair. 'Futile! Utterly futile! What profit is to be got from a diagram none can see? We who can see it are powerless to put it to use!' and he threw his drawing on the floor. The Residents looked down at it admiringly, wistfully. Eugenius was quite right, of course. The arch would never be built. They had never truly supposed it would.

Miss Melluish, though, hurriedly snatched it up and smoothed it. She said that it was a thing of great beauty in itself, and asked if she might keep it, folding it up small and slipping it inside the cover of her poetry book.

'She fancies you,' murmured Mikey, nudging Eugenius.

'And you are an uncouth boy,' said the builder-of-piers.

'Where is the Quilt going?' asked Roland Oliver.

'I'm going to see Tintin and ask him to build it,' said Gracie.

'My dear child . . . ' Lily laid a hand on her arm which Gracie threw off.

'You say people only saw me because I was happy, right?' Gracie snarled. 'So? I'll be happy. I can do happy,' and she slammed the foyer door on the way out.

The door made not a sound, and remained open. Miss Melluish said it was the saddest kind of happy she had ever seen.

❧

Gracie went first to the Yes-We-Can shop to explain to Tintin about the crack in the Dress Circle and the need for RSJs, acrows, some wrought-iron, and a builder.

He was reading a western, and broke off as soon as she entered—but only to shut the door. He generally let it stand open in summer, but suddenly found himself in a bitter draught. Chilled, he went to make himself a coffee.

While he was gone, Gracie scribbled on his library book with a gel pen. *Help us! The theatre is falling down!* Bob returned with his coffee, finished reading the page and turned it. No dayglo scrawl offended his tidy mind.

Gracie tried to pull the bottom can from a pyramid of baked beans, to bring them crashing down—as the Dress Circle might one day crash down on to the audience below—but her fingers could find no grip on the sleek metal. Aluminium, it seemed, could defy germs, decay, and ghosts.

And of course, yes, she shouted at him as shrilly as any bullying, badgering, eleven year old can shout, '*You can see me! Stop pretending! You can hear me! You can! You can! You can!*' But though Bob the Yes-We-Can Man felt a sudden unaccountable pang of sadness which he could not shake off for the rest of the day, he never realized he had had a customer, or how much he was needed.

Like a Mongolian warlord Gracie invaded the Bong Shop. She rampaged among the geegaws, gargoyles, and gaudy souvenirs, setting the fumes and vapours a-swirl, changing the shape of the blobs in the lava lamps. The thermometer-wind-chimes tinged disconsolately. The spider-crab in the aquarium moved an antenna. But Trelawny (who was minding the shop for his brother) did not look up from the *Sporting Times*.

And yes, of course Gracie shouted at Trelawny, grabbed for his bow tie like the emergency cord in a train crash, but she could not grab his attention, could not bring Time to a stop.

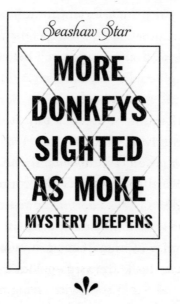

She threw herself down in the doorway of the newsagent's, her arms around Lassie, the moulded guide-dog with a slot in its head for donations to the RNIB. She told Lassie (who was an old holiday friend) that everyone, everyone, everyone in the whole world was blind. Lassie offered no guidance at all . . . unless it was to tilt her head a tiny fraction in the direction of the news placard.

Seashaw Star

MORE DONKEYS SIGHTED AS MOKE
MYSTERY DEEPENS

Frank Stuart did not want to give a lecture or he would have become a teacher rather than a set-designer and builder of elephants. 'Anyway, it is only a theory,' he said. 'Just some things I noticed.'

Gracie had returned from her trip to town and was standing on top of the piano now, like a rabble-rouser in a market square, waving her hands about. 'Tell us again why people get seen! Say what you said about Mr Turner! And why Maurice showed up in the driving mirror!'

Lily Oliver was afraid the child might be seeking a way back. Sometimes new arrivals at The Royal took it into their heads to tunnel or fly or leap their way back to life. They always failed.

'But you said! You said Tamburlaine saw me because I was so full of . . . so full-on.'

Frank Stuart, a man of few words (and no liking for saying them), scuffed one shoe on the stair. He was halfway between stage and loft, looking as if he might bolt for safety at any minute. 'I don't have enough data to say for sure . . . '

'Never mind the data. What about the donkeys? People keep seeing donkeys! It's in the newspaper. On the beach. In Primark! In Aldi! Even up the Ivory Tower!'

Frank Stuart mewed a little with shyness. Bewildered, the other Residents asked each other why an outbreak of donkeys should have brought Gracie back from town in such a state of excitement. Roland asked his wife if she could not *do* something with the Quilt until it calmed down. Lily was unwilling. At least the child had come back from town looking less broken, she said.

'I preferred her broken,' said Roland. 'She was quieter.'

'I *have* been having a think,' Frank confessed, easing himself up another couple of stairs, 'but . . . '

'About happiness being pathetic?' Gracie goaded him.

'Kinetic,' said Frank rocking from foot to foot, very much like a distressed elephant. 'When a moving object stops suddenly, energy is generated . . .'

They looked at him blankly.

'Well, then, you know frictional static—like when you rub a balloon on your jumper and it sticks to the ceiling . . .'

Half of them had never seen a balloon, let alone stuck one to a ceiling.

'Seems to me,' he said, looking upwards longingly towards the haven of his loft, avoiding their baffled stares. 'Well, look at William, there . . . '

The stares turned on the artist, who sat up a little straighter. 'Me?'

'That trip to the gallery: it bucked him up so much that he was *sighted* by a tourist.'

'I was?'

Frank applied to his notebook, like a policeman giving evidence in court. '"The Turner lookalike on the stairs—a nice touch that,"' he read out. 'I have a notion that Mr Turner's happiness that day might in some way . . .'

'And Maurice, look!' Gracie took over the assembling of scientific proof. 'Maurice. Yes, you. How were you? When you were in that car and Sapper looked in the mirror and saw you?'

'Oh tickety-boo! Tickety-boo! . . . till I realized I was lost.'

She stamped on the piano, producing a jangling cacophony of silence. '*Well, the donkeys are tickety-booing now, too!*'

Frank gave a moan and went even further up his ladder till only his feet showed. He called down, 'Donkeys are unreliable data. Donkeys don't count.' At which Lord George declared he had known a horse once that could count.

'It beat out the numbers with a front hoof.'

'What Mr Stuart is saying . . .' The builder-of-piers felt obliged to speak up on behalf of science. 'What Mr Stuart means is that we cannot measure the happiness quotient of a donkey, so that donkeys must be left out of the equation. Who can judge whether or no a donkey is happy?'

Mikey snorted. It was obvious to him: 'Wouldn't it make *you* happy to kick a fire-raiser in the head?'

'Not until *after!*' Frank's voice came echoing out of the flies. 'She would need to have been happy *before* she delivered the kick.'

The Twins, though, saw no problem at all. 'Of course the donkey was happy,' said Jim. 'She had just gone and went on an outing! Like Joanie and me went on.'

'Yes!' cried Gracie, jumping up and down on the piano. 'So *somebody!* Will somebody *please* get happy! Please! Somebody get happy enough to tell Mum and Dad about the theatre falling down! Just for a minute! Just for five seconds! Just long enough to tell them: "Go away. It's not safe." I don't care about the Circle! I don't care if the whole theatre comes down! I just want them not to be here when it does!' Her scalding tears landed without marking the shiny wood of the piano. 'Someone's got to. Because I can't. Not ever again.'

Chapter Twenty-Three
The PURSUIT OF HAPPINESS

They naturally looked around for William—searched right through the theatre. But happy or not, kinetic or not, visible or not, he was quite suddenly nowhere to be found. They supposed he had gone back to the Gallery to test out the theory for himself. His easel and paints were gone too, though, so perhaps he had left The Royal to live among the pictures that had made him so happy.

'If he has the ability we need, he must be fetched!' cried Miss Melluish decidedly, and raised a laugh. They had all lived so long with the dour and shabby version of William, in his tatty dado of a hat, that it was difficult to think of him as a fount of kinetic joy. Miss Melluish misunderstood the laughter and blushed deeply, but this once it was a blush of temper. 'Then I shall fetch him home myself!' And fastening her wild hair ineffectively into a bun, she left the theatre alone, a thing so unexpected that it drew an audible gasp from the assembly.

They held out little hope of Miss Melluish persuading William to help, so asked Maurice if *he* was still happy enough from his brush with music and tropical fish to write or speak a word of warning to Gracie's parents. The importance of the task completely overwhelmed him. He suddenly remembered watching the bomb drop from the Gotha biplane on to Windsor Avenue, and how he had willed it—*willed* it to land on the allotment, the green, the garden, anywhere except the house . . . No amount of willpower had diverted the bomb, had it? Even in his fleshly days he had not been able to divert disaster. What hope was there now? He was only a dead, one-per-cent-of-the-take-bring-your-own-banjo minstrel, after all. He flickered as he said this, like a faulty brake-light.

It was Lily who put Roland forward. The actor did seem much happier since becoming Jewish. But no one else looked very convinced. Roland was offended. 'Why should I not succeed?' he asked bad-temperedly. 'An actor inhabits his role. If he acts a king, he becomes a king! If, therefore, I fix my mind on happiness, shall I not become happy?'

And before their very eyes, he did so, flashing his eyes, flaring his nostrils and working himself into a positive rapture. His brow lifted, his pupils grew larger. The whiteness of his smile dazzled them. His chest expanded, his fingers laced behind his neck and his heels lifted off the floor. He grabbed Lily's hand and dragged her after him as far as Row H where he took her in a horizontal embrace, closing his eyes. He was reliving, inside his head, the moment at which she had fallen to her death in the Stalls and been reunited with him for ever.

'Write it! Write it down!' they urged him, this seraphic star. 'Write a message and give it to the Walters!'

But Roland, propping Lily back on her feet and sweeping his hair back over his ears, maintained he had no need of pen and paper. He would speak the words aloud, trippingly on the tongue: *This theatre is unsafe! Be gone and quickly! Leave this place until it is restored! Your daughter wishes it!* . . . Besides, there was no time to write it down. At that very moment, there came the sound of footsteps on the stairs, and they loosed Roland like a bolt from a crossbow, to intercept Ellie Walter before the moment passed. He was such a gladsome sight that his friends laughed and applauded—which made Roland happier still.

'I have never seen him so!' cried Lily. 'He really should play comedy more often.'

Within moments, Roland came back, saying that Frank Stuart was mistaken. He said that the science of frenetic happiness was nonsense; that there was no truth in it.

His acting was good, but not that good: they could see at once that Roland was lying.

The truth was, Gracie's mother *had* seen him.

At the foot of the stairs she had looked up—started backwards in fright—asked who he was—how he had got in. But in that moment, her eyes had spoken such unbearable sadness that Roland's shield of happiness had instantly vanished, and left him clutching nothing but the unhappy Truth: sometimes hearts really do break.

None of this he said aloud, for Gracie's sake. Only in touching his wife's hand did he pass to her, like a thimble, everything that had happened on the stairs.

197

'Everyone says theatres have loads of ghosts,' said Gracie accusingly. 'Not this one. Oh no. No one ever talks about The Royal being haunted. That's cos you're all too *miserable for anyone to see you!*'

They looked at her with reproach, then, they who had spilled their stories unwillingly at her feet, they who had sought out sanctuary and a pleasant routine only to have her shatter both with her questions and her outings.

'Where do all the *happy* ghosts go?' she demanded. That word again. That offensive collective noun that lumped them together as indiscriminately as 'Mods' or 'theatricals' or 'Victorians' or 'niggers'.

Lord George kept creditable control of his anger. 'Gracie is correct. We must seek out souls of a cheerier disposition than ours—those whose lives were not ended by sadness, suddenness, or misfortune as ours were. Then may we find *one* in possession of this splenetic happiness.'

'Kinetic,' said Frank Stuart.

'In Seashaw?' snorted the Oldest Resident. 'You must be joking. Miserablest place in England. Whole town's as miserable as a pub with no beer.'

'*Oh be quiet,*' said a variety of voices.

❧

They decided on the Manor House, the nearest thing Seashaw had to a stately home. It seemed the obvious place for any ghost (not partial to theatre) to head in search of comfort, space, and a little luxury. Such grand buildings are in no hurry to become modern; inside them the Past is preserved in every view from every window, in portraits and antique furniture and the smell of floor polish. They all remembered the Manor House. PC Nixon had even dined there once with his dreadful wife while she was struggling to teach him snobbery.

Gracie knew the place too and could think of nowhere better. No Seashaw holiday had been complete without a trip to the Pinkerly-Silk Manor Museum and its extraordinary welter of Stuff.

'The Manor is a museum now?' asked Shadrach uneasily.

'Oh it's not just boring old glass cases with arrowheads and flints and things,' she assured them on the bus ride out to Quark Park. 'Some old explorer brought things back from all the places he explored and he wore a pith helmet and got shot at by wolves and put in a pot by ceramicists!' Gracie had a slapdash attitude to history. It came of believing everything her father told her, and her father told terrific lies. So she knew the names of the stuffed zebra, springbok, and wildebeest, and the American bison who snowed dust if you slapped him. 'Which you mustn't,' she told the Residents.

There were several alligators who had once entered a knobbly nose competition. 'The biggest should have won, of course, but she let the little one win because the prize was a pomegranate and the big one couldn't eat pomegranates on account of the seeds getting under her false teeth.'

There were assegais and shields made of lion skin; also a stuffed lion 'who ate the people who dropped the assegais and shields and ran away, but not fast enough'. There were photographs of men with big moustaches, in arab clothing and dug-out canoes; camel saddles and the tusks of narwhals and rhinoceroses.

There was a roomful of stuffed parrots, with a sound tape running to remind the parrots if they forgot what they ought to be saying. 'Except that stuffed parrots don't say a lot because it makes them sulky, being stuffed.'

There were a penny-farthing bicycle and a necklace made out of whale teeth, the cross-section of a beehive (1907) and thirty-seven sets of antlers.

But if there was happiness on display in the Pinkerly-Silk Museum, the Residents of The Royal could not find it, and Gracie herself could not quite work out where it had gone. With her mum and dad inventing stories, and with the prospect of an ice cream in the garden outside, it had always seemed a paradise. Now, she could find neither a happy ghost nor a ghost of happiness.

The effect was even worse on the Residents.

'The moth-eaten flotsam of a bygone age,' said Eugenius Birch.

'My tiger shone like oiled copper,' said Lord George. 'Not like these.'

The stuffed bears reminded Joanie of the ones in the Hall-by-the-Sea menagerie whom she had failed to free. An elephant's-foot stool reminded Frank Stuart of Nellie, broken down into scrap.

'Dusty relics,' said Bodkins. 'Like us.'

No phantom monkeys swung through the imitation trees. No live, lithe alligators lingered near the dug-out canoes. No spirit tigers lurked in the alcoves: they had had the good sense to haunt the song-filled forests instead, or the sun-striped hillsides of their youth.

'Fusty and dusty,' said Lily Oliver, and touched her own cheek as if that too might snow dust if slapped.

A gloom settled. Gracie's expedition to the Museum had an effect quite opposite to the one she had hoped for. She who had vowed to be as joyous as a dolphin, felt herself sinking instead, as deep as any pebble. They rode disconsolately back to The Royal on the bus. Mikey briefly scented happiness, sitting alongside a dolly bird with very short skirts and very long hair. But the impossibility of chatting her up undid any kinetic magic. When he put an invisible hand on her knee, she pulled her coat tightly round her and covered up her legs against the draught.

The bus passed the beach, where donkeys were rolling on their backs in the sand and eating things out of the litter bins. But there was no point in asking them the secret of happiness. They might be zinging with kinetic joy, but they were still just donkeys, after all. The Residents, lost in their private reveries, each contemplated the fleeting nature of joy, and sighed.

'*Don't DO that!*' shouted Gracie, making them all jump. 'Whatever you do *don't sigh*! Can't you see what it does?' And she pointed to the spattering of black spoors speckling the windows of the bus, spreading out into stringy tendrils of mould.

Chapter Twenty-Four

MOVING OUT

Looking around the caked black walls of The Royal, Lily Oliver said, 'I always thought we were happy!' and gave way to tears.

'A happy community of souls, yes!' said Shadrach, 'with our plays and concerts and entertainments.' A loud crack made him squeak and jump backwards.

Lord George, armed with a circus whip he had never previously owned, stood centre-stage, plumping himself up like a pigeon in a frost.

'Nevertheless, ladies and gents! Nevertheless! It would appear that, in making the old gal our chosen sanctuary, we have blighted her fair features and marred her beauty.'

The Residents murmured and nodded. It was not a cheering conclusion but it made sense. 'We have covered "with vile and loathsome crust all her smooth body",' added Roland Oliver (which was a bit strong and made the ladies fan themselves and look queasy, but which was true).

'There was no mould when Dame Ellen Terry performed here!' PC Nixon maintained (which Roland took for a slur on his acting).

Mikey protested that he had never sighed, not ever.

'This business of fanatic happiness . . .' said Lord George.

'Kinetic,' said a voice in the flies.

'Show me the man who can make himself happy by wishing to be so! Thus came our kind into the world: actors, music-makers, painters, purveyors of books, circus and fun! To dispel the clouds of care. But we have failed, ladies and gentlemen. We have failed. Oh, not for want of talent—no!—but through keeping back our private sorrows. It shames me that I have not managed to part each one of you from the sorrows you brought here. Mr Oliver, our beloved Songbird, Mr Maurice and, at the piano, Mr Shadrach have but diverted you for a few pleasant moments. Out of good manners, out of tact, wishing not to pry, we have simply pretended your sorrows—our sorrows did not exist. We have turned up the house-lights and shut out the Past. Can we buttress up the ceiling? No! Can we mend seats, stitch curtains, put on paying shows for the living? No! And yet there is *one last service* we can do the Old Lady of Hawley Square.'

It was stirring stuff, suited to ship-launching or coronations or the lighting of Olympic flames. Shadrach improvised some rolling bass with his left hand. Roland mentally sorted through *Henry V* for a stirring call to arms. Even Frank Stuart wondered whether a Union Flag descending from the flies would add a note of grandeur. They all assumed the circus-master was whipping up some scheme to cheer everybody up. So they were as shocked as anyone by what came next.

'Up, then, and let us be gone! Let us find fresh walls to blacken, new furnishings to spoil! Let us leave The Royal and grant her peace!'

A gasp ran through the stalls. The Twins hugged each other.

'I am going nowhere!' said Lily in a rage. 'I live here!' and she ran at him, at which he snatched up a chair and, in the style of a lion-tamer, held her at bay. The Residents of The Royal stirred like bison in a thunderstorm. It seemed they might stampede at any moment.

'What do you say, ladies? Gentlemen? The sky in place of our circus tent? The stars for our limelight? What better? Moving from town to town, sighing our sighs? Why not? Have we not done enough damage to this noble old building? Must we stay and do more?' He used the chair to fend off a shower of belongings they were throwing at him. 'Again I say, leave The Royal and embrace the carefree life of the road!'

His audience were unimpressed by the joys of the road:

'I thought my touring days were behind me!'

'This is my beat and I thought always to tread it.'

'Wasn't me did all the bloody sighing.'

But they could all see he was right. If The Royal was ever to shed its canker of mildew and open its doors to a new generation of audiences, they should—they must—remove themselves and their sadnesses. They were the pollution that had killed the sparkling pond. They were a blight. Their love for the theatre had been her undoing.

'But before we go—by your leave, Mrs Oliver, Mr Oliver—one last play!' Lord George exhorted the actors. 'One last play to live in our memory when we have gone our separate ways; something to set the echoes flying around this dear theatre of ours. One final performance! And let us fill the house to the rafters. As Queen Victoria said to me on the day she gave me my Royal Warrant: Put on a show, Lord George: one feels like a good laugh. Put on a show for gawd's sake!"'

* * *

Gracie felt left behind. These were *her* ghosts. It was she who had discovered them, flushed them out, unfolded them like hexaflexagons, studied them like rare silverback gorillas. She had spruced them up, taken them in hand, shown them around, updated and comforted them. She did not like this sudden outburst of independence.

She did not want them to go away.

Anyway, how did they intend to muster an audience? 'The theatre's not open and it's not safe and who would know to come?' She took her questions and worries to Frank Stuart. 'Lord George says we have to fill the place to the rafters, and I don't see . . . '

Frank did not want her in his loft, pestering him for words in his private thinking space. 'That circus-man talks like a bulldozer.'

'But if we do put on a show who does he think's going to come?'

Frank Stuart added a last screw to the lino-printing-frame he had just invented from a tennis-racket press and a floor tile. It is hard if a man cannot be left in peace to invent a printing press in his own loft. But on and on she went, like a patchwork barn owl:

'Who? Who? Who?'

'Our own kind,' he said squeamishly. 'Other ghosts. I believe that's the scheme.'

* * *

Well, of course The Royal was not the only 'sanctuary' in Seashaw. It stood to reason. The Residents might be invisible to the townspeople, but perhaps fellow spirits from different haunt-sites would appreciate a show at the old Royal Theatre. A last show.

When the donkeys came home for a nap, Shadrach wrote on their hides (in red oil paint William had left behind) **SHOW AT THE ROYAL** and shooed them out again to spread the word.

Frank used up the rest of the photographer's silver-nitrate paper making advertising flyers to stick up in public places—the kind of places other . . . 'ex-people' of Seashaw might see them. The Residents set off in ones and twos to stick these up—in the library, The Mechanical Elephant Public House, the penny arcades, the Sea Bathing Hospital, the Town Hall . . .

Roland took a couple up to the municipal graveyard and roamed about it, looking for a spot where the maximum number of . . . *passers-by* might see it. The cemetery was a huge rambling library of life stories staffed by stone angels and overrun with squirrels. Some of the life stories were briefly told in engraved letters on the headstones: they spoke of aeroplanes plunging into the sea;

a submarine trapped on the seabed;

a lifeboat lost during a rescue;

countless young men lost to countless different wars . . .

But after an hour in this sad, solemn, masonry-strewn park, Roland Oliver brought his poster back unposted. 'No one resides there,' he told them. 'Not a soul.'

'Who would?' said his wife, tenderly brushing green moss from his sleeves. And Roland agreed. Who chose to spend their days looking at monuments of themselves and watching the squirrels pee on them? It was not entertainment, in his book.

'Too draughty,' said the Twins.

Bodkins left a poster in the Art Gallery, but saw no trace of William the Artist while he was there. (Perhaps that was why Miss Melluish had not come back to The Royal: she must still be looking.)

Maurice left one flyer near every musical place he could find—restaurants, shops, hotel lifts . . . in case there were other souls like him in Seashaw who were ravished by music. Shadrach went to the bandstand for the same reason.

PC Nixon left adverts at both Police Stations (old and new).

Mikey left one at each of the cinema screens—and this time stayed on to see the cartoon through to its end. Also the foreign movie.

Also the X-rated movie.

Also the horror movie.

(But not the rom-com because that was just puky.)

Gracie left a couple of flyers in Grosser's, because the frozen food area always felt really chilly and she wondered if that meant it was haunted.

Douglas Douglass left a flyer at the lifeboat station, in case the ghosts of his fellow crew members gathered beside the shiny new lifeboat to discuss the even shinier Old Days. He went up to the wharf, too, where a fleet of little boats had offloaded the soldiers from Dunkirk in 1940. Twenty-seven trips his lifeboat had made to France and back, evacuating torn and bloody boys from the torn and bloody beaches. Such happiness in their faces as they stepped ashore on to English soil! Rescued! Home! Alive, against all the odds! Strange, but Douglas had forgotten till now all that happiness standing around on an English wharf. He had remembered only the horror and fear and exhaustion in France. Perhaps if he had not got killed himself on the twenty-eighth rescue run he might have remembered the whole thing differently . . . Anyway, he left a flyer or two there as well. Maybe some of the boys he had rescued still visited now and then, for old times' sake, and were happy still, following a long and happy life.

Back at the theatre, the Residents racked their brains to think if there was anywhere left that they had not flyered. None of them had so much as glimpsed another ghost on their trips out. And yet surely there must *be* others out there—residents of Seashaw who did not like theatre or loved some other place more?

'What about the Shell Grotto?' said Gracie.

'Of course!'

'Why did I not think of that!'

'It was there in *your* time?'

'It survived the bombing?'

'The Quilt knows the Shell Grotto. How extraordinary! It must still be there!'

Only Miss Melluish would have asked where they meant: in her time the Grotto had not yet been discovered. But Miss Melluish was not there to ask.

'Surely the Grotto will have Residents like to us!' declared Eugenius Birch.

So they rose as one and went off to visit it.

The Shell Grotto was a renowned Seashaw mystery, stumbled upon by accident and visited ever since by curious tourists. Archaeologists and historians had visited too, but could not agree on its age or who had built it. Some said the Romans, others the Victorians.

Made up of several large excavated chambers, the Grotto was an underground hollow, like a badger's sett or a church crypt—except that its walls and ceilings had been exquisitely decorated, every centimetre smothered with scallopy fans, blades of razor shell, pearly troca, mitre, and cockle and mussel shells. It shone with mother-of-pearl. It was a fairy cavern of prettiness, old and strange and unexplained.

And that, of course, was where they found the people they had looked for in vain at the graveyard, Tesco's, the cinema, Gallery, and lifeboat station.

Its rooms were crowded with Roman soldiers and pirates, women in swimming dresses and farmers in smocks, seed merchants and merchant seamen, farriers and carriers, fishgutters, gaiter-makers, bakers and bicycle builders. There were clerks and clerics and clockmakers. There were a dozen eighteenth century Catholic priests who must have hidden there from persecution. Archaeologists who had failed in life to solve the mysteries of the Grotto had naturally returned after death thinking everything would finally become plain. But the builder of the Grotto (who was there too, of course) sat in a niche in the wall, wrapped in sheepskins, eyes closed and a smug smile on her silent lips, having vowed never to answer a single question.

Every murmur, every song, every hiccup and belch bounced and rebounded off the shell-lined walls, floor, and roof so that the whole place reverberated with noise.

Only the arrival of strangers caused a gradual silence to fall, the busy movement to slow. The faces all turned in the direction of the visitors.

'Hello!' said Gracie. 'Do you stay here always or do you go out? We're from The Royal Theatre. Do you know about kinetic happiness? We've come to tell you about . . .'

Eugenius Birch put a curbing hand on her shoulder and said, '*Festina lente,* child.' A Roman legionary shot him a startled look.

'Where are your manners? A visitor should not call unexpectedly on his neighbours. He should first leave a calling card.'

Whereupon the Residents of The Royal, in the best traditions of Victorian and Edwardian etiquette, handed out the last of the flyers advertising the forthcoming play:

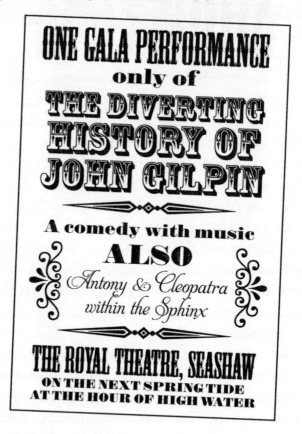

ONE GALA PERFORMANCE
only of
THE DIVERTING HISTORY OF JOHN GILPIN

A comedy with music
ALSO
Antony & Cleopatra within the Sphinx

THE ROYAL THEATRE, SEASHAW
ON THE NEXT SPRING TIDE
AT THE HOUR OF HIGH WATER

and left the Shell Grotto.

Chapter Twenty-Five

SHOWTIME

It seemed a lot to ask of cracked bricks, plaster, and paint to support the weight of two hundred people, and yet the Dress Circle was full on the night of the Gala Performance. So too were the Stalls and Upper Circle and even the boxes with their velvet chairs and little lamps. Latecomers stood in the aisles and at the back, and a family of tinkers settled into the pit having never been offered a seat in life and not expecting one now they were dead. The temperature dropped so far that dregs of beer in the Stalls Bar froze in the pumps.

And still they came: an audience so vast and so strange that those who had invited them were stricken with stage-fright—even the resident audience who were all backstage lending encouragement.

Behind the mould-blackened curtains, there was a strong smell of panic as well as donkeys. Roland Oliver had locked himself into his dressing room and was refusing to come out. Not that a locked door represented much of a handicap, and his friends passed to and fro through it to try and reason with him.

'How was I to know that full moon would fall on a Saturday!' whispered Lord George.

Given the lack of clocks at the Shell Grotto, given that calendars and British Summertime were meaningless to Romans, George had suggested the wording on the flyers. He had worded 'curtain-up' time in terms the people of Seashaw had always understood: Tide Time. High water during the highest of spring tides had proved to be five o'clock on a Saturday afternoon: an excellent time everyone had said. Everyone but Roland. Now they had a play to put on and no actor—or actress, come to that.

Roland Oliver said he was sorry, said that he sympathized, but the fact remained that he could not perform.

Lord George slapped his own forehead and cursed the acting profession for a bunch of high-strung whippets. This lost him the sympathy of Lily Oliver who said she did not believe for one moment that Queen Victoria had granted her Royal Warrant to a man who carried a set of cutlery in his breast pocket and did not like Chekhov. 'Roland is very upset—we both are. He conned the parts in four days and was most eager to play them. Oh dear. I do so wish Miss Melluish had left behind her smelling salts!'

Anxiety set like cement, pinning the Residents to the spot. When they looked through the crack in the curtain, they could see an excitement of laundresses, a crew of Napoleonic sailors, a band of Tudor fish-gutters, all waiting to be entertained. Anxious feet scuffed out the neat chalk marks put down to remind Roland where to stand onstage.

'Is it cos Mr Oliver's *scared*?' asked the Twins.

Hearing this, Roland stood up, rolled his head on his neck, pulled himself up to his full height and stalked on to the stage. His pale hands quivered by his sides.

'It goes against all my instincts. It appals me to disappoint an audience. And in general I quite agree: the play must always go on. But for this reason and for this reason alone, young persons, I cannot perform today! *It is Shabbat!*'

The Residents ducked their heads, winced and ushered Roland back to his dressing room, rightly afraid, for the first time in a century, that his words might be heard by the audience.

'What's Shabbat?' asked the Twins, trotting along behind.

'It's a holy day,' Lily explained. 'A strict Jew does not work Saturdays.'

Maurice offered to run to the synagogue and ask for special permission for Roland to perform—to which Shadrach said that rabbis were not like vicars and could not just bend the rules to suit.

'Sarah Bernhardt played Saturdays and she was Jewish!' declared Lord George. 'The biggest audience of your life awaits you, man! Will you send them away wanting?'

Lily peeped into her husband's face to see if he was tempted, but he turned on her such a look of reproach that she immediately sat down, hands folded in her lap.

'I could just tell Mr Roland he isn't really Je—' said Gracie before Eugenius clapped a hand over her tactless mouth and removed her to a safe distance.

Then, in an act of such astonishing nerve that Roland himself came out to see it, Maurice the Minstrel stepped through the curtain, gave a small bow, and began to play 'Way Down in Dixie' on the banjo.

The silence, when he finished, was as profound as at the bottom of the sea. His friends were waiting when he slipped back between the mildewed curtains.

'How was it?' asked Bodkins, breathless with admiration.

'No worse than machine-gun fire,' said Maurice.

Up till then, PC Nixon had been planning to arrest Roland Oliver for failing in his duty as an actor. Now he turned instead to Bodkins and said: 'How are you on *Iolanthe*?' And they treated the Saturday matinee audience to a taste of Gilbert and Sullivan, singing alternate verses of 'When Britain Really Ruled the Waves'.

When Mikey took the stage, no one could imagine what he might do. Perhaps even Mikey himself had no idea, beyond the fact that he was part of a team once more and playing in failing light and needed to give of his best. The piece of chalk used to mark Roland's moves still lay on the stage. Mikey picked it up and chalked three stumps on the side wall of the proscenium arch. Then he reached into his pocket and (knowing it would be there) brought out his best Lillywhite Frowd cricket ball and bowled yorkers, short hops, flippers, leg breaks, spinners, googlies and bouncers at the chalk stumps.

'You are an entire mystery to me, lad,' said Douglas Douglass afterwards.

Mikey shrugged: 'Well they must've liked it. They kept bringing the ball back.'

The arrival of donkeys in the auditorium delighted all the children in the audience, but annoyed the adults who had been trying to hear Shadrach play 'Wedding at Trondheim' on a silent piano. But there was uproar a moment later, as the Seashaw beach donkeys were followed in by a cavalcade they had recruited themselves.

Watching from the loft, Gracie thought for a moment that the exhibits had escaped the Pinkerly-Silk Museum, but the tigers who bounded from seat to seat, from Upper to Dress Circle, from Dress Circle to Stalls, from pit-rail to stage, shone like oiled copper. No taxidermist was responsible for the horses, who sported nodding plumes and high-stepping heels, and scattered any standing spectators out of the aisles. The haughty lions that stalked as far as the pit then leapt clear on to the stage were not sawdust-stuffed but sawdust trained and bred.

'Light the spotlights and give me a drum roll!' declared Lord George. *'My beasts have come back to me!'*

Beneath the S-shaped flourish of his circus-master's whip, Lord George raised his shining top hat to the audience, bowed, then put his animals through their paces. In the absence of his wife or lion-man, he draped Lionel the lion around his own neck. In the absence of his sequin-clad riders, he set his own horses circling. And though the stage was neither round nor as large as a circus ring—though the music came only from Shadrach hammering on his piano lid and Maurice plucking furiously on his banjo—the horses pranced and danced and twirled their way through a magnificent display. They had to contend with a bedlam of donkeys who bucked and bucketed about, braying like trumpets. Somehow, somewhere, the Seashaw beach donkeys had come to think themselves as noble and talented as any Lipizzaner stallion.

Last of all (because they were slow moving and stopped off to sniff members of the audience) came two gigantic bears. Up in her box, Joanie was first to see them loping down the aisle.

'Oh!' she cried, clutching her brother's arm. 'Oh, they are loose, look! They are free!' And the Twins rose and applauded furiously. The bears, once they reached the stage, did no more than stand on their hind legs, amid the whorl of horses and donkeys, drool leaking from their prodigious jaws. But, as Maurice said, they looked 'as grand as President Roosevelt and twice as big'.

The animals no sooner arrived than they were gone, led astray again by the hooligan ghost donkeys of Seashaw. And though the show had lasted only an hour, Lord George was minded to announce the National Anthem and be done. There was lion hair on his tail-coat, and the stage was lumpy with dung. His heart felt suddenly flattened, too, like a circus tent after a stampede: so many reminders of past friends! So many days dwindled into history.

So he was bewildered when, with a soft, soughing crescendo like an incoming sea, the audience stirred on its seatbacks and began to point. Something new had arrived onstage. It was only small and, from the topmost seats in the Upper Circle must have been hard to identify. But as the thing plodded into the ghost-light's silvery flare, a single wondrous word washed backwards through The Royal from front row to back:

'ELEPHANT!'

A small mechanical elephant toddled, with lifelike dignity, across the stage from left to right, passed from darkness into lime-light and back into darkness, head turning, trunk waving and a look of beady intelligence in the small washer of its eye. It had been built from the scrap memory of metal dustbins no longer seen in the back yards of Seashaw. It had been wired with the memory of watch springs no longer used by modern digital watches. It had been stuck together with fish glue from fish no longer caught by Seashaw fishermen. It ran on the kinetic power of pure genius: an elephant built from memories of a town which no longer existed, using craftsmanship that does not exist any more. The audience watched it, smiling broadly with fascination, charmed by the cat-sized elephant. And when Gracie offered to teach them 'Nellie the Elephant', they did not resist. The Royal had worked its usual magic.

❧

The singing resounded around the Circle Bar where Roland Oliver and his wife Lily now sat observing Shabbat in accordance with their religion. If Roland's refusal to perform had upset his fellow Residents, that was nothing compared with the torment the actor himself felt. Contrary to every law of theatre, he had disappointed an audience. The fact that the show seemed to be doing very nicely without him only incensed his sorrow. That remark about Jewish Sarah Bernhardt performing on the Sabbath wormed its way through and through his brain, but he knew it was just Satan tempting him to sin. *Remember the Sabbath Day to keep it holy.* No doubt Lily despised and resented him; he had deprived her of the biggest audience of her life—of her very *last* performance in her most beloved theatre. And yet, and yet . . . *Remember the Sabbath Day, to keep it holy.* He closed his eyes.

'You go, Lily,' he said. 'You can lead them in a sing-song, at least—or give them a piece of *Saint Joan.* You were always the better actor of us two.'

Her hand came to rest on his yarmulke. He thought for a moment she meant to pull it off in irritation. 'For a sing-song I should break Shabbat? For a soliloquy I should desert my husband? What a klutz you are, Roland Oliver. Not for top billing at the Aldwych would I do such a thing.'

The circular window in the Stalls Bar, which looked out on to Addington Street, twinkled like an eye as the street lights outside came on.

'Go to the window,' said Roland suddenly. 'Tell me what you see.'

'Why?' Lily pressed her nose against the dirty dimpled glass of the window. 'A tree, a motor ve-hickle? A lovely evening.'

'Are there clouds?'

'Yes, there are clouds. Pretty pink clouds.'

'But can you see between them? Look, woman! Can you see any stars?'

Lily counted four, (though the fourth was moving rather fast and had its landing lights on). 'Yes. Yes! Yes I can, Roland! I do!'

'Then say Havdalah and crush me a grape, beloved! Shabbat just finished!'

❧

And so, after a starter of circus turns, songs, and speciality acts, the largest audience The Royal had ever seen were treated to a performance of *John Gilpin*; also *Antony & Cleopatra*. And though many had never seen theatre in their lives before, though the shipwrecked crew of Dutch sailors in Row N spoke not a word of English, though it meant perching on a row of upholstery tacks for two more hours, not a soul left early. There was a listening hush as great as after snowfall, followed by applause and cheering that washed through the ancient space like a tidal surge.

A Roman centurion was so intoxicated with his first experience of theatre that he glowed with kinetic happiness. Gracie spotted him at once. 'Write "Mum, Dad, get out now!"' Paper and chalk were thrust at him and though he looked back at her rather blankly, Gracie shouted at him until he began to scribble. But whatever he did write, it was of no use. It was in Latin.

The Twins, too, were so extraordinarily thrilled by the matinee that they materialized as brightly as salmon leaping out of a stream. Paper and chalk were put into their warm little hands . . . But sadly, in life, people had never wanted to bother two such poorly little children with schoolwork. 'I'm sorry, Gracie,' said Jim. 'No one ever taught us our letters.'

Still the cheering and applause continued round about them. No one cycling past The Royal with a takeaway supper heard a sound. No lovers necking in the alleyway felt the ground tremble with the appreciative drumming of feet. No one taking a short-cut through Hawley Square to the all-night chemist gave a second thought to the darkened, derelict theatre on the corner. But beyond its padlocked doors, the walls themselves trembled and quaked to the echoing cheers of the long, long dead.

Chapter Twenty-Six

Miss MELLUISH MEANWHILE

Florence Melluish, in her determined search for William the Artist, came to the beach below Marine Parade. She had gone first to the Gallery, of course, assuming he had gone to live there. If, when she found him, he was still happy enough to be leaving palm prints on the world's windows, she would ask him to write a warning note: warning the Walters against Sapper, warning them of the crack in the Dress Circle. Her own brush with poverty and sudden death made her sympathetic to Gracie's point of view: better the child's parents should abandon The Royal than be crushed to death or suffer the shame of losing all their money and having to live in 'reduced circumstances'.

But William was not at the Gallery. She looked in every room several times over and, visible or invisible, there was no sign of him. She trawled next the artistic quarter of the town where all the potters and painters and jewellers and candle-makers and driftwood sculptors struggled to make a living. She rather hoped William had *not* visited the craft shop, *China Cuties*: Mr T was not a man blessed with tact and he would have been sure to say something rude about the quality of the art.

She looked for the boarding house where William had spent each summer, but the building had long since gone, pulled down to make way for modern times. So Florence was reduced to wandering the streets, in the hope of spotting the artist by chance. Naturally her feet carried her back to her own little boarding house in Temperance Street, and the spot in Pump Street where she had worked. But the chemist and circulating library had not outlived the tidal surge any more than she had.

She visited the modern library out of curiosity, and though it was marvellous and had one whole shelf of poetry, the books could not be lifted down with spectral hands or opened with spectral fingers. The high bookshelves proved no more than cliffs barring her way to knowledge and joy. At nightfall, the comfort and shelter of The Royal called to her across the rooftops. But Florence had set out to find William, and a certain steely pride forbade her to go back there without finding him.

So Thursday found her walking the beaches between the Clock Tower and the Lifeboat Memorial, studying the faces of passers by, looking out for easels. After all, the seafront is the best place for painting the sea and sky.

A string of donkeys were making an equally fruitless journey—fifty metres one way, fifty metres back, while small children clung to the pommels of their well worn saddles. These living beasts watched, with open jealousy, a string of bare-backed donkeys clambering about on the rocks. Children with spades and buckets and shrimping nets tried sporadically to clamber aboard these feral donkeys, but they did not stand a chance. (It would take a magic Madonna from the Bong Shop to mount a reinless, stirrupless, ghost beach donkey.) Only once did the bare-backed donkeys venture on to the sand, and that was to circle Florence once before trotting back in the direction of the rocks. She followed almost without realizing it, and found herself walking a good mile beyond the lido, beyond the holi-daymakers, beyond the parish boundary, beyond the confines of Seashaw itself. Whenever she was tempted to stop, the donkeys would turn back and circle her, like sheepdogs whipping in a rogue sheep. She began to feel rather afraid and took off her coat and flapped it at them, until the coat slipped out of her hands and fell on the sand.

A man came to her rescue, shooing the donkeys away. He picked up her coat and held it open so that she might slip her arms back down the sleeves. Florence thought she might die of shame (were she not already dead). To be seen in her drawers by a middle-aged man while unchaperoned on an empty beach! What would her mother have said? Worse still, *his* feet were bare and his trousers rolled up to his knees!

His clothes were at least respectable—a rather fine tweed Norfolk jacket and white flannel tennis trousers. His hatband sported a couple of pheasant feathers and a pencil. He lifted it as he said, 'John Davidson, beachcomber, philosopher and erstwhile wordsmith. It would greatly honour me to know your name. It is such a long while since I saw guipure lace, and it fills me with happy memories.' They both looked down at the white lacy trimmings on the cuffs of her pantaloons.

'Are you looking for driftwood?' she asked.

'Not at all, madam. I am looking for words.'

❧

John Davidson spent his days among the guipure lace of the sea's foamy shallows. He netted the bubbling rockpools and sifted the whispering surf. He picked up and popped the bladderwrack seaweed; he added punctuation marks to the looping, lapping waterline that scrawled sentences along the wet sand every time a wave withdrew. Above all, he listened to the temper tantrums of waves breaking over the stones and shells and worm casts in an endless clamour.

'Welshmen pan their rivers for gold,' he told Florence. 'I pan the sea for words. It can be done anywhere, of course; the oceans are so full of words, what with all the drowned villages, the mermaids singing, sailors leaning over the rails of their ships speaking of their loved ones or spitting curses . . . but there is nowhere quite like the Seashaw sands. You may not know this, but a circulating library in Seashaw was once carried out to sea by a tidal flood. Imagine! The words within the pages of its books wash up still with every tide. Listen yourself if you do not beiieve me. Allowing for long-shore drift, I find this the very best beach for gathering my ingredients.'

'Ingredients?' said Florence lying down amid the bladderwrack to listen. 'For poetry?'

'What else?' said John Davidson. 'Ten thousand words a day tumble ashore here. Why good gracious, madam, your rampant hair has quite the quality of the Biblical mustard seed. It "becometh a tree, so that the birds of the air come and lodge in the branches thereof". Would you like me to hold it up out of the sand?'

Chapter Twenty-Seven

CLOSURE

William and Ellie Walter, after a July night so freezing that their bones felt buckled by the cold, emerged from under their heaped clothing and agreed, without a word spoken, to leave Seashaw and never come back.

Their mystery backer had been out to cheat them. They had had to send back his money and cancel the insurance. A fire-raiser had narrowly failed to burn them to death in their beds. Neither the banks nor the Council seemed capable of reaching a decision. The smell of manure grew stronger every day, and the indelible black mould (they were convinced) had begun to cling to their very souls. A building they had remembered with affection and joy seemed, on better acquaintance, to be saturated with sadness.

'The place has a death wish,' said Will, 'and I don't want to be here when its wish is granted.'

Even an insistent finger pressing the doorbell could not stir them to answer the door in a hurry.

It was Mr Letts from the Council.

'We have it!—you! I mean *you* have it! We are there!' he said, tripping over the doorsill and into the office. He tried to suppress his excitement for long enough to make a more formal announcement. 'I have the great pleasure to inform you that Seashaw Borough Council have approved your application for the lease of The Royal Theatre, subject to a structural survey. British Heritage are funding refurbishment, and the Bettison Bequest have come up with a one-off gift of £50,000!'

They wanted to stop him—to tell him they had made up their minds to go, but Mr Letts was too excited. He was not alone, either: he had brought with him his dachshund Billy. 'Sorry, sorry! I know it's Sunday. I shouldn't disturb. But I was walking the dog when I got the phonecall and I just had to tell you at once. Also, Billy wants to see what all the fuss is about.' And away he went, so familiar with the layout of the theatre that he led the way along the maze of corridors to the auditorium.

For a moment, they all three thought the street doors must have been forced open in the night, and were letting in the sunlight: the auditorium was so bright. Will groaned. More intruders?

'Have you had the seats re-upholstered?' asked Mr Letts in a voice that suggested it was a reckless way to spend their own money before being sure of the lease. Will did not—could not—answer, but then he did not need to: Mr Letts had just worked out why the theatre was so bright. '*The mould!*' he cried, like

Alexander Fleming discovering penicillin. 'You solved the mould! Look, Billy! They solved the mould!'

No. Sonic vibration had not loosened it. Then it would simply have slithered unpleasantly down to the floor to lie in pats of black slime. The shabby carpets were not splattered with nastiness.

No. Like hoarfrost, the mould had simply melted away, evaporated, leaving the white-and-gold magnificence, cob-webbed but glorious. The stucco lion and unicorn and helmets and garland swags had all thrown off their mucky cankers. The chandelier, though dusty, was not strung with slime. The red curtains were a brighter scarlet. Even the lampshades in the boxes shone brighter.

What sighing had stained, gales of laughter had scoured clean.

'How—?' said Mr Letts.

'Oh, you know . . . ' said Will, who never undermined a good mystery if he could help it.

'Maybe the Old Lady just put on her best face for you and Billy,' said Ellie, laying a fold of the curtain to her cheek. 'But Mr Letts, I think we ought to tell you . . . '

Again the doorbell rang in the office.

'Oh! Oh!' said Letts. 'That will be the structural engineer! I forgot to tell you, didn't I?' To save time Mr Letts had organized the necessary visit by the Building Inspectorate. 'As soon as he issues a Certificate of Safety, we can get the lease signed and you're away! Even he didn't mind turning out on a Sunday. Everyone loves The Royal, don't they?'

Billy the dachshund, who had been happily trotting about the Stalls, suddenly lay down and began to bark uneasily, and to hyperventilate. Mr Letts barely noticed. After seeing the auditorium with its face washed, he feared nothing the day could throw at him. As far as he was concerned, a brighter day had already dawned in the history of Seashaw. He was dimly aware of his heart beating too fast, but then theatres always had that effect on him, even before curtain up.

❧

On stage, shoulder-to-shoulder like riot police expecting trouble, the Residents of The Royal stood and watched Mr Letts introduce the structural engineer. Their pride in achieving a houseful of happiness the night before, their delight at its effect on the plasterwork, turned to dismay. There is a terrible inevitability in watching a man with a clipboard go looking for fault, knowing the fault is there and that he will find it.

'He is very young,' said Lily Oliver. 'A full head of hair, look. He may not have the wisdom to see the cracks.'

'He is Jewish,' said her husband. 'He will certainly be too intelligent to miss them.'

❧

'Let us begin under the stage,' said Mr Goldwyn the structural engineer. The understage, yes: seat of the fire, scene of the crime, nest of viper-black wires that had melted into a tarry mat; the place where a bonfire of costumes had gone up in flames. What an excellent place to start.

Mr Goldwyn stood halfway down the wooden stairs and surveyed the swept floor, the newly creosoted joist and props, the ancient mechanism of the stage-trap shiny with easing oil.

'We are re-wiring down here,' said Will to explain emergency lighting.

He had spent the day before cleaning away all trace of the arson attempt, for fear the blame fell on them. Now he and Ellie exchanged looks which said *'not a moment too soon'*.

As he toured the theatre, Mr Goldwyn found patches of damp, leaking u-bends, spongy woodwork, a shortage of smoke alarms, some asbestos lagging; he found a warped door, a service lift that did not work and insufficient access for wheelchairs. He found silverfish in the Gent's toilets. But although the list on his clipboard grew and grew, neither his voice nor his face expressed the least worry. He even said, 'What do you expect in a three-hundred-year-old building?'

Climbing up to inspect the fire trap in the roof above the stage, he recoiled in momentary fear from a spectral white shape suspended in the eaves. But on closer inspection, it turned out only to be an enormous decaying wasp nest.

Waiting at the foot of the ladder, Mr Letts remarked jokily, 'Your first "ghost", eh, Mrs W?'

'No,' said Ellie, but did not go on. She was afraid that the handsome, blond apparition she had met on the back stairs was proof she was going mad. She had decided not to mention it, even to her husband. Mr Letts might have pressed her to explain, but he had just trodden in something on the stage that took his mind off ghosts. 'Haven't swept up this morning,' said Ellie with a slightly wild-eyed smile, and went to find a broom.

Descending the ladder from the fire trap, Mr Goldwyn paused to look out at the spectacular auditorium. 'I have been to so many plays here,' he said affectionately. 'I never thought to be on stage at The Royal. Quite a thrill really.'

His head tilted, first one way, then the other. He climbed carefully down the rest of the rungs and over the edge of the stage, hurrying up the centre aisle. Like a man caught out in the rain, he took shelter under the jutting shelf of the Dress Circle, looking upwards, scowling, banging his clipboard against his thigh over and over and over.

Will said: 'How wonderfully expressive the human body is. Not a word spoken and Mr Goldwyn has just said everything that needs saying.'

❧

'With immediate effect,' said Mr Goldwyn gruffly. He could not quite bring himself to look any of them in the eye. But he had a strong sense of duty, and it was his professional and civic duty to declare The Royal Theatre a dangerous structure, chain its doors, and ensure no member of the public entered it. He was good at his job—had already worked out the cause of the cracks in the Dress Circle—but that only made matters worse. If the side walls were sinking, then the safety of the whole building was in jeopardy.

'That is to say . . . ' said Mr Goldwyn, but did not. The Walters and Mr Letts did not need him to go into detail. The Council could not lease out a dangerous building. 'Should I send my survey report to you, Mr Letts?' he asked, but got no reply and, frankly, could not wait to be gone. Retreating, embarrassed, towards a hasty exit, he was hit in the back by the door opening.

Bob from the Yes–We–Can shop was in such a state of excitement that he had let himself in through a padlocked door. (To Bob, the only secure place was the inside of an aluminium can; anything else could be opened with a hairpin.)

'It is all in hand!' he said without preamble. 'I emailed a copy to the Worshipful Company of Metallists. (Not the note, obviously, cos that's a bit on the arty side and there's some as don't trust arty types.) Me I'm broad-minded. And it's beautiful—the blueprint I mean. Beautiful. Commonly, I'm not a man to use "beautiful", but there's no other word for it: *beautiful*. Corinthian! Next to Doric you can't beat Corinthian!'

'Sir, I'm afraid I must ask you to—' began Mr Goldwyn, anxious now to empty the buildings and put chains on all the doors.

' . . . And wrought-iron!' Bob hurtled on. 'Haven't seen wrought-iron put to good use since I don't know for how long. I blame the war. All those Spitfires. But wrought-iron and steel! Beautiful! Revolutionary!'

❧

The day before, Bob, the Yes-We-Can man, had been reading *The Canmaker* magazine when the shop door opened. He looked over his shoulder at the poster on the wall and then back at the wild-haired woman in front of him, smiling broadly.

'My daughter sent you, didn't she?' he said, chortling. 'She did, didn't she, soft article.'

'No,' said Miss Melluish. 'Necessity sent me—and my friends at the theatre,' and she spread out on the counter a sheet of paper.

'Music?' said Bob.

'Oh! Silly me,' said the woman, and turned the paper over.

Bob was only mildly startled by the woman's provocative clothing and her hair brushing his face as she leaned forward. But he was deeply stirred by the diagram she had spread out in front of him. For some time after she had left, he sat looking at it, tracing

the pencil lines with his fingertip and marvelling at the fact someone would entrust him with the task of getting it built.

❧

'First off, I thought she was a kiss-o-gram or something,' Bob told
the Walters. 'Such a one for a lark, my daughter. I thought she'd sent
me a can-can girl, what with this woman being stood there in her
knickers, saying not a lot. Then I realized she must be one of yours.'

'Mine?' said Will.

'His?' said his wife.

'An actress, I mean. So then I took a look at the drawing.
Beautiful. Bang-on bloody beautiful. The Worshipful Company
of Metallists was riveted when I faxed it to them. Hundred per
cent riveted. It'll cost a packet, but your woman in the knickers
says there are grants, so . . . '

The structural engineer eased the blueprint out of Bob's
hand and unfolded it:

Diagram for the support of Lower Circle
Royal Theatre Seashaw

'So you knew of the cracking already, Mr Walter?' he said.

'Oh yes!' said Will who had been to drama school so lied better than most.

'And you have already set work in hand to remedy it?'

'Naturally!' said Will. If he could make small children believe
he was an ewok, what could he not do? 'There's nothing Tintin
here doesn't know about metalwork. I trust him implicitly. Not to
mention the Worshipful Company of . . . things.'

232

'In the in-between,' said Bob, flushed with pleasure to think he had been nicknamed Tintin, 'I've brought along my coffins and a few acrows to stop things getting any worse. They're in the truck outside.'

'Coffins?' The structural surveyor looked around for someone who might explain, but his eyes lighted only on Ellie holding a broom and a fire bucket full of manure.

'Oh this?' she said, glancing down. 'It's good for the roses.'

'What roses?'

'In the square.' Ellie too had been to drama school. As the menfolk struggled to offload eight aluminium coffins, she filched the note sticking out of Tintin's rear pocket. It was written on the flimsy flyleaf of a poetry book, in spidery, almost invisible pencil:

Hi thee, Bob, unto the Royal
And show unto an engineer
The rigid steel, the pleasing coils,
The titan strength of this fair pier;
And say unto him, 'Be but loyal
To all the measures written here
And ye shall save the noble Royal
Which is to us so very dear.'

'Tintin keeps coffins in his attic,' Will was saying, both hands firmly in his hair by this time. 'Aluminium, naturally. It keeps out germs, you know. We had hoped to have the work done and finished before your visit, but Mr Letts rather sprang it on us . . . Can you truly spare your coffins, Mr . . . er . . . Bob?'

Tintin threw open the street doors, letting in the sunshine and the noise of a truck left running in the alleyway. He knew he was in silhouette. He knew this was the dramatic moment he had waited years for. Pulling in his stomach, he said, 'Yes We *Can*, Mr Walter! *Yes We Can!*'

❧

Roland Oliver turned on his wife in a jealous rage.

'He said "actress"! You visited this Tintin without my knowledge?' He raised one hand to strike her down. 'And in your underclothes?'

Lily giggled coquettishly and snuggled in under his arm. 'I did no such thing. It was not me. It was Florence Melluish. You *know* I never wear undergarments when I am acting. Only my corset,' and she kissed him on the mouth.

'Our Miss Melluish has clearly discovered happiness since she left us,' said Eugenius placidly, 'and a resourcefulness I did not know she had.'

❧

'Wait up,' said Mr Letts. 'Where's the money coming from for all this?'

'We have a patron,' said Will, quick as a wink.

His wife steered him aside. 'No we don't have a patron,' she hissed.

'I thought I could maybe blackmail Mr Sapper. No? Threaten to tell the police he tried to burn the place down?'

'You would end up buried in concrete under a shopping centre or something.'

Will returned to the man from the Council. 'We don't have a patron after all,' he reported. 'We could sell our internal organs on eBay if there are no insertion charges this weekend?' The day had taken on a surreal quality. He felt he had stumbled into a play by Pinero and had no idea what was going on. But he had been to drama school, and if drama school had taught him one thing, it had taught him never to ask what was going on. That just made people think you were ignorant. His wife began to cry.

'Make tea or sell tickets or something,' he suggested, giving her a hug. 'The day is young and we're probably dreaming, so what the hell? Oh look. Here's Tamburlaine the Bong Man now. What do you think he's brought us? A flying carpet to escape on?'

But it was not a carpet Tamburlaine and his brother Trelawny were dragging into the theatre through the street doors. It looked like a used lining from the cage of a giant budgerigar.

'Well, we brought it. Where do you want it?' said Tamburlaine.

'That depends what it is.' Ellie was wary.

'One backcloth, circa whenever. As per the note.' And he gave a fold of paper to the surveyor, who was nearest to hand. 'Them across the road weren't keen on us taking it, so I told them you'd pay them fifty quid for it and re-felt the cycle shed. Seemingly the shed's the only bit left of the old building. Used to be a stables, did you know? It's old, you can say that for it. Couple of hundred years of cobwebs on that there.' And he nudged the canvas with the toe of his boot.

His brother Trelawny seemed less happy about coming half-way across town to strip the roofing felt out of a cycle shed right behind the theatre. 'I found myself asking: *why can't they get it themselves?*'

'We don't mind,' said Tamburlaine affably. 'We only wondered.'

So Will gave them £20 and Ellie gave them carrot cake and promised them free tickets when the theatre reopened. He did not try to explain the inexplicable.

'Tell us about it some time,' said Tamburlaine taking both slices of carrot cake since his brother ate nothing orange on principle. His hands were black from the canvas. His eyes were blacker. He took in the serried row of aluminium coffins, the surveyor with his clipboard, Mr Letts from the Council, the white splendour of the auditorium. But Tamburlaine never questioned other people's lives. That way, he felt no need to account for his own. 'Heard about the ghosts. Nice. Good for trade, I should think, a few ghosts. Everyone should have some. Kid all right, is she?'

The plate of carrot cake fell from Ellie's hands to the floor and shattered. Luckily the roll of canvas caught most of the cake. 'No. Not really, Tamburlaine. We lost her.'

'Shame. Well, tell her hi from me when she turns up.'

❧

The canvas was far too big to unfold in the aisle. They dragged it outside again and unrolled it in the alleyway, kicking litter aside to make room. A backcloth, painted with a stormy sea, lowering clouds, the hint of a shipwreck . . . It was cracked along the creases and had ragged holes along the top edge where it had once been roped into the flies. The letters 'JMWT' were scrawled on the corner in red paint.

Mr Goldwyn, meanwhile, unfolded the note Tamburlaine had given him—'Extraordinary handwriting!'—and read it aloud.

In 1789 the young Joseph William took work at the Royal Theatre painting a backcloth for a production of The Tempest which regrettably he was never to see performed. (Accounting ledgers show that he was paid the sum of 4 shillings).

'But his current backcloth is *so* much nicer. You should sell that one,' remarked a young woman walking past them as they gazed at the sad remnants on the ground. She turned in at the scenery door. The sun momentarily shone through her massed glory of wiry hair. Her long coat failed to conceal that she was, in fact, wearing no skirt, only long pantaloons trimmed with guipure lace.

Goldwyn pursued her into the theatre to tell her it was off limits—out of bounds—unsafe. But coming out of strong sunlight into the dark momentarily blinded him, and when his irises opened again, there was no sign of the girl in the long coat.

He did, for the first time, take in the backcloth hanging behind the stage—a crude but enthusiastic representation of a structure—like an arch overrun by jungle. He looked at the blueprint, then again at the backcloth. 'Good heavens.' Clearly Mr and Mrs Walter had painted it themselves then had an architect translate their daub into a workable blueprint. It could not be a coincidence.

He moved further off. Not so crude, after all, perhaps. From a distance the work looked almost convincing. The style was a passable imitation of something by the smoke-and-fog man. Perhaps they were planning a 'local-interest' play—about Seashaw's very own local hero—to re-open the theatre . . . Yep. There it was in the corner. An imitation of the great man's signature. JMWT. '*JMWT!*' Mr Goldwyn ran outside shouting it. '*JMWT! JMWT!*' He looked at the note, at the backcloth, at Will, Ellie, and Mr Letts sitting around it eating cake crumbs off its unhygienic surface. 'Good god alive, people!' cried the surveyor. '*Don't eat off it! It's a Turner!*'

❦

Afterwards, Mr Goldwyn of the Buildings Inspectorate walked only as far as the little park at the heart of Hawley Square, and sat on a bench there until his legs stopped shaking. He had the oddest feeling he had just taken part in a play.

For the fiftieth time, he studied the blueprint for the retaining arch—

Diagram for the support of Lower Circle
Royal Theatre Seashaw

It was an extraordinary mixture of old and new, like something from an Arts and Crafts mansion. He wondered who Messrs Birch & Stuart were, and whether to write and compliment them on their beautiful draughtsmanship. It made him strangely happy to think such architects still existed.

The arch's elegant wrought-iron tendrils reminded him of roses round a door. And being reminded of roses, he looked around him at the square. There were no roses. A donkey was scratching itself against the parking metre in the street. But, as he had thought, there were no roses.

Chapter Twenty-Eight

The WHEEL TURNS FULL CIRCLE

PRICELESS OLD MASTER
FOUND IN CYCLE SHED

Windfall for Historic Seashaw Theatre

The papers said at first that it was a gigantic hoax to get publicity for the theatre's reopening. Fortunately, the old accounting books from among the archives for 1789 showed not only the payment of four shillings to JMWT for the painting of one backcloth, but the theatre's outlay of five shillings the following year to replace the roof of the adjoining stable.

So, two hundred years on, the backcloth—oldest existing work by the nation's most famous painter—sold for rather more than four shillings. Quite a lot more. Enough, indeed, to refurbish The Royal, staff it, and finance several seasons of drama.

❧

'It was of no great merit,' said William. 'At the time I did not take it much amiss that they lined a stable roof with it. Some art endures. Some is fleeting.'

'Theatres aren't,' said Gracie decidedly. 'Theatres go on and on and on and on. Look at The Royal.'

'Ah me! There you are wrong,' said Lily Oliver wistfully from overhead. 'Theatre is the most fleeting art of all. Every performance is lost for ever as the curtain falls . . . though of course the next performance is a chance for it to be better yet.'

They were riding the Big Wheel, the very first of the rides to be installed at the new Funland. As the wheel turned, each pair of riders reaching its summit could see the whole of Seashaw spread out like a map, and beyond it the sea. Despite all the traffic, the whispering rain, the workmen busy down below installing the carousel and the chair-o-planes, it was still easy to hear the background music of the sea. Maurice said it was playing the Blues.

'I told you Funland was coming back!' said Gracie delightedly. 'You wouldn't believe me!'

A lot of things Gracie had said the Residents had doubted: the return of Funland, the merits of venturing outdoors, the splendour of modern day Seashaw. They had resented, too, the way she ferreted out their secret sorrows. And yet it had somehow loosed history's grip on them, prised open the steely fingers of the Past and let them squiggle free.

William T had had terrific fun riding buses around town reading newspaper articles about his 'Priceless Old Master' over people's shoulders, spotting errors in the journalism. 'One paper said I was born in Seashaw. One that I dwelt at the Victoria Public House! One says that the backcloth showed Nelson's flagship! Another hints that I butchered small animals to grind their bones into paint. They all call me "Joseph" and yet was I never called "Joseph" in my lifetime but always "William"!'

The mistakes did not seem to upset him. William had emerged from under his curtaining black hat as from under a thundercloud, and everything was a source of amazement or amusement to him now. Realizing that he could save The Royal had amazed and amused him enormously.

After delivering to the Bong Shop his all–important note regarding the old backcloth, he had even plucked off Tamburlaine's sheepskin hat—the one with the earflaps—telling him, 'Do not go blinkered through this world, boy! You may miss some glimpse of Beauty in the corner of your eye!'

'Right,' Tamburlaine had responded, as underwhelmed as ever.

And if happiness caused William to flicker into visibility from time to time as he roamed about the town, those who saw him assumed he was employed by the Tourist Board as a Turner-lookalike. Assuming he was an actor, they did not give him a second glance.

'Do you have more to show us, young lady?' Eugenius called across to Gracie.

''Course I do. There's a man at the Mad Hatter Café who only wears yellow ever—except on holiday. Then he wears red.

And he keeps his Christmas decorations up all year round because he likes Christmas best. The Golf Club has a signed picture of Tiger Woods on the wall.'

'Who or where is Tiger Woods?' asked Lord George, whose soul was ravished by tigers almost as much as by elephants.

'It's a who. I don't know, but he signed the photo himself, which has to be good.'

'Ah! The ink I expended in autographing my photograph for admirers!' mused Roland.

'And there's a clock that tells a different time from everywhere else in the country!' declared Gracie, getting into her stride.

The Residents all looked at their timepieces. 'Of these we have several,' said Eugenius, suppressing a smile.

'There is Miss Melluish, look!' said Shadrach pointing towards Lido Beach. 'I wish she had come with us today!'

From the summit of the Big Wheel, Florence could plainly be seen riding a donkey through the surf, her bare feet trailing in the water, her hair a cloud of waywardness and fire.

❧

Florence Melluish had called only that once at the theatre, just to check that the blueprint had reached its destination—to be sure that Mr Birch's beautiful arch would be built. It was instantly plain to her friends what had equipped her with enough kinetic bliss to deliver the diagram: Miss Melluish was in love. Apart from the obvious fact that she was visible, there was a brightness about Florence like the glitter off the sea on a sunny morning. She hugged Gracie tight, in that way people do who want to share their happiness: one candle tilting against another to light its wick.

243

'Darling John is very partial to cricket, you know. We play French cricket on the beach most days. Do come, won't you? It is greatly enjoyable. John has a theory, you know, and I lean towards it. In truth, I lean towards everything in Mr Davidson . . .' She smiled rapturously and lost the thread of her argument for a moment among a multicolour tangle of other threads. 'Where was I? Ah yes. It is commonly thought that we people of . . . "*little substance*"—have been left marooned in the world by some tragedy or the manner of our death. Some disaster or misery or violence that has *wedged* us in the aether. Yes?'

'Like shrapnel,' said Maurice.

'I suppose I too have always accepted this notion of things. But Mr Davidson does not agree. He tells me that when a vital day's cricket at Lord's Cricket Ground is spoiled by rain—the last day of a Test Match, for example, which is greatly important . . . (Did you know this? I fear I did not . . .). Where was I? Ah yes. When a vital day's play is missed, then free "rainy day tickets" are given out to those who have suffered the disappointment of a wasted journey. (Darling John himself was deeply unhappy in life.) He now believes that we phantoms have been, for some reason, issued with . . . a rainy day pass. As compensation for a life . . . well . . . *rained* upon.'

'A mighty big compensation!' said Bodkins with a sceptical snort. 'Were you not at The Royal for two hundred year and more?'

'Indeed, Mr Bodkins! And yet in all that time I barely made use of my rainy day pass! Too afraid or too ashamed, I have simply hidden from the Past. Mr Davidson believes our "extra day" only begins when we have learned how to use it! Fine as your company was, pleasant as the entertainment, until now I was not making proper use of my good fortune! Now is come my time of sunshine and good sport and jolly company and strawberries for tea.'

'You mean, we get extra time until we've had our fair share?' said Gracie.

'*I* haven't had my fair share!' complained Mikey.

'Then go out and get it, boy!' said Miss Melluish, and gave him the money for a candyfloss.

'But then what?' asked Gracie. 'What when you've used it all up? Does the pass run out? Do I have to go? I don't want to go. Who wants to go: none of us want to go! I want to stay here at The Royal and be near Mum and Dad and watch over them and . . . You don't want to go, do you, Miss Melluish?'

Florence stretched her arms over her head, breathed in deeply the smell of carpet newly laid throughout the theatre, and examined a rainbow cast by the chandelier catching the sunlight. 'It depends what comes next, does it not?' she said dreamily. '. . . But John will be missing me. You must excuse. Have fun, everybody.'

And ever since that last visit, Florence Melluish had been roaming the beaches with Mr John Davidson, quite ninety years her junior, scandalously unchaperoned, assembling poems from words the sea washed up, and selling them, like sticks of rock, to fellow ghosts in need of poetry. The two of them spent the proceeds on candyfloss from a ghostly booth near the clock tower. (They had crowned their donkeys with bonnets of guipure lace, to keep off the wasps.)

❧

The mizzling rain was a blessing. Every few moments, each pair of riders on the Big Wheel—

Gracie
and William,

PC Nixon
and Bodkins,

Lily
and Roland,

Douglas
and Mikey,

Maurice
and Shadrach,

the two brown
bears . . .

Frank
and Eugenius,

The Twins

Lord George
and his lion,

would see something, recall something or share a joke that caused the air to crackle. Had it not been for the rain, any one of the workmen down below might have glanced up and seen freeloaders riding the Big Wheel without a ticket. And the safety certificate had not even been issued yet.

'Strictly against the by-laws,' said PC Nixon and blew his whistle for the sheer hell of it.

The builder-of-piers had been thinking the matter over. He took issue now with Lily Oliver. 'It is not true that a play is lost for ever when the curtain falls,' he said. 'It is not lost from the memory. People remember the plays they have seen. Some plainly remember them a great while.' And he looked above and below him at the Residents whose happy recollections had brought them all back to the shelter of The Royal.

'In that case,' said Lily, 'people are like plays. Even when their lines are spoken and their moves are made, they live on in the memory.' As she loosed her corset, the artificial flowers in her bodice sprinkled down on to Gracie in the car below.

'You think?' said Gracie, looking up. 'We stay remembered?'

'Undoubtedly,' said Roland. 'Especially actors and quilts.'

Chapter Twenty-Nine

BETTER DAYS

In any theatre there is a ghost-light. After the footlights are out, after the spotlights' white puddles have evaporated, while the lighting gantry is still clicking as it cools, the ghost-light stays on. The stage-hands think it keeps them from being plunged into darkness: after all they still have a set to strike, props to gather up. But the actors know that the light is not really for the stage-hands—nor for the cleaners sweeping ice-cream cartons from between the seats. The little light left glimmering above the stage is for the ghosts, of course, as they sit about discussing the performance and, little by little, reclaim the empty auditorium.

❧

The theatre on the corner of Hawley Square does not look much from the outside. The unprepossessing concrete floats bracing both sides of the building do not help (though the tub roses will mask those pretty soon). No, the full glory of The Royal is all on the inside, where a brilliant chandelier hangs from the roof illuminating three terraces of white and gold plasterwork, a sea of red seats, a swash of scarlet curtain, a hum of anticipation, the hoppity-hop of people moving sideways into their seats. There is a smell, peculiar to theatres, of upholstery, hot lighting gels, perfume, shoes eased off, scenery paint, sawdust, peppermints and glossy programmes. There is a Christmas feeling of unwrapped presents, too: behind those closed curtains anything might be waiting.

It surprised everyone how quickly all of these things returned, once The Royal reopened for business.

Of course there are ghosts—every theatre has ghosts, The Royal more than most. A host of ghosts. Occasionally, on birthdays and anniversaries, they amuse themselves selling programmes to unsuspecting playgoers or licking the ice-cream off a plastic scoop somewhere between tub and mouth. They have a particularly unpleasant attitude towards children who fidget, talk, cry, or demand to go to the toilet during the first half. When the interval arrives, they sit down behind the children and spit in their ice cream. But that's just Seashaw: it may not happen in other theatres.

The acoustics are strange. Even when there is a small crowd in, on a wet matinee say, the applause sounds startlingly loud. Actors in particular notice this, and say that it feels like playing to a full house.

From time to time a familiar face disappears from among the family of Residents, leaving behind a warm swash of air. It is rarely commented on, for the prospect of leaving—change—moving on—can be frightening, especially if you have lived in one place for a century or two. But the alarm is tinged with a tingle of excitement because, as Miss Melluish said, 'It all depends what comes next.'

❧

Will Walter does not greatly encourage the parties of ghost-hunters who sometimes ask to rent out the theatre for the night. For one thing, he does not himself believe in ghosts. For another, he prefers (as he puts it) 'live' theatre. He wants The Royal to be a place people come to see the living, not look for the dead.

Now and then, Ellie still dances at night on the silvery disc of light cast by the ghost-lamp. But the old frenzy has (like the mould) unaccountably melted away lately. Or perhaps her imagi-nation has improved. For it often seems that her dance has an audience, and that a glance into the flies, the little opera boxes, the wings catches her daughter watching, a smile (or a question) forming on her lips.

After the curtain has fallen and the punters have left; while the ghost-light is still burning, Will and Ellie have been known to sit in the auditorium feeling the sheer age of the place. They cannot help but sense the talent and laughter and music and applause and words and happiness that have soaked into the fabric of the build-ing over the course of three centuries.

Ellie says she can still smell the occasional donkey.

Will says, 'I can deal with that, can't you?'

'Oh yes. I was just saying.'

'The bear stink was a bit rich, but that seems to have passed.'

'Bears would be ridiculous.'

'Yes. But the occasional donkey?'

'Not important in the great scheme of things.'

'I think Gracie would quite like parfum de donkey.'

'You reckon?'

And Gracie says, 'Believe it.'

AUTHOR'S NOTE

As you will guess from the dedication at the front, this book was born in Margate. The idea came, in fact, from Will Wollen, Artistic Director of Margate's beautiful Theatre Royal: a book in praise of the town, past and present, created with the help of the local people.

After he got in touch, I began to read up on my subject. I came across such excitements as bombing, fires, storms, libraries washed out to sea, lions on the beach and mechanical elephants stalking the promenade. Mods and Rockers held running battles along the seafront. Turner returned time and again to paint 'the finest skies in Europe'. Dreamland (Funland) thrived, faded, closed . . . but is coming back to life. And two centuries ago, the sea came ashore, in the most catastrophic tidal surge in Kent's history.

Dozens more stories jostled for my attention—lifeboat rescues, runaway trams, the winter the sea froze, pirates, crashing aeroplanes . . . but I'll have to leave someone else to write those: there was simply not space for them all.

Of course, there were some things I could not find out from books and the internet. So I took myself off there—to its Museum, its beach, its sights and sounds, its shops and schools. And the people of Margate were kind enough to supply the most important information of all: the reasons they love the town the way it is now.

They told me about the mysterious Grotto with its shell-encrusted walls, the caves, the cupcake shop, the man who always wears yellow, the arcades, the parks, the joke shop, the skating rink, the shop that only sells cans. And, of course, the Theatre.

(I supplied the donkeys myself: my favourite part of any seaside holiday.)

❧

So why did I change the name of the town to ❧❧❧ 'SEASHAW'? ❧❧❧

Up and down the coast of Britain, seaside towns whose glory days were fifty or a hundred years ago sit looking out to sea and brooding on what the tide of Time has washed away. Their people feel the same fierce pride in their town as Margatians do. Each townscape is constantly changing: ageing, decaying, shrinking, sprawling, building afresh, reinventing itself. Unique as Margate is, it is not the only town with stories under every flagstone, with memories of worse and better times, with bizarrely wonderful characters. Every one of those towns deserves a book of its own. In the meantime, each one will recognize something of itself in the fictional town of Seashaw.

Also, this is a *made-up story*. I invented its plot and I invented the people, too.

Yes, George Sanger did winter his circuses in Margate. Mr Birch did design its pier, and Tamburlaine's Joke and Bong Shops do exist. But I have taken shocking liberties with these people's natures, lives, looks, opinions and by putting my words into their mouths. George Sanger would not mind—he told whopping lies all the time—but then he was a showman. Gracie Walter is alive and well, and understands about theatricals and story making. But others might not take it so well. You and I might mind very much if a stranger drew sketches of us that did not look anything like us.

The Theatre Royal in particular I have slandered unforgivably! It is not falling down and never has been. No mould grows on the gilded walls; no donkeys poo in its dressing rooms . . . And who am I to say what ghosts haunt its beautiful auditorium? I have not had the pleasure of their acquaintance.

But one day soon, this story may appear as a play on its stage. So maybe you and I (and they) will be there together to see it.

Adventure in New York · 1001 ARABIAN NIGHTS ·

THE ANGELS · The Canterbury Tales · THE STORY

CHRISTMAS · A PACK OF LIES · St George and th

· FIRES' ASTONISHMENT · The Princess and the M

Deep Blue Sea · Vainglory · GOLD DUST ·

· Blue Moon Mountain · STORIES FROM SHAKES

BAABRA LAMB · Good Dog Gregorie Peck · ON

The Golden Hoard · WIZZIWIG · THE DEATH DEFYING

· THE SILVER TREASURE · Moby Dick · King A

The Bronze Cauldron · GOD'S PEOPLE · Greek Gods

· CYRANO · The Crystal Pool · THE IDEAL

NEVER LET GO · SMILE! · Sky Ship · NO

Aesop's Fables · THE STONES ARE HATCHING · Always

· Roman Myths · Beauty and the Beast · THE

SHEEPLESS NIGHT · PLUNDERING PARADISE · 101 Great

LOVE AND FRIENDSHIP · How The Reindeer Got Their

· The Great Chase · THE KITE RIDER ·

CAT AND RAT FALL OUT · Gilgamesh the Hero · SIX STO

THE WORLD · THE HEROES: Hercules Perseus Odysseus

· Oxford Treasury of Fairy Tales · SHOWSTOPPER! ·

WENCESLAS · Fig's Giant · THE WHITE DARKNESS

AND SON · The Nativity Story · PULL OUT A

AND THE DRAGON, KING ARTHUR . . . AND A WORLD OF

My Grandmother's Clock · The Nutcracker ·